The Sedumen Chronicles Book 6

Firebird Champion

Orren Merton

ISBN-13: 978-0-9906936-9-7
BISAC: JUV037000 (Fantasy and Magic)

Cover Illustration by Dusan Markovic
Cover Design by Michelle Merton
Internal Design by Orren Merton

Special thanks to Jools, Cathleen Small, and Barry Wood

1st Printing.

This is a work of fiction. Any resemblance to any living person, demon, angel, extra-dimensional beings, or events is purely coincidental.

For those who feel the world on their shoulders

1

"CAN YOU TELL WHAT THEY'RE CHANTING behind that door?" Rachel points straight ahead toward the end of the basement corridor.

"Not yet," I shake my head.

The closer we get to the steel reinforced door underneath this huge office building in downtown Madrid, the louder and clearer the chanting becomes: it sounds like many voices, all chanting what sounds like "L'reek...L'reek..."

I don't know what or who "L'reek" is, but it doesn't sound like a Spanish word. It doesn't sound like a friendly chant, either. The voices sound almost dazed, like they're under a spell or something.

I spin my head around.

"Ready?"

Rachel and our forces all nod.

I hunch down and slam my shoulder against the center of the door. The reinforced steel bows inward like putty. The hinges burst apart and the door falls into the room.

No human could have popped that door off the wall like that—but I'm not human, I'm a Seduman. That means I'm half-human, and half-Sedu. A Sedu is a being from a parallel universe entirely composed of spirit. They longed to experience physical existence, so they manifested bodies which resemble demons from human folklore and mythology. My dual parentage lets me pass myself off as Alexandra Gold, a typical nineteen-year-old, pale, blue-eyed, brunette, and then reach into my "Sedu self" and become Firebird Alex, the "demon" warrior with flaming hair, eyes, and really sharp teeth.

After the door crashes to the ground, scores of startled people sitting on thin metal folding chairs in the center of the room turn and stop chanting. There's got to be at least fifty people staring at me, looking confused and scared.

I spring through the open doorway. Inside the room stand two Nephilim armed guards on each side of the door, two at the back of the room, and probably a dozen of them at the front. Nephilim aren't fully human, either. They have four eyes on stubby eyestalks, nostrils but no nose, and nasty razor-sharp teeth. The Nephilim don't openly display their features—they cover their heads with masks and hide their eyes in oversized, steampunky goggles.

The Nephilim right next to me aims his pistol at me, but I'm not concerned. My trench coat protects against VATS, which stands for Viscous and Terrible Solution—yeah, I know, sucky name, but hey, we didn't come up with it. It's basically a super-corrosive substance that the Nephilim use inside of their shotgun rounds to eat away our tougher-than-human skin.

I grab the Nephilim by the throat. I pull him closer to me and breathe fire on his head. His ski mask erupts in flames. I smash him into the wall hard enough to crack his skull. He falls limp to the floor as my thirteen-year-old niece and soul-sister, Rachel—known to the world as my shield maiden, Stinger —steps into the room and fires two bolts from her double crossbow at the Nephilim at the back of the room. I don't need to turn toward them to know they're dead. Stinger doesn't miss.

Stinger's also a Seduman, wearing the same Team Firebird uniform I am: long, red, hooded, leather-like trench coat with my firebird insignia, black pants made of the same protective material, black boots, and fingerless gloves. Whereas I'm from a Sedu line that fashioned themselves as demons out of Western mythology, Rachel's father, my adoptive Sedu brother Vetis, is from a line of insect Sedim. That's why under her hood Rachel has huge, oversized glowing red eyes, and her skin consists of hard, shiny, dark-green tinged insect-like plates.

I focus on the front of the room and realize who the cult members were chanting to. There is a grotesque-looking monster at the front of the room holding in its four gray, clawed arms a screaming, horrified young woman. He's holding her tiny body off the ground and up to his head. As he inhales, tiny rivulets of flesh and blood are being visibly sucked off of her body and into his open, sharp-toothed mouth.

This creature looks something like a Rishon, a spirit being from another part of the spirit universe known as The Firstlands. Like the Sedim, the Rishonim were spirits from the spirit universe who wanted to experience what it would be like to have physical forms, and manifested physical bodies. Since those spirits formed their realm and bodies long before the human race evolved, their forms were inspired by far older, huger, creepier eldritch horrors from other worlds. But the Rishonim made a fatal mistake—they made their forms too large, their realm too big, for their spirits to maintain, and The Firstlands crumbled. All the Rishonim decayed and disintegrated or went insane.

That's what we thought, at least. Turns out, a couple of the Rishonim escaped to Earth God-knows-how-many millennia ago. H'ythiis, a huge, twelve-foot-tall, four-armed, two-legged, winged Rishon with tons of eyes on eyestalks and her mate escaped, and they started the Cult of the Watchers.

The being in front of me seems like a Rishon, but kinda looks...different. Small. He's bigger than a human, but for a Rishon he's downright scrawny, maybe even less than seven feet tall. Taller than the maybe five-foot-tall woman he's holding, but way smaller than other Rishonim I've seen. There aren't the traditional Rishonim tentacles around his mouth, either. He's only got four eyes on tiny eyestalks, unlike the other Rishonim I've seen that have dozens of eyes on longer eyestalks.

"L'reek!" I shout. "Put her down!"

The monster turns to me. I unsheath my curved Sedu blade and will it to ignite with blue flames, a special power only my Sedu blade has. The look of surprise in L'reek's eyes tells me that even if another Rishonim told him about me, seeing me up close and personal freaks him out.

Good. I can use that.

He throws the girl against the wall and howls, then shoves the Nephilim standing with him at me.

The Nephilim swing what look like submachine guns around from their backs and start shooting. When they start firing, the cultists snap out of their reverie and start shrieking. Some people dive to the ground; others get up and are cut down by the Nephilim's bullets. See, that's the kind of bastards these Nephilim are. They don't care how loyal their worshipers have been; they'll kill them too.

Rachel and I didn't come alone. With loud battle cries, six of our Mazzikim charge into the room toward the Nephilim. Mazzikim are quite a fearsome sight: they are spirit warriors from Sediin that aren't as large and powerful as Sedim, but still really fierce. Some are four-legged creatures with horse legs and rhinoceros heads, others two-legged beings with gorilla bodies and crocodile heads, but all have solid red eyes and wear leather-like armor with the symbol of the House of Keroz that protects them from the VATS bullets the way our uniforms protect us. Those Mazzikim with arms wield shields and swords.

Racing into the room but stopping next to me is the beloved Mazzik captain of my guard, Zaebos. He's shaped like a dog the size of a small bear. He has rust-colored fur under a canine-shaped, red Team Firebird coat, and two rows of shark-like teeth inside his long muzzle. He loves me dearly and fights with me against all enemies, but he is even more invested in destroying the Nephilim. They murdered one of his young puppies, the brave Zaev, who died protecting me. Zaebos crouches and growls next to me, his red irises blazing, his razor-sharp teeth exposed.

I sprint toward the closest Nephilim. My jacket is pummeled with small-caliber bullets, but they don't even slow me down. The Nephilim starts to draw a knife when I close on him, but it's too late. I slice him from shoulder to hip with my Sedu blade and kick his body out of the way. The Nephilim next to him is already on the ground, his throat ripped open by Zaebos.

Another Nephilim sticks a knife into Zaebos's shoulder. Zaebos rears and howls, spinning toward the attacker. I inhale deeply and breathe a jet of flames on the Nephilim's head. While he does the "holy shit, I'm on fire" panic dance, Zaebos takes him down.

As the Nephilim drops, L'reek unfurls his wings and glides over the

Nephilim corpses. I inhale to breathe fire on him too, but he kicks me in the head first, knocking me backward. L'reek lands next to me and slashes at me with his dagger-like claws. I jump backward, but not before he slices the left sleeve of my coat.

With two of his four arms, he pulls long knives out of his belt. I stab at him, but he twists sideways and I miss him. He grabs my arm with one hand and stabs me with one of his knives. With my heavy coat and hard skin it only sinks a couple inches into my side—not fatal, but it stings like nobody's business.

With a battle cry as fierce as a thirteen-year-old girl can muster, Stinger, a blade in each hand, leaps a good twenty feet across the Nephilim corpses, throws both blades into L'reek's chest, and lands on top of L'reek, having drawn two new blades. She plunges both of them into his back. She may only be five-foot-three, but her momentum is enough to knock him into the wall. He winces from the pain but effortlessly bats Rachel off of him. The two blades didn't seem to do much damage, and he flicks them out. Rachel shakes herself off and spits an acid stinger at him. It hits his arm and his flesh begins to sizzle. That makes him grimace and wince.

I take the opportunity to stab again, this time piercing his stomach. As with Rachel's weapon, mine doesn't pierce very deeply; it feels as if something is trying to push my blade out of his body, fighting against me. The blue flames are clearly making him uncomfortable, at least. I breathe fire on his chest—that affects him. As with Rachel's acid, I can see his skin begin to burn and blister from my spirit fire.

He screams. With two arms he slices at Stinger, with two other arms he slashes at me, and then he flies up to the top of the twenty-foot ceiling and crashes through a window into the darkness outside.

2

"Zaebos, please tell our Mazzikim we're staying until the human authorities arrive to help the injured."

Zaebos bows his head and turns to the nearest Mazzik.

I stride over to Rachel and put my arm around her. She returns the side-hug as we assess the situation.

"You okay, girlie?" I ask.

"Yup. You?"

"Yeah, I'm okay. That was some amazing fighting, by the way. Throwing knives in midair? Your training with Lord Stygg is paying off!"

"Thanks!" Rachel beams. "Lord Stygg pushes me hard, but it's been worth it. I'm getting way better at fighting mid-leap! But I'm still not as good as I need to be." Rachel points her head toward the window. "Did we know there was another big nasty? And by we, I mean you."

"No," I sigh. "You heard them chanting 'L'reek,' right?"

"Something like that," Rachel nods.

"I think that was him. He looked like a Rishon, but a runty one."

"Yeah," Rachel agrees. "I'd thought H'ythiis and that Good-son-turned-Rishon bastard were the only two. So now there's three? Are there more?"

"God, I hope not..." I exhale. "Maybe these cult members know more. First, let's help out that girl L'reek was trying to absorb."

"Good call." Rachel closes her eyes and concentrates. Soon she returns to her human form: skin tone not nearly as porcelain-white as mine, long wavy brown hair way nicer than mine, with huge brown eyes, way too big for her head. She's cute, don't get me wrong, but she does look a bit bug-eyed—go figure. Still, she's far less scary-looking that way. We both pull our hoods and masks back.

The girl stares at us, bleeding and shaking against the wall where L'reek threw her. I look around the room. Our Mazzikim have blocked the door so the cult members can't leave. Most of the cultists are huddled in the middle of the room, their chairs pushed every which way, some staring at us in awe, others shaking and terrified. I see a few wounded people and a few dead, but they'll have to wait. This girl is their victim, and helping her comes first.

"Hey there," Rachel bends down and speaks in soft, reassuring tones. "Can you speak English?"

"Poco...little bit," she forces out as she tries to control her breathing. "Hurts..."

I kneel down and touch her arm to offer her some comfort. I rein in my flaming eyes and hair, and retract my sharp teeth and fangs. Nearly every inch of her exposed flesh has small, cigarette-burn-sized holes, all bleeding a little.

"What was it do to me? Will I dead? Nothing hurt so much in whole life..."

"I know..." I nod sympathetically. "I've felt it too. I'm so sorry..."

"What happen?" she implores again.

"I'm sorry if my words confuse you, okay? But I'll tell you what I know." She nods.

"These beings are from my universe. It takes a lot of energy for them to keep their bodies on this universe. The only way they can keep them is to drain living souls—kinda like the way we use batteries. That's what L'reek was doing to you."

She shudders. I understand the shudder. The way the Rishonim inhale a body completely, like sucking soda through a straw, hurts just as much as you think it would—it's like getting every single inch of your skin and bone ripped out of your body. And just as bad, as your spirit is sucked into them, you forget everything, where you are, who you are, everything but pain.

I hope she doesn't ask me about how the Sedim and Mazzikim keep their bodies, because it's basically the same. The Sedim, Mazzikim, and Ruhin feed off human souls to power their bodies and Houses as well. They don't go to Earth to feed of humans who are alive, however—they wait until humans die, and their spirits disconnect from their physical bodies and wander Gehenna, the realm of disconnected spirits. The beings of Sediin found that the easiest way to "harvest" human spirits from Gehenna was to look and act like demons who'd come to collect them for punishment. That's why Sedim and Mazzikim look like demons, and have demon-like powers. Even though they don't murder or absorb living, innocent humans, I can't imagine telling this girl any of the above would make her feel warm and fuzzy about us.

"But I no die?"

"You're not going to die," I reassure her, relieved she doesn't want to pursue how I know any of this, or how it relates to me and my warriors.

I kneel down next to Rachel and the girl. "I can try to heal you faster than your body will heal on its own, if you want me to. But I need to tell you: it will hurt. A lot."

The girl stares at me wide-eyed. Rachel puts her arm around the trembling girl's shoulder sympathetically.

"I'm not trying to scare you. My House in my universe, the House of Keroz, has a motto: *there are no lies in the House of Keroz*. I'm just being honest."

She looks at Rachel, then up at me, takes a deep breath, and tries to nod, but she's so freaked out it's more of a head twitch.

I inhale and close my eyes. I place a hand on her so I can feel her torn flesh. I imagine her blood vessels repairing themselves. I concentrate on communicating the image in my mind to her cells.

Being able to send images like this is new to me. Recently, my body was nearly destroyed in kind of the same way that this girl was being absorbed. When the House of Keroz put me back together again, I found that I could communicate with all the flora and fauna around me. I'm literally asking her cells to heal, and her cells are responding.

The girl tries to keep it together as long as she can, but the pain of her nerves firing and cells healing is too much. After what I can tell is an agonizingly long time for her, she breaks down and wails, shaking like a leaf.

"Not long now," I hear Rachel whisper to her. "You're so brave, you can do this...."

In my mind, I finally get some feedback from her cells. They don't "talk" to me or send me images; I just feel a sense of calm emanating from them, like her body is working normally again. I open my eyes to see that all of the girl's wounds are now scabbed over.

"Are you okay, sweetie?"

"Itchy," she trembles. "Gracias."

"I'm glad to help," I smile. "I'm Firebird Alex, and this is Stinger."

"Juanita."

"Hi, Juanita," I offer my hand. "How did you get here?"

"I wait for bus," she explains. "Yesterday. I alone at stop. Get on bus. From behind, someone put bag over my head, then...how you say...knock over..." she mimes her eyes closing and her body going limp.

"You were knocked out?" Rachel prompts.

"Ya. Smell something, then knocked out," Juanita confirms. "Woke up in dark room. No food, no toilet. Two of those...things," she waves a shaky hand at the corpses of the Nephilim, "tie me, take me here. No understand to what they say—too scared. Then that thing breathe me in."

"Your body should be okay, but we'll get you to a hospital just to be sure. Would you like that?"

"*Sí*," she nods. "Very much, yes."

"Before we go, would you be willing to speak on a video we make, to tell the people what happened?"

She inhales deeply. I can feel her getting anxious. I don't blame her. She just wants all this to be over, and here I'm asking her to relive it all in front of the entire Internet. But this is how we get the word out, tell people how to keep safe and what to look out for, and how we keep the Nephilim and their damn cult on the run.

"Can I speak Spanish?"

"Of course."

"Then, okay. I do it."

"Good," I pat her arm. "First, I need you to tell me if you can see the bus driver in the crowd. Even if he's one of the dead people, please let me know."

Juanita nods and looks over everyone. "At back," she points around and over the crowd. "In brown jacket."

I rise. Rachel looks at me, a smile creeping across her face.

"Sento," I call to a Mazzik with the head, chest, and arms of an orangutan but the body and legs of a horse.

"Yes, my lady?"

"Bring *that* one to me," I scowl, pointing toward the man in the brown jacket.

Sento nods and turns toward the terrified man.

3

"DO YOU SPEAK ENGLISH?" I demand of the large, shivering, heavyset man Sento roughly shoves to the floor in front of me.

He just stares.

"Inglés!" I shout, letting a few flames shoot out of my eyes just to be a bitch.

"N-no Inglés..." he stammers.

"Please inform him," I turn to Juanita, "that he's going to tell the world what he did and why, and then we're going to call the policía and have him arrested."

She looks at me, wide-eyed and nervous. I try to offer a sympathetic expression, assuming the idea of talking to the police makes her nervous. Then I notice she's staring at someone behind me.

"No need to call...I'm already here. I speak English."

I turn around to see a burly, tall, dark-haired man sitting on the floor, his eyes staring at the ground.

"Dammit, another cop in the cult," I shake my head.

"Not just any cop. Chief Inspector of Policía Municipal de Madrid."

"Seriously?" I huff. "What the hell? You're supposed to be protecting people, not rounding them up so that monsters can suck them dry!"

"Sí," he nods, his head hanging low. "I know."

"Looks like I'll be exposing you, too," I seethe.

The Chief Inspector stops nodding, sighs, and finally looks up at me.

"Do you understand what you're doing?" He doesn't sound angry or accusing, just dejected and sad.

"Of course. I'm driving the Nephilim into the open and destroying them."

"But do you understand what is happening? In the world, I mean, because of you?"

"Because of me?" I shout incredulously. "The Nephilim hide in shadows and travel underground in tunnels they dig and through sewers. They've been operating at the fringes of human society for, what, thousands of years? And they got away with all this kidnapping and killing because of people like you!"

Even though I'm fuming, I know what he's referring to. Nobody outside of the Cult of the Watchers knew who the Nephilim were, what they looked like, or what they were doing. That all changed a few weeks ago when I unmasked one on the streets of London. Now everyone knows what they look like—and the Nephilim hate me, my family, and all the Sedim and Sedumen more than they already did.

"How many sacrifices do you think the Watchers kill a year? A hundred people? A thousand?"

"Do you know how many of those Watchers need fresh bodies and souls?"

"There are three," he says. "So even if they needed a person every day, that's only, what, one thousand people in a year?"

"That's a lot of people!" Rachel jumps in.

"*Sí,*" he nods. "But how many people die, globally, every year? Is a thousand so many? Every time you expose leadership—a police force, a government, whatever—the people don't know who to trust anymore. And when people don't trust the law, who do you think they go to if someone robs their store or attacks them? You? Can you be everywhere? Do you see? Society breaks down. You're creating anarchy around the world."

"You should have thought of that before—"

"How many people do you think will die in riots and violence now? A thousand a month? A day? How many deaths will *you* be responsible for, Firebird lady?"

"I..." my words catch in my throat. I hadn't thought about the repercussions of our actions beyond clearing the world of the Nephilim and Rishonim. I just assumed that everything would continue as normal. But will it? I don't know what to say.

"That's not a reason to let the Watchers keep eating people!" I insist.

"Maybe," he shrugs. "I've made...regrettable choices. Some to give my wife and my boy nice things. Others...just for me. But I never stopped believing in law and order. The Cult of the Watcher maintained the existing order. You are destroying it."

"*You're* destroying it, dickhead!" Rachel spits. "You should have thought of that before you sold your soul to these evil bastards!"

"She's right," I nod to Rachel. "Your false gods more than murder people; they've been draining everything, the souls of people, the life force of the planet, you name it. Eventually they'll destroy everything, leaving nothing but dust. They're a disease."

"Maybe," he shrugs again. "Sometimes it's better to manage a disease if the cure can kill you."

"I have faith in humanity. No matter how selfish and scared people are, if you lead them into the light, they'll follow," I say proudly.

Rachel exaggerates a bob of her head to show her agreement.

"Maybe. But you're just young girls. I've seen—"

"Oh, shut up already!" Rachel bugs out her already huge eyes. "Alex, let's do this."

"Sento, not another word from him until the authorities take him," I point at the chief inspector.

Sento bows and kicks the chief inspector in the head hard enough to knock him out.

"That's not quite what I was thinking," I chuckle, "but it'll do."

Sento looks at the inspector's crumpled body, grunts, and walks back to the huddled cultists.

The truth is, the inspector's words hit me deep. I want people to be safe, comfortable, to be able to live their lives and love each other and have opportunities and all that good stuff. The last thing I want is anarchy and mass panic and death. He may have just been lashing out, but that doesn't mean he was wrong. There's no way that the small number of warriors and Sedim in our House could police the whole planet. Besides, we insist in our videos we don't want to take over the world. Being global cops would sorta go against that.

"Hey..." Rachel says, her arm around Juanita to comfort her and a sympathetic, thin smile for me. "Don't worry. We'll work it out."

I smile. Rachel always knows what to say.

"And hey, we learned there's a total of three Rishonim. That's worth something."

"True," Rachel says. "Time for me to get the secure phone?"

I nod and squat down next to Rachel and Juanita.

"Juanita, I'm going to explain what happened here, and then I'm going to ask you to explain what happened to you. Don't worry, you can talk in Spanish, whatever is comfortable. Then I'm going to make the bus driver speak. Finally, I'll say a few words at the end. Then we'll get all this sorted out. Is that okay?"

Rachel reaches into a zipped pocket of her coat and pulls out a special, secure phone.

Juanita inhales slowly, bows her head, and sighs.

4

"I'M COMING TO YOU this Tuesday night from the basement of an abandoned office building in the AZCA financial district of Madrid, Spain," I begin, standing in front of the huddled cult members and Mazzikim, with Juanita to my left and Zaebos by my right, standing as tall as he can so that his face— scary double rows of shark-like teeth, blazing red irises, and all—are in frame. I have reined in my pointy teeth and fangs, but not my flaming hair or eyes.

This makes our third video in two weeks coming from somewhere else. I figure I should probably explain, at least a little.

"I know I've been coming to you from a lot of different places recently: first Mobile, Alabama, then Mexico City. We can go around the world so fast because we can open portals between anywhere on Earth and our House in Sediin in only minutes."

That's true, but it's not the full story. In our House in Sediin, we have a portal mirror. A Sedu or Seduman can think about anywhere on Earth we've been, and the mirror will change to that location. Then we can step through the portal to that place. Rachel and I haven't been to all these places ourselves, but between my Sedu brothers and our Sedim allies we can pretty much go anywhere in the world.

"Stinger, my warriors, and I thwarted another gathering—this time, just as the Nephilim were feeding this lovely young woman to one of the cult's Watchers. I'll let her explain."

I gently rub Juanita's arm. She inhales slowly and exhales even more slow- ly, her arms trembling slightly and her eyes glassy. But after just a moment she rallies, brave girl, and starts softly, haltingly relating her story in Spanish. Rachel slowly moves a little closer to make sure we can hear her over the back- ground noise of people shifting, muttering to each other, Mazzikim guarding them, and all that.

At one point, she looks away from the phone, to her right. I don't speak Spanish, but her words sound more angry than anxious.

That's my cue.

"Sento, bring him."

Sento drags the bus driver over and drops him on his knees in front of me. Juanita involuntarily shudders. I lift him by the shoulders high enough that his head will be in frame. The scared driver tries to squirm out of my grasp, but I'm so much stronger than he is it's not even funny. He can't budge.

"Tell us your name and what your orders were," I demand.

I turn to Juanita. She translates for the driver.

When the driver doesn't comply, I will my hands to heat up so that they start warming his shoulders through his coat. He figures out what's happening and quickly starts speaking in a pleading tone, volunteering his name and other information. When he stops talking and starts whining again, I nod to Sento, who picks him up in his orangutan arms and hauls him off camera again.

"Is there more to your story?" I ask Juanita.

"*Sí*," she nods and turns to Rachel's phone to continue her tale. At one point I hear her utter "Firebird Alex" and "Stinger" with grateful tears in her eyes. I can't help but smile, even though I'm not sure what she's saying. After a few more sentences, she stops talking and turns to me.

"Thank you," she says.

"Of course," I smile.

I exhale slowly. Okay, time for my final words. I'm not a natural public speaker—truthfully, it was less than two years ago that I was a nearly silent goth girl who just wanted to hide. Here I am now, a public figure, a supernatural heroine, speaking to the world. I want to address the chief inspector's warning to me, but I'm not super confident what to say. Hopefully something is better than nothing.

"I know this is terrifying. Anyone can be in this cult. Right here, in fact, we have the chief inspector of Madrid's police force." I motion to Sento with my head and then point my head toward the chief inspector. Sento lifts his limp form off the ground. Rachel holds the phone up to Sento and the inspector, then nods. Sento drops the chief inspector back to the floor once Rachel points the phone back at me. I exhale and give myself a moment to think.

"Dismantling the Cult of the Watchers isn't gonna happen overnight, so please use your heads. If you see the police trying to maintain order, they probably are. We're going to call the policía and ambulances to take care of the injured here; their leader may be bad, but most people are still good and still want to help. But while the Nephilim are still running around, don't go out alone. Watch out for people who ask you to do things that don't feel right. Stay safe, and stay smart. Chaos will only make our job harder."

Okay, time to wrap this up. "We'll beat them. We can't bring back the people we've lost, but we can stop them, and we can make sure that this kind of thing can't happen again. If you see or hear anything, be sure to let us know on the Lady Firebird social network accounts. They're always monitored. Thank you."

I lower my head, and Rachel stops recording.

"That was great," Rachel says, swiping a few more times on the phone and then handing it to me. "Do you want to check it out?"

"Nah, it's still kinda weird seeing myself on video."

Rachel smirks and playfully shakes her head.

"I'm just going to send it on to Jake, then give him a call."

"Cool," Rachel says, then turns to Juanita. "Juanita, do you want to help me call some ambulances and the police? Don't worry, we're all gonna stay here until everyone is taken care of."

Juanita nods, and she and Rachel walk toward the cultists to see who's wounded. I step over the busted door and into the hallway so I can have a tiny bit of privacy.

Jacob Harman is my tech-guru-hacker-extraordinaire fiancé. We met not quite two years ago, when I was so distraught over the death of my mother that I was terrible company. He stuck it out while I came out of my shell, and we fell in love. He knows exactly who I am; he accepts my life as Firebird Alex and all my commitments and flaws. He asked me to marry him a few months ago when we were on a romantic getaway in Paris, and that may have been the happiest I've ever been in my life.

Jake not only accepts that I'm Lady Firebird, but he's learned to appreciate all the crazy spirit beings that are part of my Sedu family. And my brother Garz—perhaps the fiercest warrior in all of Sediin—accepts Jake, too, even though Jake's skinny as a stick and not a fighter. And right now, Jake's using all of his hacker brilliance to help us hunt Nephilim.

Mort Stygg, the billionaire defense contractor and Seduman son of Lord Stygg, put Jake to work at one of his security contracting offices in Washington, D.C. There, Jake has access to next generation secret spy technology. He's been trying to tune some satellite equipment and create sensors that can detect Nephilim movements based on their unique radiation signature. At least, that's how I think he explained it. I've gotten way better with understanding technology since being with Jake, but sometimes I still mix up what he tells me.

As I leave the room, Zaebos quickly follows.

"You're not going to let me out of your sight, are you?" I grin.

"Absolutely not."

I gently scratch the rust-colored fur on his neck as I rein in my Sedu self. I send the video we just made to Jake's phone, then tap the button to video chat, and a moment later I see Jake smiling back at me.

"Can you see me okay in the weird lighting, or do you need me to go Sedu?"

"You're great," Jake says. "I guided you guys to the right building?"

"Yeah. You should have seen it, all these Spanish people in suits totally freaking out as we appeared out of nowhere in the middle of the street and ran into this office building."

"I'll bet," Jake chuckles. "I got your video."

"Two of the people in it are speaking Spanish. Can you get a translator to add subtitles?"

"Too bad Godinez is in hiding." He curls his face.

"Yeah," I sigh. "Translation app?"

"I hate to rely on algorithms; their translations can end up so stilted. I should be able to find someone in the office who can speak Spanish," Jake says.

"That's good. You know...the chief inspector of the police was in there—"

"Seriously?" Jake shakes his head.

"I know, right? Anyway, he said some things that really...it got to me. Since the Cult of the Watcher is so integrated into the global economy, governments, police, all that, he told me that I'm risking creating global anarchy by bringing down the cult. On that video I say a few things at the end trying to keep the peace, but if you can come up with any ideas, too...."

"I will," Jake immediately gets it. "That's exactly what we don't want. I think that Mort can really help out here. He's not just tied into the ruling class, he's been around since the late 1800s, and that's a lot of experience."

"See, you've already come up with a great idea," I smile.

I hear commotion above me.

"Hey, I hear what I think are EMTs entering the building. I should really help sort things here."

"I'll clean up the video and get it subtitled, and then get it out. It's only two in the afternoon here in Washington, so there's still time for our media relations people to hand it to the news and other media today."

"Yeah, and send it to Wyatt and Raya, too," I add. "I'll call him next to let him know it's coming."

"Smart," Jake compliments me. "Wyatt can send it on to his firm's PR and media department, and they can help spread it."

"Yeah, and Raya can get it out to the shelters and her nonprofit network," I add.

When we bought the house we named "Firebird Manor"—a gorgeous beach house in Corona Del Mar, a very expensive seaside town in Orange County, California—we worried that we'd terrify the community and never fit in. Then two of our neighbors, Wyatt and Raya, surprised us by coming by to say hello and getting to know us. Wyatt is a surfer and associate lawyer, and his girlfriend Raya volunteers at local Orange County soup kitchens and homeless shelters and works as a pottery instructor. When the Nephilim burst into Firebird Manor, it was Wyatt who alerted the police.

"Oh, here's something else: we ran into another Rishon, named L'reek, who might be the offspring of H'ythiis and Goodson. When I'm done here, I'm going to talk to Kesed and see what he might know."

"Another Rishon? Goddammit," Jake sighs. "Yeah, if anyone knows about the Rishon, it would be Kesed the Greater Rishon, wouldn't it? After I send the video, I'm basically done here. How about I meet you at the House of

Keroz?"

"I would love that," I grin. "I'd really, really love that."

"Me too. I've even got something for Rachel."

"Really? What?"

"I got a package from Judaica Online. It was anonymous, but I know it's from Josh."

"Bat Mitzvah books?"

"Yup, the meaning of the ceremony, coming of age as a Jew, that type of thing." Jake confirms.

Jake sent Josh, his younger brother, away with their dad because the Nephilim knew about them and where they lived. Clearly Josh had been thinking a lot about Rachel while in hiding. All of us—me, Rachel, Jake, Josh—are Jewish. Rachel was supposed to have her Bat Mitzvah as soon as she turned thirteen, with her adoptive father, Rabbi Norman Hirsch, doing the service. But before she turned thirteen, her father was murdered, then she found out she was a Seduman, and now all this insanity has put her Bat Mitzvah on hold.

Judaism is really important to Josh—probably more central to him than the rest of us. And he's got a wild, mad crush on Rachel. He's cool with her being a Seduman warrior, but he's always trying to appeal to her human side. I'm sure the gift books are intended to do that. Making online purchases could be dangerous if it revealed their location, but luckily Jake schooled him on how to be anonymous and use prepaid cards.

"She'll snicker at them but secretly love them," I smirk.

"I'll bet you're right. See you soon. Love you, Alex."

"Love you, too." I disconnect the call.

I swipe until I get to Wyatt's contact info, then call the direct line to his office at Duncan & Goldfarb.

"Hello, this is Wyatt Bennett; can I help you?"

"This is Alex, and I think you can."

"Dude!" I can practically hear Wyatt's huge surfer grin over the phone. "Good to hear from you, m'lady! More baddies trampled under your boot?"

"Yup. And there's gonna be video coming your way from Jake."

"Oh yeah?" I hear his leather-backed chair squeak as I presume he sits up straighter. "What do you need? Distribution?"

"Exactly. We want to slingshot it to everyone we can. And not just to let people know we're on the job. It was brought to my attention that if I do this wrong, people will lose faith in institutions, and that will just make things more of a mess than they already are."

"I can see that," Wyatt agrees. "If you can keep people chill, it won't just keep them safer, it keeps them out of your way when you go after these guys. It would—okay, cool," Wyatt cuts himself off, as if he's having a discussion with himself. "I'll forward your video to our PR administrator and tell her to send the video along with a note that it's in our clients' interest that they keep on keepin' on, and not panic or do anything out of the ordinary. I'll ask her to send it to her media contacts as well."

"That would be perfect, Wyatt. Hell, I'd almost believe you're a lawyer." I crack.

"Aw, we can't have that, can we?" he laughs. "Anything else?"

"Can you get it to Raya, too?"

"You bet."

"Thanks," I sigh.

"My pleasure. You can always count on me to stand up. And hey, remember: I have faith in you. The world has faith in you. I know they hit you hard, and they're not done yet. But you got this, Firebird Alex. You got this."

5

"YOU KNOW I LOVE YOU," Rachel wheezes and doubles over on the floor of the portal room in the House of Keroz. "But you can suck it."

The movies make walking through magic portals look as easy as stepping out of the shower. Unfortunately for a Seduman, that's not how it works. Pushing through a portal between Earth and Sediin is more like slogging through a swimming pool filled with wet concrete. And when you come out the other side, it's a total shock to your system. Since Sediin is a universe made of spirit, there's nothing material here; everything that feels real, isn't. That means there's no atmosphere to breathe, atmospheric pressure to keep our bodies in shape—all the stuff we rely on without thinking about it. If a human off the street were to step through a portal they'd instantly disintegrate. Sedumen can survive because our spirits are partly from here, but our bodies have to get used to holding themselves together and having no air in them. The transition is really rough physically, with intense sweating, uncontrollable muscle spasms, and the horrible sensation of suffocating until our lungs get used to contracting and expanding without actually filling with anything. Thankfully, after a few minutes, we're okay. But those few minutes are total hell.

Well, it's hell for Rachel. When my House healed me from nearly being absorbed, I was left with the powers of a full Sedu. But unlike other Sedu, I wasn't an original spirit here from the time of Creation or born of two Sedim mating; I was created by the union of a human mother and Sedu father. So I'm a Sedu, but still kind of a Seduman. I dunno. It's weird. I'm the only being like me in either universe.

But it does mean that like a full Sedu, traveling through portals isn't quite as tough on me anymore. I still feel all my muscles tense up and that unsettling feeling of having nothing to breathe in my lungs. But I can keep on my feet and push through it. Still, I've only had the powers of a full Sedu for a month or so, and I remember the full shock and trauma Rachel feels like it was yesterday.

"If I could make you a full Sedu too, I would."

"Good answer," Rachel pants, curled on the ground. She reaches up her hand to me, and I pull her up and out of the way of our large portal mirror so that we're not blocking the way for our Mazzikim as they return through the portal.

"My mistress?" A two-foot-tall Ruhin—the smallest and least powerful spirit beings on Sediin—who looks like a cross between a raccoon and a monkey stands in front of Rachel with an open bottle of spring water in his hand. There is no food or water on Sediin, but for us, they keep a ton of water and non-perishable food that they bring from Earth. We've found that a few sips of water helps us recover faster, so the Ruhin always try to have some bottles in the portal room when we arrive. And my brother always has two Ruhin stationed in the portal chamber round the clock for whenever we decide to return.

Rachel looks up and tries to smile, but her expression ends up like more of a constipated grimace. She reaches a trembling hand to the bottle and uses both hands to bring the bottle to her lips and take a sip.

"My lady?" Another Ruhin, this one looking like a bipedal ferret with a lizard head, hands me a bottle.

"Thank you." I tip my head as I take a sip.

"I shall fetch the Sedim." The ferret-lizard Ruhin bows low and runs out of the room shouting "Lady Firebird and Stinger have returned!" somewhat frantically. I can't help but chortle a bit.

"How was your raid, my sister?" Garz asks as he walks into the portal chamber with Vetis.

The two brothers make quite an amusing pair. As it happens, Vetis is a good thousand Earth years younger than Garz, but the height difference alone is enough to make Vetis look like his "little" brother. My red, extremely muscular half-brother Garz stands around eight feet tall and has huge, sharp horns and teeth, burning red eyes, and a humanoid shape with somewhat reptilian features. We share the same fire-based powers of igniting things with our hands, burning eyes, and breathing fire. Vetis, on the other hand is originally from the House of Es, a House of insect-based Sedu. He's got gray-green insectoid skin, four praying mantis–like arms ending in claws (although one claw was severed, and has been replaced by a silver prosthetic claw), a dragonfly-like head with huge eyes, and a small, lipless mouth. He can leap like a grasshopper and spit acid stingers. And Vetis is no taller than me, at around five-foot-nine.

Garz and Vetis used to look a bit more similar. Both Garz and Vetis have this in common—they were not among the initial Sedu spirits. Each was born from the mating of a male and female Sedu. I'm sure that's why Vetis is tiny for a Sedu. And Garz used to only be about seven feet tall, with stubby little horns. When our father, Keroz, sacrificed his own life to save mine, that left Garz as the head of the House; the spirit of the House filled him and he grew a foot taller, and his horns grew long and sharp.

Trotting along next to Vetis is Zogo, our loyal servant and the only other being left alive from Vetis's original House. Zogo is a Ruhin, but he's taller than most Ruhin at about three feet. He looks almost exactly like a humanoid, bipedal turtle without a shell. Sediin is a world in which most beings are afraid to show affection for fear that others might see it as weakness, but Zogo very obviously loves us all. He dotes over Rachel and me whenever we're around, and can be downright bossy to the other Ruhin if he feels like they're not paying us what he considers our due deference.

"Hi, everyone," I greet them. "It went pretty much as well as could be. We rescued a human woman and didn't loose any Mazzikim."

"And of the Nephilim?" my brother prods.

"We got 'em all," Rachel pants out, clearly feeling more like herself. Her father and Zogo walk over to her.

"Excellent," Garz offers with the tone of a proud uncle.

"We did see another Rishon, unfortunately. A new one. L'reek, they called him," I say.

"Another Rishon?" Garz narrows his eyes.

"Yeah." Rachel grimaces.

"But a scrawny one," I add. Garz and Vetis look at us with puzzled expressions.

"As scrawny as me?" Zogo asks.

Rachel laughs. "You're not scrawny! You're huge for a Ruhin!"

Zogo stands up a bit straighter, a smile of pride across his short beak.

"Here's what I mean," I begin, and explain the entire raid to Garz, including dealing with the rescue personnel and police before we left.

"Now I want to talk to Kesed about L'reek, see what he can tell me," I finish my retelling of events.

"A solid plan." Garz nods.

"Do you know if he's here?"

"Kesed and Zedek both are here," Garz says. "I'm sure Kesed will be pleased to be useful to you. You know how guilty he feels about his part in this."

I nod. Kesed was the Greater Rishon of Mercy. That means that he's larger than the Rishonim—about twenty feet tall to their twelve or so feet tall—and it was his task to watch over the Rishonim and make sure that with all their great strength and vast spirits—way vaster than Sedu—they were merciful. For a while, he did. But when The Firstlands fell apart Kesed suffered too, and his guilt and shame and loneliness resulted in his fusing to his throne in his ginormous palace as the Rishonim died.

At that point, he stopped watching over the Rishonim. He had no idea that a couple managed to escape destruction through a portal to Earth. He blames himself that they've been free to absorb living beings on Earth without mercy for millions of years. We've all insisted it wasn't his fault, but Kesed still beats himself up for it. I know how that goes—I beat myself up for absolutely everything. I love my life right now, I feel useful and loved, I've found an amazing family and friends, but I still worry that I'm going to do something stupid and ruin it.

"Would you like some food before you consult with Kesed, my lady?" Zogo asks. "A full meal? A snack? A nibble?"

"I'm going to go straight to Kesed, but you gave me a great idea. Jake is going to return to the House of Keroz as soon as he's finished in Mort's office, which shouldn't be long. Could you ask the kitchen Ruhin to assemble a spread of snacks for us—cheeses, crackers, fruits, nuts, chips—along with some water?"

"Of course, my lady!" Zogo beams, clearly happy to be of service. "I'll have the dining area—"

"Actually, we'll eat our snack in my chamber."

"Oh?" Zogo seems confused.

Rachel shoots me a wry grin and shakes her head.

Zogo looks quizzically at Rachel.

"Ohhhh!" His eyes go wide as he gets it. "Of course, my lady!"

"Thank you, Zogo."

Zogo bows to us, then runs out of the portal chamber, already shouting orders even though he's nowhere near the kitchen and they'll never hear him. We all chuckle.

"My lady." Zaebos lowers his head as he comes through the portal mirror with a few Mazzikim. "All the Nephilim have been burned. The rest of the Mazzikim will be following in a moment."

"Excellent." Garz bows his head to Zaebos.

"Zaebos, why don't you relax with Daeba and your puppies?" I caress his back. "I'm going to talk to Kesed, then spend some time with Jake."

"Thank you," Zaebos says. "But please, my lady—"

"I won't leave the House without you, I promise." I chuckle.

"I want to train some more," Rachel says. She turns to her dad. "Are you up for returning to the House of Stygg?"

"Of course," Vetis puts his two right arms around his daughter. "Let us gather Qwyll and a few Mazzikim and we'll be off."

Qwyll has the body of a five-foot-tall albatross, the legs and arms of a chimpanzee, and the head of a mountain lion, all covered in beautiful white fur. As one of our bravest flying Mazzikim, he has taken it upon himself to be Rachel's "in air" trainer for when she jumps, because she can get airborne up to twenty feet or so. Qwyll has also become her dear friend, the way that Zaebos is a dear friend of mine. He accompanies her not only because he wants to be part of her training, but because, like Zaebos, he doesn't want to let her out of his sight. If anything ever happens, he wants to be right there to protect her.

"When you're done, Jake says he has a package for you."

"For me? From who?"

"Who do you think?" I playfully shove my shoulder into hers.

"Well...yeah, I mean...okay." Rachel starts blushing.

"Anyway, you have fun with Jake." Rachel smirks at me as she and her father leave the portal chamber together.

I shake my head and Garz and I follow them out.

6

"KESED? ZEDEK? MAY I COME IN?" I shout as I bang on the thirty-foot tall, thick brown door.

"Please, dear one!" Kesed says. "Join us!"

I shove open the extremely heavy door to the massive chamber.

Unlike the Sedim, the Greater Sedim have no Houses of their own. At first, the only Greater Sedu was Zedek, the Greater Sedu of Righteousness. He has a form like a twenty-foot-long purple-skinned bearded dragon.

He used to just fly around The Nothingness, going from Sedu House to Sedu House to try and enforce righteousness among the Sedu. When my father was alive, he opened our House to Zedek, whenever he wanted a place to stay put. When Kesed, the twenty-foot-tall, purple skinned humanoid with three-fingered hands, three eyes, and delicate, feminine features, finally broke free of his decaying palace in The Firstlands, he came here and met up with Zedek, who had been his soulmate, the love of his life, long before either had manifested bodies.

Recently a third Greater Sedu has sprung into being: Kenuut was created with the memories of our father, who despite his brutality, was the most honest Sedu in all of Sediin. As Greater Sedu of Honesty, Kenuut enforces honesty among the Sedim and acts as our liaison to Merkaba, the realm of blessed spirits, where souls that were kind and decent in life congregate and enrich each other.

Garz, aware that these three Greater Sedim had no residences of their own, offered them a home in the House of Keroz—and not just because Kenuut reminded us of our father. Garz sees the House of Keroz being the center of Sediin—the Palace of Glory. He knows that I have dedicated myself to trying to be the best person I can be, and that has inspired him to remake our House with that end. He has the ability to draw from the spirit of the House and reform the grounds into anything he desires, so he created a huge palatial wing large enough for cavernous rooms for Kesed and Zedek to share, and one for Kenuut.

Kesed and Zedek's chamber is decorated sparsely. Kesed's remaining aquamarine runestones from the ruins of his palace adorn the walls. A giant couch fills the middle of the room. On it, Kesed lounges with his back against the red velvety armrest and his purple, twenty-foot-long frame draped across, while Zedek's twenty-foot-long reptilian body curls around Kesed. Kesed's arms embrace Zedek's two upper limbs and wings, and Zedek rests his head on Kesed's chest. I'm used to seeing Kesed either manic or miserable. Seeing his soft, feminine face looking so serene, his two aquamarine eyes looking happy and his third eye softly glowing red, is nice. Better than nice.

And I feel like a dolt for walking in on them.

"Hey, if you two—"

"Sit with us," Kesed removes one of his arms from Zedek's wing to wave me toward the couch. Zedek smiles at me and uncoils himself from around Kesed. He lowers himself to the floor and sits in front of the couch.

"Hi, Zedek," I begin. "I'm sorry for interrupting your private time. I didn't know—"

"Nonsense, dear one," Zedek brushes off my concerns. "We have eternity to enjoy each other's embrace. You need to talk with Kesed now. We both welcome you."

"Thanks." I exhale, more than a little relieved.

Zedek wraps one of his front claws around me and lifts me onto the huge couch, for which I'm thankful; the seat is over my head and without Zedek's assistance I'd have to climb up to sit with Kesed. Zedek deposits me next to Kesed, then curls himself on a very large plush red cushion near the side of the chamber.

"So how goes your mission?" Kesed asks as he hugs me. "Tell me! Tell me! Tell me!"

"We busted up a meeting of the Cult of the Watcher and freed their prisoner, Juanita."

"Great job!" Kesed gently squeezes.

"Thanks! We saved her from...a runty Rishon, we think it was..."

"A 'runty' Rishon?" Kesed giggles like a little girl conspiring with me to do something slightly naughty. But mid-giggle, he suddenly stops, goes quiet and wide-eyed. "There—there is *another* Rishon?" he stammers.

When The Firstlands crumbled, Kesed fused to his throne, unable to move, for billions of Earth years. I can't imagine what that long unable to move or to do anything other than think would do to a mind. When we discovered Kesed nearly an Earth year ago, he was pretty much stark-raving mad. But Zedek loved him as much then as he did at the beginning of time, and together they've worked on calming his thoughts, making him sane again. He's way more stable than he was when we found him. But his lightning mood shifts can be pretty unsettling if you're not expecting them.

"We're almost certain." I nod and tell him about the entire event.

Kesed and Zedek both listen silently, grimly.

"So I think he's a Rishon named L'reek," I conclude.

Kesed sighs and closes his two lower eyes.

"I do enjoy 'runty Rishon,' though." Kesed opens his eyes and giggles.

Then just as quickly, his face reverts to his solemn expression. "But I fear you are right. There is another...but this one, I would not have known."

"Why?"

"Because I believe that L'reek is the offspring of H'ythiis and her Rishon mate, born on Earth."

"Do you think he's a runt because he was born on Earth?"

"No. He's a runt because the Rishonim didn't know any better."

"Um...I have no idea what you mean by that," I shrug.

"Have you ever wondered," Zedek joins in the conversation, "why even though the Sedim have such powerful, idealized forms, their offspring tend to be...lesser?"

"Yeah." I nod. "I have. And Mort told us how Lord Stygg's Sedu wife Bleega was infertile. If the Sedu manifested their own bodies, why wouldn't she manifest a working reproductive system?"

"That's just it." Zedek points a claw at me to emphasize his point. "When a Sedu manifests a form, that Sedu must imagine into being every aspect of their form, not just their external appearance, but what internal systems they would have as well. So if they imagined a reproductive system incompletely or couldn't imagine one at all—"

"They couldn't reproduce. That makes sense."

"The Sedim had chosen to manifest bodies after they had come in contact with human spirits already," Zedek continues. "So they knew about sex and pregnancy and birth. But they didn't necessarily understand about the minutiae that goes into the reproductive cycle. So nearly all Sedim were able to create some sort of reproductive ability in themselves, but it wasn't perfect. And some did not even try, or tried and failed."

I nod.

"H'ythiis and her mate escaped to Earth long before the days of mammals," Kesed continues. "I don't know when they decided to manifest gender and reproductive systems, but I'm guessing neither really knew what they were doing, and so the result is a 'runty Rishon.' And that Rishon was probably closer to an Earth being than a Rishon from The Firstlands, and could reproduce with human women to create the Nephilim."

"But if L'reek is the father of all the Nephilim, how can there be so many? I mean, we've faced hundreds of them when we fought them at their stronghold on Hannity Hill in Tanzania. Do you think one Rishon..."

"His life, like his parents, is sustained by living spirits," Zedek says. "This would make his life long. And that's a lot of years—"

"To rape hordes of women," I huff as I lower my head.

"Perhaps, but not necessarily."

"You think women volunteered to have L'reek's babies?"

"They are worshiped, yes?" Kesed intones softly, knowing that I don't want to hear what he's suggesting. "Wouldn't carrying the offspring of your god be a great honor?"

I'm about to protest when I remember something that the Nephilim prisoner I interrogated in Poland said to me. That Nephilim was trying to get under my skin and told me that his mother had a far better death than my mother did. Maybe that's what he meant, that his mother knew what she was getting into and willingly submitted to L'reek. My mom had no idea Keroz was a Sedu because my dad had assumed human form and called himself Keith.

"It's still squicky." I curl my mouth in disgust. "Okay, so all that makes sense, but how can the dead—well, the not alive, I guess—create life?"

Now it's Kesed's and Zedek's turn to look at me with puzzled expressions.

"You know I can sense living things, right? Well, those Rishon are completely empty; I sense nothing, like they're not even there. And the Nephilim only feel half alive to me, like a dying creature."

"Even the life that L'reek creates is death." Kesed lowers his head in shame.

Great. Now I've just gone and made a Greater Rishon miserable. That was so not my intention. See what I mean by screwing everything up?

"Hey, Kesed." I rub his arm compassionately. "None of this is your fault. You know that. I'll find them, and we'll stop them together."

"Yes, we will." Kesed offers a faint, melancholy smile.

"But finding them can wait a little while." Kesed leans in conspiratorially as his third eye starts to glow bright red. "Jake has just arrived."

7

I push open the heavy door to my chamber on the second floor of our House. All the doors are like this—a Sedu can create rooms and the facsimile of objects, but not machines or anything with complex internal moving parts. So no doors have spring-operated locks. Most are just really heavy so that they stay closed, while others like the main gate have latches.

"Fancy!" I smile.

"Isn't it?" Jake agrees, sitting at the small round table currently overflowing with the snacks that Zogo and the kitchen Ruhin brought for us.

My room is significantly smaller than the huge palatial space that Kesed and Zedek share, but it's still the size of a gigantic living room. My four-poster, queen-sized bed is in the middle of the room, and next to it a large silken rope descends from the high ceiling. The rope connects to a bell hanging in the hallway so I can call for Zogo or another Ruhin.

I walk over to the opposite wall, which features my dresser, clothes racks, a full-length mirror, and the door to Rachel's adjoining room. I see Jake placed the Judaica Online box Josh sent Rachel on top of my dresser. I strip out of my heavy Team Firebird coat so that I'm just in my black leggings, long-sleeved black cotton shirt, and boots. "I'll be with you in a sec. Gotta pee first."

"Take your time."

Behind my bed is a doorway covered by rows of horizontal beads instead of a heavy door. I push aside the beads and step into my bathroom, such as it is. It's got a metal-like toilet that is pretty much just a seat over a hole. The Sedim have brought gallons and gallons of water from Earth and make sure we always have a few buckets of water in our bathrooms. I miss running water; in Sediin "flushing" consists of dumping water into the toilet ourselves so that the contents of the toilet are washed through a pipe and out of an opening in the side of the House. It's not awesome.

In addition to the toilet and water buckets, the bathroom includes a standing iron bathtub, a basin to pour water into, towels, and a mirror. After I'm finished I pour some water into the water basin to wash my hands, then head over to the table.

"It's the water poured into wine glasses that really makes the spread," Jake quips as he holds up his glass to me.

"Aw, Zogo tries," I laugh. "When I told him I wanted to meet you here privately, he got all excited."

And boy, Zogo went all out. We've got dried fruit; crackers; bread; hard, aged cheeses; and some dry salamis all sliced and organized into pretty swirls on large wood planks.

"He's pretty awesome." Jake smiles.

"You're pretty awesome..." I bend down and give Jake a long, deep kiss, letting the softness of his lips and the taste of his breath wash over me.

I plop down into the chair next to Jake, pick up the other glass of water, clink it against his, then empty the whole glass.

"Thirsty?" Jake smiles as he takes my glass and refills it from the large pitcher that Zogo placed next to the snacks.

"Oh yeah," I chuckle. "Thanks, love. It's just great to relax for a moment, after..."

"Wanna tell me about it?" Jake takes another sip from his glass.

"I do, but I know talking about it will get me all upset again," I sigh.

"I can imagine." Jake nods. "No rush. Time is so fast in Sediin that we can sit here for an hour and it will be just over a minute on Earth. Just kick back, take a load off, and we'll talk whenever you're ready. We have time."

I smile and look deep into Jake's ocean blue eyes. He returns with one of those ear-to-ear grins that lights up not just his face, but the whole room. The way he's sitting now, the spark in his eyes, the confident and loving curve of his smile...

"You know what I'm ready for?"

I slide off my chair and onto his lap. He lets go of his water glass and puts both of his hands around my back. He's tall enough that I barely need to bend my head down to lock my lips to his. He opens his mouth enough for our tongues to entwine. He tightens his grip around me.

I reach under his T-shirt as he wraps his lips around my neck. "We have time..." I whisper as my hands gently caress his nipples...

"Okay, now I really *am* hungry," I exhale, smiling and sweaty. I roll over until I'm on top of Jake again and kiss him hard enough to shove his head back down onto the pillow. "But I also feel like we should probably talk about what happened in Madrid."

"Yeah," Jake breathes, kissing me again. "Would you like me to bring a snack to you in bed?"

"Mmmm, that sounds great, but I should probably get up and get dressed if we're going to talk about this stuff."

"Why?"

"I dunno, it's silly. I feel sort of exposed talking about our enemies when I'm naked. Stupid, I know."

"Nah, I get it. They've hurt us, and it gets under our skin. Just don't make me wear a tie or anything."

"Oooh!" I playfully slap his shoulder. "Just for that..."

All Sedim have the ability to shape the spirit of their own House into the appearance of material things. Garz, as the head of the House, can rearrange the entire House of Keroz. But Vetis and I can create smaller objects. I sit up and focus on an image in my mind of a tie. I concentrate on the color and width of the tie, the material it's made out of, the pattern of the stitching, everything. In a moment, the spirit of the House swirls around me, and a thin black silk tie with a slight embossed striped pattern appears on the covers between Jake and me.

"So can I wear just the tie—and nothing else?" Jake smirks.

"As cute as you'd be like that, you don't have to wear it." I lean over and give him a peck on the lips.

We get out of bed, put on our clothes, and return to the table. I pick up his chair, which I'd knocked over in my passion. I feed him some grapes as he puts together a small cheese and salami sandwich and hands it to me.

After I down the sandwich, a few more pieces of dried fruit and crackers, and nearly an entire pitcher of water, I start talking about the raid on the cult meeting in Madrid in more detail than I had before. Especially the words of the police chief.

"I know what you said on the phone, but I'm still worried that by saving people from getting murdered by the Rishonim, I'm going to cause a global catastrophe," I finish.

"You're not." Jake shakes his head. "People are more resilient than that. Governments go through crises of confidence, have corrupt governments, and manage. Seriously, think of how many shit leaders have run countries, been protested, all that. It's not like every time a city's police chief is fired or a president sucks or gets toppled, the entire country falls apart."

"Yeah, but do you think there's been anything as global as exposing and hunting the Nephilim before?"

"Probably not," Jake admits. "But don't forget all the billionaires like Mort Stygg who don't want global chaos, because then they might lose their holdings. They'll be propping things up."

"That's true, unless some of them are in the cult too."

"I asked Mort about that. He doesn't think so—people at that level are so obsessed with power, they refuse to give any up, so they're not easy prey for the promises of the Nephilim. There's no room in most of their hearts to worship anything but themselves."

"That makes sense." I nod. "Thanks for the pep talk."

"I mean every word. Keep telling people to stay alert and calm. You just worry about cleaning up the system. Let the system worry about regaining the people's trust."

"Will do," I smile. "So next I—"

"My lady?" Zogo bangs on the door. "Are you two...may I..."

"Thank you for knocking first. Come on in, Zogo. The food was perfect, by the way," I add as we both turn our chairs toward the door.

"I'm so glad, my lady," Zogo says, but without his usual bounce. "Mort Stygg has returned from the House of Stygg with Mistress Stinger's party. Their expressions are...not joyful..."

8

JAKE AND I hurry downstairs to the main doors of the House of Keroz, where Rachel, Vetis, Qwyll, Mort, and some of his Mazzikim all stand around talking. Pyza and few of our Mazzikim accompany Garz.

It's great to see Pyza there, and with Garz. Pyza is the last remaining of the original female Sedim. There were never many—most Sedim chose to manifest male bodies. She's thousands of years old and was friends with Garz's late mother, Ryka. To hear Pyza tell it, Keroz had his choice of either Ryka or Pyza—and Pyza was the more beautiful Sedu—but Keroz went with Ryka, who was more selfless and kind.

Once all the other females were murdered, Zedek helped Pyza escape to Earth; she only returned to Sediin to help us when Earth was threatened. She wasn't sure she wanted to stay and has always been hesitant to get too involved in House affairs. But Garz and Pyza have clearly become closer, and Pyza hasn't left yet. I think it's adorable. They make a cute couple—like Garz, Pyza has red skin and red eyes. Hers aren't flaming like Garz's eyes though. Pyza also has gorgeous long brown hair. Pyza's older than Garz, but hey, what's a thousand-year age difference when you're both over two thousand?

As soon as Rachel sees me, she gives me a tight-lipped, pensive smile— enough to let me know she's happy to see me, but that all is not well.

"Hi, Uncle Mort." I offer a slightly wider smile than is probably justified, to try to lift the mood. That's also why I call him "uncle." He's not related on either his human or his Sedu side, but he's been so good to Rachel and Jake and me, he's like an honorary uncle.

"Always a pleasure," he says with almost the identical smile to Rachel.

"How was training?" I ask Rachel.

"I'm getting better." She reaches into her backpack and pulls out her golden double crossbow and holds it up to her face. "Today Lord Stygg has been teaching me to aim while jumping. I'm still no good—"

"She's being modest," Vetis jumps in. "She hit the target over half the time."

"Yeah, but when I'm on the ground I hardly ever miss," she counters.

"Hey, one outta two when you first pick up a new skill is pretty awesome," Jake adds. "I'm really impressed."

"Aw, thanks Jake. I'm really impressed with your tie." Rachel tries to suppress a grin.

"It's an inside joke," Jake chuckles, tugging on the black tie that hangs loosely over a light gray button-down shirt I created for him before we left.

The idea of wearing the tie amused him, so I made the shirt to go with it. He left the top button open, loosely put the tie on, then tucked the shirt into his blue jeans. He looks kinda silly, but kinda hip too. Which is funny, because my dork fiancé is not a hip person, but neither am I, so it works out.

"Uh huh..." Rachel smirks with that I-don't-know-what-you-mean-but-I-bet-it's-sexual tone of voice. She looks at me and raises her eyebrows.

"By the way, Josh anonymously sent me some Bat Mitzvah books for you," Jake says.

"Oh?" For the first time, Rachel's mood seems to lift—and then drops again. "That's really cool. Thank Josh for me, if you can reach him. I just don't know when..."

"Is it that bad?" I turn to Mort.

"I hate to be the bearer of serious news," Mort begins. "But as I told Rachel and Vetis at my father's House, G'suul has released a video to the world, and it is addressed to you."

"G'suul?" I exclaim, because nobody can restate the obvious like I can.

"Would that be Adam Goodson's Rishon name?" Jake asks, because he's way quicker on picking up these things than I am.

"I'm certain of it," Mort says, his face tight. "You should see it firsthand," he insists. "In my office."

"Okay. Let me just get Zaebos. I don't know if he'd forgive me if I didn't bring him."

"It would take time, but I probably would, my lady," Zaebos says, walking up to us from behind with my honor guard and Leeik. Leeik has the head and body of a huge, muscular gorilla with brown fur and lizard-like arms and legs. He is one of the very strongest Mazzik warriors we have.

"Come." Garz holds out his arm toward the portal chamber.

9

I shove my way through our portal mirror and come out of a portal mirror in a big, spare office. A large window overlooks downtown Washington, D.C., and the wall perpendicular to the mirror is filled with dozens of monitors, each showing something different—some code, some news, some views from security cameras. As each of us shoves our way into the office, we spread out so we're not crowding the mirror. After Mort has recovered, he walks over to his desk.

"I'll put the video on the center screen," Mort says.

We all nod.

After a couple of swipes across a tablet on Mort's desk, the center screen fills with a frightening image. A huge head and shoulders of what is clearly a Rishon fills the center of the video. Gray-green and shaped like an up-side-down pear, it has no nose or nostrils; a dozen red, glowing eyes on each side of its head; and what looks like a score of short, thin tentacles on the front of its face, covering what I assume is a terrifying mouth filled with razor-sharp teeth. Immediately behind and to the left of him is L'reek. And behind the both of them is a wall of Nephilim, all in black trench coats, ski masks, and huge, steampunky goggles. It's like a Nazi rally of monsters.

"Humans, I am G'suul," the Rishon head in the center snarls. His two dozen eyes all glare menacingly into the camera. His mouth tentacles sway and shift with his words, exposing some of his short-but-sharp teeth.

"This is my offspring, L'reek. We are the Watchers who have kept watch over humanity these long centuries. We have been the glue that has kept your societies together, kept you housed and fed. In return, your numbers have fed us."

"Firebird Alex and her band of criminals—"

"Go to hell!" Rachel shouts at the screen. I can't help but snicker.

"Have sought to bring down the webs we have woven to keep your society together over the centuries. They do this for their own ego. Humans, they do not care about you."

"Oh, and you do?" Rachel spits.

"They have taken my wife to their universe for the express purpose of torturing her. This is their true reason for opposing us. Torture is their only true joy."

I swallow nervously. Of course the stuff about me or Team Firebird enjoying torture is bullshit. But we did capture H'ythiis and hand her over to Lord Stygg, who wanted revenge for H'ythiis's murder of his wife. I've never asked how Lord Stygg was treating H'ythiis, but I knew. Sedim have been torturing prisoners for millennia. Including my own House. My own father wasn't just brutal, he was known as the Butcher of Sediin. I feel it even in myself—when a Nephilim blew Rachel's chest open with VATS goo that nearly killed her, I wanted to make him suffer in horrible ways.

I want Sediin to be better. *I* want to be better. It's slow going, but it's working. That doesn't change the fact that Lord Stygg wants revenge, and I pretty much know he's not being gentle about it. G'suul is trying to make us look like we're villains, sure, but there's just enough truth to make that one sting.

"Your reign of terror ends now."

"*Our* reign of terror?" Rachel's huge eyes widen with indignation.

"You will return H'ythiis, and then you and all of your House, as well as the Houses of all your allies, will surrender to us."

"I will enjoy tearing each one of his eyes out of his head," Garz seethes.

"As long as you live, we shall unmake the very society that we helped build, demolish entire regions, in order to feed ourselves with enough souls to enter your universe and take what is rightfully ours. Remember, Firebird, every human death, every one, is on your head."

Rachel's, Jake's, and my jaws all drop.

"Look upon me...and despair," G'suul says, and then the video ends.

"Well, that's pretty shitty," I frown.

"Of course, you know that whatever devastation he and his Nephilim cause is not your fault," Mort says.

"But—"

"There's no 'but,' Alex," Rachel cuts me off. "They've been killing people forever. They'll keep killing people forever. We're stopping them. We're the good guys."

"But he just threatened to kill lots of people," I point out. "Before they just killed one or two at a time. So if they do that, the change is my fault."

"Of course it's not," Vetis shakes his head. "He is the one deciding to kill, not you. They are murderers, Alex. They could have committed mass killings in the past, and we'd never know. They could make the decision to mass murder humans in the future as well, for any reason, whether we had discovered them or not. The fact that at this moment he's trying to pin this on you doesn't make it your doing."

Please listen to them, Garz thinks to me. Sedim can send thoughts to other Sedim in their family, so Garz and I and Vetis can communicate silently if we want to. *I know that your nature is to blame yourself for everything. You are not a murderer, no matter what they do. You are simply in their way.*

I turn to Garz and offer him a tight half-smile. I know he's right, I just can't feel good about it with so many potential victims on the line.

"Remember," Jake adds. "Disguised as Adam Goodson, G'suul read your report. He knows how to push your buttons. He's the kind of asshole who doesn't care who or what he destroys just to get under your skin."

"Agreed," Garz says, "G'suul knows that there's no way so many Houses in Sediin would all agree to surrender to certain death in order to preserve human life. G'suul simply mentioned it so that the more desperate the humans become, the more they'll blame you."

"Besides," Mort joins in, "we know they surprise regions by pouring out of tunnels under the ground; it will take them so long to dig tunnels under a town or village we'll have found and destroyed them by then."

"But what if they already have the tunnels?" I say. "The Rishon have been around Earth for, what, millions or billions of years? The Nephilim probably hundreds or thousands. That's a lot of time to tunnel."

Mort is about to counter when I turn to Jake.

"Speaking of time, how old is this video?" I ask.

"Well, YouTube says that it was uploaded a couple hours ago," Jake points at the screen.

"No, I mean when was it created?" I ask again.

"Let's check the time stamp in the video metadata," Jake says to Mort.

Mort nods and swipes around on his tablet as Jake looks over his shoulder.

"Oh God..." Mort and Jake both say, their eyes wide.

10

"MONDAY," Jake frowns.

"This is from yesterday?" I nearly hyperventilate. *Of course* they only posted this now. They want to make a big splash with whatever they're going to do. "They've been on the move all this time, I'm sure of it! We've got to figure out where—"

"Alex..." Mort nearly whispers and points to the screen at the top left of his wall.

The handheld mobile video of people running is extremely shaky, like the person holding the phone is panicking. The people are all dark-skinned with wavy black hair, like they're from the Near East somewhere, but the area looks completely unfamiliar to me. The script on one of the walls I see in the background looks Eastern or Asian, but it's not one I know—I can read Hebrew thanks to years of going to Hebrew school and having a Bat Mitzvah, and I know what Arabic looks like, but not that writing. Mort turns up the volume, but I can't understand what they're saying.

Then the pavement and asphalt evaporates beneath their feet and they fall into a pit. A man in a trench coat with a ski mask and huge goggles grabs the camera and the image goes black.

Mort swipes around some more and replaces the central screen feed with an English language news feed that says "Live from India" across the bottom.

"More reports from Kota in Southeast Rajasthan," a blond reporter with a British accent says. "As the ground falls away, the villagers fall with it. Those who try to throw ropes or help them out are being pulled in themselves."

"Some have said that they have seen the Nephilim—the creatures that Lady Firebird first exposed in London and then fought in Tanzania—pulling in and carrying off people," her male co-anchor, also British-sounding, adds.

"Other reports are the Nephilim are simply shooting—"

"We have another amateur video," the man interrupts his co-anchor. "Apparently showing one of those Watchers. Let's see if we can load it..."

First in a small corner of the feed, then taking over the whole screen, is a very distant video of what clearly looks like a very large leathery-winged beast flying around, picking people up and ripping them apart.

In the same video, just as distant, another larger leathery winged creature picks up a person and holds it up to its face. This person isn't ripped or dropped. The person seems to flail desperately and disappear, only clothes remaining.

"It's not clear what is happening..." the female anchor says.

But it is to me.

I feel sick to my stomach.

I lower my head.

"The Indian army has reported shooting a few of the Nephilim, but they say that the creatures have already left the area."

I raise my eyes as the video changes to a soldier's shoulder cam. It shows the body of a fallen Nephilim, its acid blood eating away at the grass.

"This seems to be the first of the promised reprisals against humanity for Lady Fireb—"

The feed dies. We all turn to Mort.

"I think we've heard enough," he says softly.

Garz and Vetis nod.

"Oh God... Those poor people... So many people..." I rock back and forth as both Jake and Rachel walk over and each holds one of my hands.

"This has to have left a massive chemical or radiation signature," Jake says, his voice clearly broken up.

"I'll get on it. Right now." Mort grabs his tablet from his desk. "Excuse me."

"See," Jake says as he squeezes my hand. "We're not going to let them get away with this."

I feel my phone vibrate in my pocket.

I pull it out and see that its Raya.

"Hi—"

"They're here!" she shrieks. "They're massacring everyone! Your creatures—there's not enough! Wyatt! Wyatt! Oh God, hurry! Wyatt! *No! Wyatt!*"

"We're coming!" I scream as I turn around and dive into the portal mirror.

11

WE ALL PORTAL BACK to the House of Keroz. Time moves much faster in Sediin than Earth; an hour in Sediin is only a minute on Earth, so we take the time time to don our combat gear and prepare for battle. Though we lose a couple of Earth minutes, it's worth it to be able to charge right in, ready for anything.

At least we have an idea of what's happening. A dozen armored Mazzikim are stationed at all times around Firebird Manor. As soon as the Nephilim came out of the sea, one of our Mazzikim jumped into the Firebird Manor portal mirror to alert the House of Keroz as to what was happening. Another dozen Mazzikim grabbed the remaining armor Garz kept around and returned to Earth to try and save the humans on the beach and repel the invaders.

Once Rachel, Jake, Zaebos, and I are dressed head to toe in Team Firebird uniforms, we shove our way through the portal along with another dozen Mazzikim wearing new armor Garz created while we were getting ourselves ready. Garz stays behind to create more armor for Mazzikim and send them through. If we're going to face an army, Garz wants us to have an army of our own.

I'm the first to step out into the remains. We're too late. The support beams and remaining walls of Firebird Manor have been completely blasted to rubble. Even the perimeter walls barely stand.

Just as I can sense living beings around me, so can I sense those spirit beings connected to my House. I close my eyes and reach out, trying to feel all the spirits tied to the House of Keroz. I shudder. I feel only Rachel, Zaebos, and the Mazzikim who came with me. None of those who were already here.

Sedim, Mazzikim, and Ruhin are normally eternal. Death in Sediin isn't permanent for a spirit being. A spirit being "dying" in Sediin means that the physical body the spirit manifested dies, and the spirit returns to its House of origin. There it can re-form a new body. That's one of the reasons they kill each other so regularly in Sediin. It usually just means they re-form even more pissed off.

But that's only if they die in Sediin; a spirit being that is killed in our material universe is truly destroyed, lost forever. All those Mazzikim that died fighting the Nephilim gave up eternity out of loyalty and love for me.

I inhale deeply as guilt, sadness, and rage fight to overwhelm me. The plaster and splintered wood all around us makes it hard to walk, but Jake cautiously finds a path over to me and puts his arm around my shoulders. He's clearly as downcast as I am. This was his home as much as mine. We've lived here together since he asked me to marry him. We both loved Kesed's Greater Mazzik servant, Galdyr, who died saving our lives in this house. He loved Zaebos's puppy, Zaev, and he loved our Rottweiler, Jesse. And it was here that I discovered I had a relationship with the life force of all living things when I asked the grass and dirt for permission to bury our loved ones, and the ground spontaneously opened and welcomed them by itself. The complete destruction of Firebird Manor feels like desecration of holy ground.

Rachel twitches and spasms on the floor silently. Her eyes are shut tightly, I'm sure because she's crying. She didn't live here full time, but I know how much Firebird Manor and all its inhabitants meant to her. She always told us how after she turned eighteen, she was looking forward to moving in with us. And she still will—we're going to rebuild. We're not running away. But it won't be the same.

We wait until Rachel has recovered enough to walk on her own. Silently, she stands. When she's ready, she offers us a single nod.

At that moment, a rip appears about six feet up in the air right next to us and continues to the floor. A searing light as bright as the sun blinds us for a moment as Klara—our blonde, statuesque, eighteen-year-old housemate, Seduman daughter of our closest ally Lord Gryx, our Ukrainian bestie, and the fourth indispensable member of our group—tumbles out of the portal dressed head to toe in her own Team Firebird outfit.

"*Bozhe moi*," she wheezes out, crying as she seizes up. "*Bozhe moi*... This was my home...our home..."

Rachel squats down and puts her arm around Klara. Klara twitches, sweats, and cries in the rubble as she recovers. Finally, she recovers enough for Rachel to help her stand.

"I had to come," she tells us. "This was my home, too. So many memories..."

"We'll build new ones," Jake says. "And we'll get these bastards."

Klara nods.

Rachel nods.

I turn to Zaebos. "Let's go."

We step through one of the blasted openings in Firebird Manor's outer wall and before we even reach the steep walkway down to the protected, reclusive Little Corona beach, the chaos and sadness deafens us. As soon as we reach it, we are confronted with the horrors we were too late to prevent. Everything is destroyed—trees are blasted, grass is dead, the sand is littered with bodies of adults and children lying in pools of blood. Some of the shot and sliced people are moaning, some mothers are crying. The sun begins to set over the Pacific Ocean on a beautiful evening with near-perfect weather, but there's too much death and destruction for us to appreciate it.

As we continue walking toward the beach into the heart of the devastation, I begin to see some of the partial bodies of our dead Mazzikim. Mazzikim maintain their bodies with their spirits; when they die there's nothing left to sustain their physical forms, and the empty bodies slowly disintegrate into nothing. I see the left half of a Mazzik that might have been an eagle head on some kind of bipedal alligator-like body crumbling into the dirt next to a Nephilim with no eyes. Closer to the beach, what was probably an apelike Mazzik with very little left decays in the middle of a pile of Nephilim carcasses, clearly having taken many down with him. I'm sure many of the Mazzikim bodies have already evaporated, and I'll never even know them.

"I'm sorry," I whisper. "I'm so sorry."

"Not your fault," Rachel says, her eyes red and glassy.

"They knew what they were doing," Zaebos says. "They knew the risk when they made the choice to defend this place."

"Doesn't make me feel better, though," I sigh.

"On your left," a male voice shouts from behind. We all stop walking and step to our right as a dozen EMTs race to the beach with gurneys.

As we stop, I see Raya sitting on the dirt, where grass and a bench used to be, crying into Wyatt's surfboard. Her sleeveless orange chiffon sundress is soft and beautiful, her sobs loud and ugly.

We walk over and Jake, Rachel, and I sit next to her. Our Mazzikim form a protective ring around us, facing outward. The people either running down to the beach with medical equipment or beginning to gather to see the carnage give them a wide berth, which is fine by me. I'd like some privacy.

"I came as soon as you called," I say.

Raya looks up at me, her face streaked and crusty with the tears she's already cried. "I know."

I don't want to push her, so I just sit silently. Everyone with me takes my lead. I close my eyes and focus on trying to reach out to all life, to see what's left. The life in the soil screams to me. Even the crabs and mussels on the beach that aren't dead are terrified. I shudder so violently that it takes both Jake and Klara to hold me steady.

"Don't..." Rachel whispers to me. "There's nothing you can do."

"They came from the sea," Raya begins, talking so quietly through her sobs we all have to lean way in until our ears are practically touching her lips. "Not from boats. They just rose out of the water. Those Nephilim with goggles. They started shooting..."

"You saw it?" I ask.

"I was sitting on a towel, waiting for him. I like watching him surf, you know..." She rests her head on his still damp surfboard, sobbing.

I put my hand on her arm, trying to give her some of my strength.

"Wyatt had come out of the water. We were getting ready to leave..."

Raya's face tightens with the pain of the memory.

We sit quietly until she's ready to continue.

"I folded up the towel and we left the sand and started up the walkway to Ocean Street. That's when they just popped out of the water and started shooting people on the beach. It was...so much screaming. Some scattered, others froze..."

Raya reaches out and grabs my arm. "Your Mazzikim were so awesome, Alex. Truly. They raced down and tried to protect us. They rushed those Nephilim, took bullet after bullet, and tore the Nephilim apart, until they were overcome themselves. And then...and then..."

Raya breaks down again. Klara reaches over and starts caressing her hair. Raya's lips untwist from their quivering to offer her a tiny smile of appreciation.

"Two huge beasts...those monsters from the video—the Watcher things—burst out of the water, straight up, flying. They landed on the beach. Each of them grabbed somebody, and...and...sucked their whole body into their mouth, like inhaling air from a balloon."

Rachel nods sympathetically.

"They turned to the two of us. We were goners, I knew it. I grabbed Wyatt's arm and tried to pull him off the beach...not brave, I know but I just thought, maybe, if we were fast enough, we'd get away. But Wyatt...he..."

She starts bawling so loudly the Mazzikim, who have been facing outward guarding us, all turn around to make sure everything is okay.

"He calmly handed me his surfboard," Raya wails. I hold her while Klara keeps caressing her hair. "He said that I would die—that everyone on the beach would die—if someone didn't give them time to get away. I screamed and I screamed...I begged and I begged...he kissed me and told me to run here and wait for him."

"Wyatt wanted you safe," Rachel nods.

"As I ran up here," Raya sobs, not even acknowledging us, "Wyatt strolled right up to those Watcher things and demanded that they leave. I couldn't believe it. Even the Nephilim stopped to see what Wyatt was doing. People were grabbing their kids and scattering...I just stared at him from up here, unable to move or make a sound."

"You did the right thing," I reassure Raya. "There's nothing you could have done."

Raya raises the corners of her mouth slightly, then continues. "The taller one bent over Wyatt and waved its mouth tentacles around and tried to scare him. Wyatt shook his head and said he knew that they could kill him, but he wouldn't give them the satisfaction of being afraid. Wyatt told them they wouldn't gain anything by killing him or anyone else, and they should go home. The big one laughed, stabbed him through the gut with a claw, and then...and then...it inhaled him."

I caress Raya's arm as she cries, my own eyes getting glassy. Wyatt...not Wyatt...

"It was so horrible, Alex! His body just flew apart, like he was being ground up in a blender and sucked into its mouth. He screamed...Oh Goddess, his screams..."

She starts screaming herself. Rachel, Klara, and I all hug her. She puts her arms around us all, her head between us crying onto the dirt.

"Where are the Rishonim—the Watchers—now?" Jake asks once Raya has calmed down a bit.

"As soon as they killed Wyatt, the beach was mostly empty. The people who weren't killed had made it away, and the Nephilim were mostly killed by your Mazzikim. Those things took off on their huge bat wings to Firebird Manor and blasted it with lightning or lasers or something from their mouths. When S.W.A.T. and ambulances started to arrive, they were already gone."

"Wyatt saved you, and he saved a lot of people by giving them time to run away," Rachel says, taking Raya's hand. "He's a hero."

"As much of a hero as anyone on Team Firebird," I add.

"But why did my hero have to die?" Raya weeps.

Why did any of them have to die, dammit?

"It's my fault they came for me here before, and it's my fault they attacked here again," I tighten my mouth to keep my voice steady. "The Nephilim and Watchers have been killing and controlling people for thousands of years or more. Now that I know, I won't let them anymore. So they declared war on me, all my loved ones, and all of Sediin."

Raya wipes her eyes. "Wyatt loved you all like family and believed in your mission. I know he'd be glad you guys are still alive."

Raya leans against me. I caress her back as Klara keeps caressing her hair and Rachel pats her arm.

"The Nephilim and Rishon are poison to the whole Earth. They destroy everything, everywhere they go. And we're going to stop them," I promise. "No matter what."

"Wyatt would want that," Raya sobs. "Up in heaven, I'm sure Wyatt is proud of you."

I hold Raya, my glassy eyes giving way to rage. No, he's not. If he had just been killed, I could have sent our Mazzikim to find his spirit in Gehenna and guide it to Merkaba, guaranteeing he would end up with the spirits of his ancestors. But by being absorbed by G'suul, Wyatt was completely destroyed, body and soul. There's nothing left; his eternal spirit is now fuel for G'suul. It is truly a fate worse than death.

I'll never tell Raya that. I'll let her think that her love is looking down on her. But I'll make these Rishonim pay for what they've done to Wyatt.

For what they've done to my friends. For what they've done to us. For what they've done to everything. We just need to find them.

12

MY SECURE MILITARY PHONE starts buzzing under my coat. I assume it's General Patrick; the only other people who could call me on my unknown, unlisted phone are sitting with me.

"Something's come up?" Raya sniffles. "I can see how you tensed. It's okay if you need to go."

"Don't worry about it." I caress her arm. "My phone's buzzing. There's no way I'll be able to undo all the zippers and straps of my Team Firebird coat here, so I'm not even going to try. I'm here as long as you need me to be. You can come with us if you want."

She looks at me, and for the first time the hint of a smile is visible. "You know that I don't blame you, right? Any of you." She makes eye contact with each one of us. "Wyatt didn't either. Even if you are their excuse, it's all on them."

"Thanks, Raya. But that's not why I offered—"

"Oh, I know." She shakes her head. "I just don't want you to feel guilty."

"Too late," I sniff out a melancholy chuckle as I lower my head. "I've been blaming myself for everything that's happened since they murdered Agent Susan Weaver."

"Don't, sweetie." Raya touches my face.

I raise my eyes to hers. I swear, she looks like an angel, sunshine itself, even in tears.

"Thanks," I force out.

Rachel rubs Raya's knee in thanks.

We sit silently for a moment as Raya composes herself. She inhales deeply, then exhales slowly. "There's an officer taking statements down the walkway. I should really give one."

"Are you up for it?" Jake asks. "It's okay to wait a little longer."

"No, no, I should." She nods, agreeing with herself, psyching herself up. She slowly pushes herself up off the ground. I hover next to her, ready to support her if she stumbles, but only if she needs me to. I want her to feel strong.

We all rise with her. "Would you like some company?"

She smiles and nods, wiping a tear off her cheek.

"Zaebos, we are going to talk to the human law enforcement."

Zaebos turns to me and bows his head, then addresses all the Mazzikim. "Duigan, Sento, Pelegor, we shall walk beside them. All others walk behind— as casually as possible."

They all acknowledge Zaebos's instructions, and we start walking back from the dirt planter to the sidewalk and down to the beach.

As we walk, I unzip the top of my jacket, undo the side straps, and reach into the zipped inner pocket. I pull out my phone—I was right, it was the general. I return the call.

"Alex," General Patrick exhales as he answers my call.

"Your timing—"

"Yeah, I know what happened," he confirms. "News travels fast. Bad news does, anyway. How's you're team? You all okay?"

"The Mazzikim who were guarding Firebird Manor and the reinforcements that came are all destroyed. When my team got here, the damage was already done. We're accompanying our neighbor to give her report now."

"She rattled?"

"Yeah..."

"Christ almighty, I'm so sorry your friends, household, and neighborhood were hit again. As soon as Mort hooked me up to his live satellite feed and I saw Firebird Manor blown to shit, I knew this would be horrible."

I just sigh.

"Well, I have some...I can't call it good news, but at least it will make things a bit easier from here on out. The Pentagon has officially declared the Nephilim and Watchers terrorists. That means the US military is now officially charged with defeating them, and I can offer you any aid you need without having to circumvent orders."

"That is helpful. I have to admit, we're not sure what our next move is yet. I think tracking them just got harder; they burst out of the ocean as easily as they come out of tunnels in the ground. But I have faith in Mort and Jake finding a way."

Jake turns to me and gives my arm a quick caress.

"People I trust in INSCOM and the CIA are working on it too," General Patrick says.

"I'm glad. Oh, General—speaking of trust, the chief inspector of the Madrid Police said something that kinda rattled me."

"What did he say?"

I tell the general what the chief inspector said about my actions resulting in more deaths than the Nephilim and Watchers combined.

"Nah," General Patrick says.

I can't help but sniff out a slight chuckle at how quickly he dismisses the police chief's idea. I wish I could let it go that easily.

"Alex, I understand why you'd be upset by the chief inspector's concerns, but he's either trying to get under your skin or Spain has a more fragile government than either of us know. Remember, power abhors a vacuum. If one police chief is jailed, another will take his place. If one president is toppled, another will be appointed or elected. And that person will swear up and down that they're not part of the Cult of the Watchers."

"But what if the replacements are cult members?"

"Then we'll take them down, too—and after that, the replacement will be replaced, until eventually they find someone who isn't a cult member."

"Are you sure?"

"I'm sure. To really destroy an entire society's infrastructure, you'd need to destroy all of it at once, or at least so much at once that they can't plug all the holes. You're not doing that. We're not doing that."

"Thanks, General. Is there anything you think I should be doing?"

I can hear him breathing as he thinks of what to say.

"The videos are good," he says. "It all works together: the sweep and clean operations, along with the video you released in Madrid asking the people to stay calm, be vigilant, and trust in society. Coming from you, that helps. Show them that as chaotic as things are right now, they can still trust their neighbors."

"Will do. Thanks, General."

"When you need us, just call," General Patrick says.

"I will," I promise. "Thanks for checking up on us, and thanks for the pep talk."

"I wish I didn't have to give them. Keep me in the loop, Alex. We'll get them."

"Yes we will, General. Talk to you soon," I sign off.

Raya is already talking to the officer, who is recording what she says and gently giving her an arm to lean against. He seems kind and earnest. That's nice. The Mazzikim are all milling around on the dirt and rocks next to the sidewalk. I'm proud of them—they have cleared the sidewalk so gurneys and people can get by without having to walk around them, and they're trying to look as unthreatening as possible. Who knows, maybe some people feel more secure with our presence around. I hope so.

Jake looks over at me with a compassionate, tight-lipped smile as I put my phone back in my jacket. I hope my expression shows how grateful I am that he's with me, but I think I probably just look pained and sad. That's how I feel, anyway.

"Excuse me! Miss Firebird!"

We all turn around and see a woman in a business suit with a cameraman behind her. She's about five feet behind us, waving at me.

"Yes?" I raise my eyebrows.

"Orange County Herald. May I ask a few questions?"

"I guess." I shrug. "We just got here, so you should probably ask one of—"

"Had you thought about the possible repercussions of your actions when you declared war against the Cult of the Watchers? Did you think it through?"

Goddammit. I *so* don't want to deal with this line of questioning now.

"How stupid are you?" A very angry Rachel steps forward. I can see by the hint of red glow sparking in her eyes and the slight hardening of her skin that she's barely able to keep from going full Sedu on this reporter. "Would you rather that they just keep murdering people for centuries, because everyone is too chicken shit to do anything about it? What if you were one of the people that they murdered, huh? Or your mother? Brother? Sister? Kids? How would you feel then?"

I can't help but smile at my soul sister. You go, girlie.

"Someone would have exposed the Cult of the Watchers," Jake continues. "Their rituals look Satanic, and their kidnappings may have been covered up, but people did notice. Someone would have pursued it—maybe a journalist like you—the Nephilim would have been exposed, and they'd be in the same position they're in now, the Watchers forced to feed in the light."

"At least this way, we're on the job. Remember, our Mazzikim died saving as many human lives as they could," I add.

"Okay, well, now that you're on the case, Lady Firebird, what can you do?"

"I—"

A man shouts with pain below us on Little Corona beach. Instantly we all flip around and look toward the sound. I see a police officer next to the body of one of the Nephilim corpses, plopped down on the sand, holding up his hand like he got a nasty burn.

I run down to him. From the sounds behind me, I can tell that all of Team Firebird and probably the reporter are jogging behind.

"What happened?" I ask as I squat down next to him.

The officer, a tall, Hispanic man, grimaces in pain as a sizable patch of skin on his back of his hand blackens and bubbles before his eyes. He's clearly a tough guy, but his hand is shaking and you can see the strain on his face.

"I...we gotta move these bodies off the beach. I grabbed his arm...my hand brushed his blood..."

"The Nephilim blood is toxic. It burns everything it comes in contact with. They destroy everything, all life, the ground itself," I say.

"Can they patch me up at the hospital?" he winces.

"I can help. May I?" I hover my hands over his.

He nods.

"I'm sorry—this will hurt."

"Can't feel much worse than it already does." He tries to smile.

I close my eyes and focus on the cells of his hand. I imagine his healthy cells carrying the dead and damaged cells away, replacing the necrotic tissue with living tissue. I imagine the Nephilim blood that seeped into his system being absorbed and destroyed by his own blood and immune system. His grunts and stifled moans let me know I'm succeeding.

I'm so focused I lose track of time until I hear him say, "Well, I'll be damned."

I open my eyes. There is a fresh layer of new, pink skin over the burns on the back of his hand. I notice my Mazzikim and Team Firebird have formed a loose ring around us as a crowd has gathered, including the reporter.

"You'll want to go to the EMTs up there to get that treated and wrapped."

"Lady Firebird, I...thank you," he says, gratitude and disbelief playing on his face in equal measure.

"I'm just glad I could help." I answer and help him to his feet. I turn to the Nephilim corpse. They're a danger to everyone here. Their toxic blood will burn the beachgoers, the beach itself, and the sea life.

"You were right, Officer. We have to get rid of these corpses."

I reach into myself and pull out my flaming eyes and hair. I inhale deeply, lean down, shove his machine gun out of the way, and breathe a long jet of spirit fire onto the body of the Nephilim. Sedu fire is far hotter than earthly fire, and in no time, the pooling blood and the entire corpse—clothes and all—are nothing but ash, leaving only his machine gun on the sand.

I rise and turn toward the reporter who had confronted me on Ocean Street. "*That's* what I can do."

All around me, the victims, medical technicians, witnesses, and police all clap and cheer.

13

Hearing the crowd clap for me feels good. I'm still too broken up about my friend Wyatt, my Mazzikim, and Firebird Manor to really feel proud or charged or whatever, but I'm happy not to be the enemy.

Rachel, Klara, and a few Mazzikim help the EMTs pick up any remaining wounded people and get them on gurneys, while Zaebos and the rest of the Mazzikim help me gather all the Nephilim bodies. Jake calls Mort Stygg and lets him know what's happened here and what we're up to.

With all the Nephilim corpses in a pile, I inhale slowly and breathe Sedu fire on them. As my breath runs out, my head creeps forward, and I become aware of two large, apelike Mazzik hands steadying me. The timing is perfect—as I run out of breath I collapse into his arms. The Mazzik holds me up as I inhale and exhale a few times, building back my strength and oxygen supply. When I'm ready, I inhale slowly and deeply, and breathe another jet of flames.

I do this three or four more times until the Nephilim carcasses are completely torched. I let the ash blow away as I comb the beach looking for spots where the Nephilim blood has corroded the sand. I breathe on each bloodstain, cleansing the beach of their filth.

I am pleasantly surprised and heartened by those who take the time to greet or thank me when we pass. Some even point out bloodstains for me. I make a point to smile at or at least acknowledge everyone who's kind enough to say something to me. It's tough when I'm feeling this down on myself, but I'm so relived that these people don't hate me after all this. They'd have every reason to—yeah, I didn't make the Nephilim and Rishonim attack, but if I didn't live here they might have been left alone. Or maybe not, eventually. Who knows. Self-loathing is one of my superpowers.

"Thanks for cleaning up Little Corona." Sergeant Franklin's brown lips curl slightly upward in a tight but sympathetic smile as she holds out her hand. I've met her before; when Firebird Manor was attacked previously, she was the lead officer on the scene the next morning. She confronted a cult member who tried to take over the crime scene from her, at great risk to her own life.

"Hi, Sergeant. It's my pleasure." I take her hand as I finish my sweep for bloodstains. "This is my beach too. That's why they came again, to turn people against me and finish destroying my house."

"Yeah," she nods. "Well, some here might want you gone, but I think a fair number of us see your house laid waste and understand that despite their words, you're a victim in all this, too."

"I'm so sorry we weren't here sooner."

Sergeant Franklin shrugs, her shoulders barely reaching her short, straightened black hair. "We see your videos. We know you've been busy. And you've been helping people and cleaning up, so everyone knows where your heart's at."

"Thanks, Sergeant. I'd..." I trail off as I get an idea.

She raises her eyebrows and waits for me to continue.

"Hey, um, do you think it would be okay to take a moment with you and make another video? With cult members embedded in governments and stuff, I want to show that you can still trust most officers."

"Yeah..." she nods, her voice far away as she clearly is in thought. "Okay, that's a good idea. In fact, how about you give me five, and I'll get some more officers and any EMTs that haven't already split, too."

"That would be great. I'll get my team together."

Sergeant Franklin gives me a quick pat on the arm as she walks away and begins gathering her officers. I flag Jake down and he heads toward me. I scan the beach for Rachel and Klara. I see them up on the sidewalk above Little Corona. I concentrate on them, trying to call out to them silently. I can't think them my thoughts they way I can with a Sedu, but I reached out with my thoughts to Qwyll, a Mazzik from our House, and he felt my call.

After a few moments, Rachel starts looking around like she heard something, then turns around to look at me. I wave to her. Rachel points to herself then to me, to ask if I want her to join me. Klara turns around too.

I nod and then point at all the EMTs around them. Rachel and Klara get it. They turn to the EMTs and start talking to them and pointing toward me. That's my girl.

"What's up?" Jake gently puts an arm around my side and gives me a short peck on the lips. "Mort gives us his condolences, says he's prototyping something for us."

"Do you know what?"

"I think a handheld radiation detector. I'll know more when I'm back."

"Ooh, that sounds cool. So I'm going to need you to shoot some video. I'm trying to get a lot of us—police, EMTs, and Team Firebird."

"Nice." Jake grabs his phone and starts swiping away. He looks up and twists his head from side to side.

"Okay, I think the light is best if you guys are all over there, by those rocks." Jake points off toward the rightmost edge of Little Corona, where there are lots of rocks of different sizes, all the way up the rock cliff to Ocean Street above. "It'll look nice against the sunset."

"Sounds good. I'll get everyone."

Rachel, Klara, and a few Mazzikim reach the sand of the beach about the same time that Sergeant Franklin has roped about four other officers into being in our video. They see us and head for the same spot.

"Thanks, everyone, for being a good sport," I begin as we all congregate together. "I've heard...there's been complaints that I might be creating anarchy, so I want to send a video out about how we're all working together."

Everyone expresses their agreement as we get to the rocks.

"Okay, I'll need you guys to squeeze pretty tight," Jake says, holding up his phone. "We should probably leave out the Mazzikim—I'm sorry, guys."

Zaebos tips his head and directs the Mazzikim off to the side.

"Klara, do you want to be part of this?" I ask.

Klara's always been kind of shy about being officially part of Team Firebird publicly, but she's really been stepping up. I want to give her the opportunity if she wants it.

"Can we be in our Seduman forms?" she asks.

"Absolutely," I say, going full Sedu myself. Well, except for my super-sharp teeth. "It will help some of our features come through so we're more than silhouettes in the sunset, I think."

"It'll look really cool," Jake agrees.

"Yeah, rub it in why don't you?" Sergeant Franklin quips.

I don't know quite how to answer, so I smile and guide the sergeant to stand next to me. She's right, the fading light will make anyone with dark skin look even darker. But other than the flash on Jake's phone, we don't really have any other lighting source. Hopefully my flaming hair will help illuminate the people of color in our group.

Rachel and Klara both take on their Seduman forms and stand one on each side of me, with Sergeant Franklin standing next to me and in front of the taller male police officers. The EMTs gather next to and behind Rachel.

"When we start filming, if any of you have anything to say, just speak," I address everyone. "Don't worry about the timing. Jake can always do some editing before he sends it out."

They all agree.

"We ready?" I ask Jake.

"Yup. Just nod."

I inhale slowly, then exhale.

Jake looks up and nods as the flash comes on the phone.

"The Nephilim and the Cult of the Watchers have been busy. Their murdering sprees have taken them to Kota, Rajasthan, in India, and Corona Del Mar, California, in the United States. We're working on tracking them to where they hide, so we can get them before they strike again.

"Unfortunately, we can't be everywhere at once. If we're close enough, we'll work with local law enforcement and health and safety workers, like we are here, to aid them in the cleanup and whatever else we can do. Stay away from any Nephilim bodies—their blood is like acid; it will burn through anything. Leave them for the local authorities to incinerate."

I see off to Rachel's side that as I say that, the officer I healed holds up his now bandaged hand to emphasize my point.

"Even though cult members have infiltrated many aspects of life, that doesn't mean you can't trust anyone. There's only so many cult members and a lot more good, decent people like Sergeant Franklin here"—I hold my open hand out toward her—"and her team, who want to keep order and keep people safe."

Sergeant Franklin takes a step forward. "Law officers and medical personnel who are trustworthy will be happy to show you their license and give you their badge number. Their directions will make sense and be obviously in the common interest. We all want the same thing. We work for you."

She steps back and gives me a slight bob of her head.

"Thank you, Sergeant Franklin. Please don't start to fear your neighbors and your local authorities. That's what the Cult of the Watchers wants—it makes it easier for them to kidnap and eat people if we don't trust each other. Instead, be vigilant with and for each other. Post online to the Lady Firebird accounts if you see or hear something. And please, be good to each other. That's how we beat them. Thank you."

I pause and look around for a moment to see if anyone has anything else to say. Nobody does, so I turn back to Jake and nod.

Jake swipes away. "That was excellent, everyone. I'm going to send this to Dr. Stygg—our team is going to do some light sharpening and then audio processing to get the wind noise out of the video before we post it."

"Oh crap, I didn't think of the wind!" I frown.

"It won't be a problem, don't worry. I'll text him now," Jake says.

"Thanks for helping me put this together, Sergeant," I say.

"Our pleasure. It was a good idea. I hope it helps."

"Me too," I agree.

"One day, girl, we're gonna have to go out for lunch or something to—" Sergeant Franklin's radio crackles to life. She takes it and walks away.

"Oh, shit," Jake says.

I walk over. "What's up?"

"Mort just said—"

"That there's another attack. A tiny town in Oklahoma called Broxton," Sergeant Franklin finishes Jake's sentence.

"Okay, let's go." I draw my Sedu blade from it's sheath on my belt.

Klara grabs my arm. "Do we know anyone who's ever been to Oklahoma?"

Well, shit. We can only open a portal to places we've been before. None of us has ever been to Oklahoma, that's for sure.

"I..."

Klara pulls out her secure phone. "I'll call Captain Jeffers."

"Great idea." I pat her arm.

I turn to Jake. He's already talking on the phone to Mort.

Rachel walks over and sighs. She's as frustrated as I am that we may not be able to get to Broxton.

"Okay," Klara says. "If we can get to any Army or Air Force base, she and General Patrick can arrange transport for us."

"Mort can get us to a military base not too far from Broxton," Jake says, walking over to the rest of us. "He'll meet us in the House of Keroz."

"How far is not too far?" I ask.

"Doesn't matter, it's gonna have to do," Rachel points out.

14

"I have been to Sheppard Air Force Base in Texas," Mort pants, propping himself up against the entryway to our portal room. It's very improper decorum for a Sedu or Seduman to portal into another Sedu's House, even if they're allies, so as soon as Mort and Jake ended their call, Mort Stygg portaled to the House of Stygg, and then two of Lord Stygg's Mazzikim guided him through The Nothingness to the main gates of the House of Keroz.

"How far is that from Broxton?" I ask, mostly recovered.

"I think maybe ninety minutes by car," Mort says. "By plane, not long. It's less than a hundred miles."

I huff and shake my head. If Broxton is under attack right now, all the damage will be done by the time we get there.

"It's the best we can do," Jake puts his hand gently on my back.

"Garz is creating armor and weapons for our Mazzikim," Vetis informs me as he helps his daughter and Klara up.

"I'll remain in Sediin and coordinate with our allies, so they are ready to join us in battle," Vetis says, looking worried.

"I'll be fine, Dad," Rachel wheezes.

He doesn't seem convinced.

"Klara, there's no shame in staying to coordinate our allies with Vetis," I add. "Not everyone has to be a warrior. If we get lucky and catch the Nephilim before they tear up Broxton and retreat underground again, that means a lot of fighting. Don't worry, you're a part of Team Firebird even if you're not on the front line."

Klara is still tense from portal travel, but I can tell she's feeling extra tense because she's torn.

"Thanks, Alex," Klara says, more than a little nervously. "You're the best, you all are. I like being a field nurse, helping the wounded, and spiting my Sedu neurotoxin on your weapons. Especially if we're going to be late—there may be a lot of wounded. I'll trust in our Mazzikim to keep me in one piece if we end up in the thick of it."

"Okay." I offer a tight smile. I'm glad she's coming, but I'm also worried as hell that I might lose another friend.

Ten more Mazzikim of all shapes and sizes come into the portal chamber—Mazzikim with horse bodies and alligator heads, ape bodies and lion heads, you name it. All in the VATS goo–proof armor. Some of them, like Leeik and Sento, I know. Others I don't. And of course Zaebos would never let me go anywhere without him, bless his soul.

"Garz offers his apologies that it takes so much time to armor us," one of them says. "He remains to make more."

"No need to apologize. I'm grateful for all of you and pray none of you is harmed. Are we ready?"

The Mazzikim all bow. Everyone else nods as they walk toward the portal mirror.

"Be safe. And give them hell," Vetis says.

"Oh, don't worry—we will," Rachel smiles.

Vetis returns a worried smile as he stands at the doorway, along with Zogo and two other Ruhin, to see us off.

"We are all ready, my lady," Zaebos says, shuffling to my side.

"Mort, please do the honors," I motion to him, and Mort concentrates on changing the image in the mirror.

"Let's go." He waves toward the mirror, currently displaying an extremely tall chain-link fence topped with spiraling barbed wire.

We shove our way through the portal and find ourselves at the back of the base. I can't see much into the base since it's already later in the evening in Texas and dark. Since I'm in better shape than the Seduman, I help Rachel and Klara move away from the portal so all of our Mazzikim can step out of the portal as well. As soon as we're all out, a doubled over and spasming Mort raises his hand to his ear and pantomimes taking a phone call.

"Got it." I pull out my phone and dial General Patrick.

"How can I help?" he answers.

"We're outside Sheppard Air Force Base."

"And you need a ride to Broxton," the general surmises. "Captain Jeffers spoke to Klara earlier."

"Yup."

"Gimme ten minutes," he says. "I'll get you a Sikorsky S-70 to take all of you to Broxton."

"I don't want to sound ungrateful..."

"But time is of the essence," he finishes my thought. "Okay, five. You'll need that to catch your breath anyway."

"Thanks, General. And can you ask if an emergency medical team can accompany us? We might get there too late to fight the Nephilim, but we can at least help the wounded."

"Will do." General Patrick disconnects the call.

15

As soon as I put down my phone, two soldiers come around the side, shining lights on us. They both leap nearly three feet in the air when they see us; I can only imagine what it must be like to be on a routine patrol and find crazy monsters, an old man, and some teenagers staring back at you. We give them our names just as their walkie-talkies go off. We stand still and relaxed as they speak into their radios. It's pretty clear we're the topic of conversation, given how many times they look up at us.

I gotta say, the soldiers are great. They relate that their commanding officer not only told them about us, but conveyed our urgency to them. They race us through check-in at the main gate and guide us to a hangar off to our right. Once inside the hangar, the flight commander shows us to a Sikorsky S-70 helicopter and pilot. I'd asked for a medical team, but they don't have one ready and we can't wait.

The pilot does a fair job of hiding her shock at seeing a dozen crazy animal-demon-looking Mazzikim climb into the back of her chopper. But despite her nerves she's courteous and professional and gets us off the ground fast, which is all we can hope for.

It takes us over forty minutes to get to Broxton, Oklahoma—or what's left of it. The place is a ghost town by the time we arrive. Not that Broxton looks like it was ever much of a town—just a few clusters of single-story ranch-style homes, shops, and buildings that popped up around E1400 Road and US Route 281. The few streetlights are busted, and the light from our helicopter is the only thing illuminating the scene. Ditches and broken shops remain where the Nephilim collapsed the ground. Charred remains of buildings indicate where the Rishonim blasted.

Our pilot lands facing the clusters of buildings so we can use the chopper's lights to see. Smart.

"Let's look for survivors," I say as we disembark the chopper.

Once we're outside, I walk around the chopper to the cockpit. The pilot opens a side window and looks down at me. "Be ready to take off at a moment's notice—we're looking for wounded."

She gives me a thumbs up.

I rejoin my team and we head toward the trenches. Rachel holds two crossbow bolts out to Klara, who spits her Sedu neurotoxin on them. Rachel then loads them into her crossbow. I pull out my Sedu blade and will it to the size of a full-length, curved sword burning with blue flames. Jake draws his weapon of choice—his phone.

The Nephilim had collapsed the dirt on each side of the four lane E1400 Road. Most of the Mazzikim check out the leftmost trenches, while Team Firebird, Mort, Zaebos, and my guard check out the trenches on the right. As soon as we reach the edge of the trench, I squat down, hold my hands out over the hole, and close my eyes, reaching out to any life force or spirit that I might be able to detect.

The soil overwhelms me with a deep sense of fear and pain. I moan and fall backward, but Jake and Klara catch me.

"Are you all right, Alex?" Mort asks as he places a kind hand on my shoulder.

"It's as if the ground is begging me for help, to save it," I explain.

"Do you know from what? Can you get that from the soil?"

I concentrate harder on the soil giving me any impressions it can. The ground can't talk to me in words, but I do get some more impressions of pressure, of burning, of death.

I open my eyes. "I think...I think it's telling me that one Rishon was here, and its footprints burned the soil. I also feel people here, being killed. I think some Nephilim might have been killed too, and their blood burns the soil."

I close my eyes again and concentrate. "Tell me how to help you. Tell me what I can do."

I'm filled with an intense sense of burning from the ruins of a large ranch house about a hundred yards in front of us on our right. I reach out and feel a weak, human-type life force. That could either be a wounded human who's running out of time or it could be a Nephilim who's half-human, half-Rishonim—Rishonim show up as just another dead zone, an absence of life, so Nephilim feel like a person half-alive.

"There," I open my eyes and point. "Wounded human...or Nephilim."

"Can you detect heartbeats?" Mort asks.

I close my eyes and concentrate. I can feel a fair number of heartbeats—my own, Jake's, Rachel's, Klara's, and Mort's. But that's it.

"Not from the battered house." I frown. "That doesn't give me the warm fuzzies."

Zaebos calls over the Mazzikim on the other side of the trench.

"Jake, Klara, Mort, why don't you wait in the chopper with the pilot," I suggest. "There might be fighting coming."

"Or you might need a field nurse," Klara counters.

"Or to send a quick message or look something up," Jake adds.

"I'm not much good at waiting. And besides, I'm fairly spry for a one-hundred-and-eighty-five-year-old Seduman," Mort winks at me.

"I know you're all brave—"

"Or stupid," Rachel jumps in.

I can't help but let a slight, wry grin escape. "But I don't want to risk you in an ambush."

"Alex is right, especially Jake. You don't have superpowers," Rachel reminds Jake.

"Thanks for the vote of confidence." Jake smirks. "Seriously, though, I really appreciate the concern, but it's cool. We're surrounded by Mazzikim; it'll be fine."

Rachel shakes her head. I inhale deeply, praying that this is just a wounded person we can treat—or a single Nephilim we can take out fast.

"Let's go."

We cautiously approach the ranch-style home that has had its roof and windows blown out and its door charred open. Zaebos steps in front of me and I want to protest, but he shoots me a look that lets me know there is nothing I can say that will convince him to let me go in first. He motions with his muzzle to the Mazzikim and they flank him, with a few remaining behind us to protect Jake and Klara. Rachel and I enter the demolished house right behind them.

"Beware the blood," Zaebos says. I look inside the blasted doorway and see exactly what he means. There are two Nephilim bodies stacked up just inside the door, their machine guns still in their hands. Zaebos and the Mazzikim step over them, avoiding a couple pools of blood that have already eaten through the cheap shag carpet.

There's stuffing from shot up and destroyed furniture all over the front room, along with bodies of a few large men with a lot of guns strewn around them. The walls are riddled with bullet holes. The Nephilim may have killed them, but these men clearly put up a fight.

We walk into a dining area and kitchen. Another Nephilim body face down in a pool of its own blood, a long knife covered in blood still in its outstretched hand. A man, woman, and infant girl each covered blood lie sprawled out on the linoleum, all of them with open knife wounds.

"Is it one of them?" Klara asks.

"Let me check." I bend down, close my eyes, and reach out to the life forces in the room.

My eyes shoot open and I go full Sedu. "It's—"

Before I can get another word out, the Nephilim springs upon a gorilla-headed, bipedal lizard-bodied Mazzik next to Zaebos. He shoves his knife in the Mazzik's throat before any of us can react. Rachel shoots him in the head with two crossbow bolts just as Zaebos slams into him with his muzzle. The Nephilim falls to the floor. This time, he's not getting up.

As our Mazzik falls, I grab his head and torso. His form goes limp. As I feel his spirit expire, a sharp pain shoots through me. I gently lay the body down, sad and angry.

"Goddammit!" I seethe, my eyes red. Another being from my House destroyed by these evil bastards. A being that might have lived eternally, but gave its life to protect me and Team Firebird.

"Please, my lady." Zaebos gently places a paw on my shoulder. "Galin chose to accompany us here. He knew the risks."

"I know," I sigh. "But that doesn't make it weigh on me any less."

"Hey." Rachel, who has also gone full Sedu, puts a gloved hand on my other shoulder. "Listen to—"

We are all startled by the side wall on the other side of the kitchen exploding drywall and plaster out at us. L'reek breathes a pulse of what looks like blue lightning at the three Mazzikim at the back of our formation. One Mazzik's head explodes.

L'reek leaps into the middle of our group and slices Rachel and three Mazzikim with his four dagger-like claws.

Rachel screams.

I leap up and grab her.

Zaebos springs at L'reek. His teeth wrap around the back of L'reek's thigh.

L'reek flexes his leg and flings Zaebos across the room. Zaebos slams hard into the wall as L'reek slices open four additional Mazzikim.

L'reek extends his arms, but not to slice.

Oh no—

Oh God—

He's not—

He wouldn't—

He grabs Mort in his two left arms, Jake in his two right arms, and his leathery wings thrust him upward.

"*Noooo!*" I scream into the black sky.

16

I CAN'T STOP SHAKING. L'reek is flying away with the other half of my spirit, my soul.

"Rachel, here—"

Klara's words snap me back. Smart girl—Stinger had her hood over her head as soon as we were attacked by the Nephilim. L'reek only caught the side of her hood and throat. Her thick, insect-like Seduman skin was able to keep L'reek's claws from going too deep, but she's still sliced. Klara pulls off her hood and wraps a bandage around her neck to stop the bleeding.

"Thanks, Klara," Rachel pants.

Rachel nods to me.

"Chopper! Now!" I grab Rachel and bolt for the door.

What's left of our party runs as fast as we can back to the helicopter. I carry Rachel. I look into the front window of the helicopter—the pilot is staring wide-eyed at the Rishon as it recedes further into the distance.

I barely wait until I've put Rachel down and the last of our Mazzikim have arrived before I start barking orders.

"See the monster? After it!"

The pilot nods rapidly, too panicked to speak.

"Now! Now! Now!"

She nearly jumps off her chair and then turns around, her hands shaking as she starts flipping switches and pulling levers to get airborne as fast as she can. I feel kinda bad about scaring her like that, but I'll apologize later. Right now we have to save Jake and Mort.

"Stay focused." Rachel shakes my arm. "You can't freak, okay?"

I nod. I notice that the bandage Klara wrapped around Rachel's neck is saturating with blood.

I reach up to her bandage. "Let me, Stinger..."

Rachel nods.

I undo her bandage, hold my hand over the gash, close my eyes, and concentrate on her blood no longer oozing out, the cells in her thick, dark, shiny insect-like skin closing up the long gash in her throat. I can hear Rachel grunt and feel her squirm.

"Thanks, girlie," she says after a while.

I open my eyes and see a thin, pink layer of soft, human skin filling in the gash in her throat. "Any time," I answer. I try to smile, but I'm too distraught. I feel like there's an army of bees in my stomach, all trying to fly out of my throat at once.

I glance out the window. I have no idea where we are or where we're headed. I don't know if we're still in Oklahoma or back in Texas—it all looks the same to me.

I slide closer to the pilot.

"Looks like it's taking your friends to that oil refinery." She holds out a shaky finger toward what looks like a tiny wire box with four smokestacks in the distance. At least the refinery is really well lit, with lights ringing the smokestacks and strung between them. That makes it very easy to see in the darkness.

"I...I'm trying to get there as fast as I can," she swallows, her words shaky with fear. "The Sikorsky S-70 is a transport, big and heavy, not meant for pursuit."

"As fast as you can," I say in a hopefully less hostile tone and slide back to Stinger.

As we get closer, I can see the refinery sending huge, pillowy clouds of thick black smoke into the air from each corner, and intermittently flames shoot up from the middle, billowing more black smoke. We've gained a lot of ground, but not enough.

Finally, I see L'reek as he dives into the middle of the refinery.

"Follow it!" I point and scream.

"We can't go into the refinery," our pilot says. "we're too big; the propellers couldn't handle the smoke and drafts."

I turn to her, my jaw shaking. I don't know what to say. I can feel the flames shooting out of my eyes.

"I'm sorry!" the pilot practically cries. "I have to put her down in front of it."

In my frustration I slam my fist into the side of the helicopter. We all buckle. The pilot shrieks and leaps a foot off her chair, even though she's belted in.

"Alex!" Rachel yells as she points at the metal hull near my fist.

I turn to realize that I'd punched a dent into the side.

"Sorry," I say to the pilot. I slide back to Rachel. I close my eyes and tell myself not to cry. Both Rachel and Klara caress my back, trying to calm me down. All I can think about is Jake being sucked into that thing. Or tossed into a chimney. Or torn to pieces.

Dear God, please not Jake...

"This is as close as I can get. I gotta bring her down," the pilot yells back to me anxiously.

I scoot up to the front. I try to quickly scan all the metal platforms in view for any signs of Jake, L'reek, or Nephilim, but no luck. The black smoke from the refinery obscures my view.

The pilot lands us fairly hard inside the fenced parking lot facing the brightly lit oil refinery, her lights shining into it. We're shaken around, and the Mazzikim turn to the cockpit, looking pretty upset. But I don't blame her; I'm assuming I scared her into landing as fast as she safely could.

"Klara, please stay behind. You're not a warrior," I order as I leap out of the chopper.

I briefly scan the concrete and metal structure; I count at least four metal platforms that go around the entire refinery, with metal stairs connecting them. I race to the first set of stairs. Rachel leaps behind me, crossbow locked and loaded. I can hear the Mazzikim disembarking behind us as we hurry to the first metal stairs leading up to a platform. I climb the staircase three steps at a time and then bound across the metal platform, passing pipes and vats filled with God knows what.

"Do we know where we're going?" Rachel calls to me.

I slow to answer, when I hear a crack and feel hard stings on my heavy trench coat. Three bullets slam into my left shoulder and back from above. I look up in time to see a Nephilim two platforms above me turn and run toward the middle of the refinery.

"There!" I point and run in the same direction, looking for any kind of stairs up to the higher platforms. After speeding past a bunch of large vats and enclosed structures, I see metal stairs. I bound up them as fast as I can and keep running. My chest heaves and I'm boiling inside my heavy Team Firebird trench coat but I don't dare take it off—my Sedu skin may be hard enough to take a bullet, but if the shell has VATS goo in it I'm a goner.

Three more shots fired from above and behind me into my back jerk me forward and trip me up. I fall forward on my face and barely keep hold of my Sedu blade. I flip over in time to see the Nephilim who shot me duck behind two huge metal cylinders above me. I growl in frustration, spring to my feet, and keep running in the direction I was already going, still looking for another staircase to an even higher metal platform.

I find one and leap up the stairs as fast as I can. I try to keep picking platforms that take me closer to the center of the refinery. Four large smokestacks line the platform I'm on. As I run past each one, Nephilim take shots at me. I don't stop to engage them. Can't afford the distraction. I've got to save Jake.

The platform turns left. I follow it around and keep running. My chest and legs burn but I can't stop. Not now. After a few hundred feet it turns right, heading back to the center of the refinery. As I turn, I hear the sound of metal being strained and torn. I see the parallel platform to the one I'm on, about sixty feet away across the refinery. Two Nephilim hold Jake.

Jake's alive. I nearly scream for joy.

Jake. Is. Alive.

At least for now.

A deafeningly loud, buzzing alarm goes off below, and a huge plume of black chemical smoke fills the space between us.

"Jake!" I cry.

With the smoke blocking my view ahead, I look around me. The three Nephilim all have machine guns and are standing at a distance, not firing.

"Let go of me!" I hear below me.

Oh no!

In my focus on Jake, I completely forgot about my team, my Mazzikim—my Rachel!

I fold my torso over the platform railing so I can see the platform below me. Two Nephilim, one hanging onto each of Rachel's arms, keep her more or less motionless, her crossbow nowhere in sight. I scan all the platforms on my side of the refinery that I can see. I spot a few Nephilim patrolling, and I can make out what looks like the bodies of some of my Mazzikim, motionless and bleeding. Dear God, how could I be this stupid? I am the worst leader in history. Every one of those deaths is on me.

The huge plume of smoke in front of me begins to thin. I try to look through the black soot for signs of Zaebos, Klara, or Mort in the platforms beneath me. I can see Mort being held under Jake, but no sign of Klara or Zaebos or the rest of my Mazzikim.

I look all the way down and see that there's a vat of some kind of boiling greenish-black liquid that smells like turpentine mixed with motor oil or something; it's overpowering. I try to shake the smell out of my nose as I look up at Jake.

L'reek now stands behind Jake, lording over him. Three of L'reek's arms hold Jake, with his upper-left arm holding a razor-sharp claw against the front of Jake's throat.

L'reek sneers at me, gloating.

"Put down your blade now!" one of the Nephilim closing in on me orders.

17

I DON'T KNOW WHAT TO DO. I can't get to Jake. I feel more than helpless. Anything I could have screwed up, I did. I tremble, wide-eyed, staring at the claw against Jake's neck.

"I said drop it!" the Nephilim says again.

I don't take my eyes off Jake. I let my blade fall to the checkered metal platform. Stupid to disarm myself, I know—but if it buys Jake some time...

"What do you want?" I shout across the refinery.

"Look down," L'reek smiles cruelly.

"What about it? What is that stuff?"

"It is your end. I doubt you can burn...but you can drown. There's no way you'll swim in that! Throw yourself into the vat, and I will let your lover, Rachel, and Mortimer Stygg go. Refuse...and watch them die."

I look down. The blackish-greenish stuff looks viscous and nasty and horrible. He's right; the temperature wouldn't kill me, but I'd probably drown in there. I turn back to Jake.

"How do I know you'll keep your word and not kill them all anyway?"

"You don't—you simply have no choice." L'reek laughs maniacally and pokes his finger into Jake's throat. Jake winces and grunts as a thin rivulet of blood trickles down his neck.

"Stop!" I grab the rail.

"Then dive," L'reek sneers.

As angry as I've ever been, as much rage as I've ever felt, I have never so desperately wanted to tear someone apart as I want to tear apart L'reek right now. He doesn't just have the upper hand, he has the only hand. That claw is cutting into Jake's throat. There's no action anyone can take faster than he can shove it further into Jake.

Maybe I can save Rachel below me, but that means I'll watch Mort and Jake and any Mazzikim left die. If I jump, I won't watch Jake die, but L'reek won't just say, "Oh goodie, she did what I asked. Okay, you're all good to go."

What can I do? How can I get out of this with everyone alive? I gaze across the refinery at Jake. He looks as scared as I am.

I see Mort struggling to get free from his own two Nephilim captors.

"You're a bastard!" I hear Rachel yell below me. "We'll kill you all! There's nowhere you can run! Let go of me you—"

I hear Rachel being struck. I feel a cold shiver down my back. I reach out to the life around me and feel Rachel, Jake, and Mort's heartbeats, thank God. They're all still alive—with extremely fast and panicked heartbeats, but alive.

I have to do something, now. But what?

I stare desperately at Jake as Rachel pants, Mort struggles, and L'reek cackles defiantly.

"Alex..." Jake swallows.

"I'll get you out of here, I—"

"From our first conversation in the library nearly two years ago, I fell for you. I've loved you from the beginning."

My whole body goes colder than ice. Jake's heartbeat has slowed to nearly calm.

"Don't talk like that!" A tear wends down my cheek.

L'reek laughs even louder, clearly loving the fear.

"I'm so proud of who you are, Lady Firebird. You're a hero to the world. They need you. Never give up. You're bigger than any one of us."

"Jake!"

"I love you, Alexandra Gold."

Jake closes his eyes and impales his throat on L'reek's claw.

18

I SCREAM.

Blood pours out around the claw stuck in Jake's throat.

My Jake.

Bleeding out.

The world stops turning.

I grab the railing to steady myself.

Rachel screams below me. I barely hear her. My eyes burn with Sedu fire and tears of shock.

This can't be happening. Jake is fine, back in the helicopter, back in Sediin, back at home. He's waiting for me, that ear-to-ear grin that I can't resist, oceans in his blue eyes.

He's not in front of me, breathing out his last.

He can't be.

I scream.

Jake and I were going to be married. He was going to help me keep the world safe as part of Team Firebird. He was going to be the father of my children—if I could even have children anymore. We were...

We *were.*

He's really there, across the refinery, eyes closed, face blank, bleeding out on a claw. All my power, and I couldn't stop this. I've failed again. My biggest failure yet. Jake is more than my best friend, my lover, my fiancé. He's part of my soul. A part of me that's bleeding out, too far away from me to grab him and make his cells close the wound before he loses too much blood. I can't save him.

I scream.

But he knew that. He knew not all of Team Firebird could make it out of here alive. So he volunteered to die, so that we could be saved. Because that's what he always does. That's who he is.

I'm not a hero. I'm just an idiot with superpowers. Jake is the real hero. I would die for Jake, for my team—but he *did* die for Team Firebird.

But he's not dead yet. Not quite.

I stop screaming.

Jake, I don't know if you can hear my thoughts, but if you can, hang on. Please, my love. As long as you can. I'm coming for you. I don't know if I can save you. But they will not defile you. I promise you that much. I will save your body and soul from being devoured.

Jake, know that you've saved me, and that I'm going to save Rachel and

Team Firebird from L'reek and the Nephilim.

Then I'm going to kill every fucking one of them.

19

I REACH DEEPER into my Sedu spirit than I have before, more than I ever dared. I embrace the monster within—entirely.

I turn toward the three Nephilim to my left and exhale the longest jet of fire I ever have. They must be ten or more feet away, but all of their ski masks go up in flames. They drop their machine guns and grab their heads, screaming.

I pick up my Sedu blade, will it to the size of a dagger, and sheath it in my belt. Grabbing the metal railing, with a cry of fury I rip the rail in two. I grab a short length of it with both hands and push myself off the platform, swinging on the torn rail like a rope. The rail buckles and tears off of more support beams as my weight pulls it down to the level below.

Rachel shouts and struggles with all her might against the three Nephilim, one on each arm and one holding her body. She's wriggling and writhing so violently they can barely hold on. The two Nephilim holding her arms stare at me. I can't see any expressions through their goggles and ski masks, but I assume they're surprised, maybe even shocked.

I release the rail-rope, and my momentum carries me to the platform next to the Nephilim holding Rachel's right arm. I try to land on my feet, but I land hard on the checked metal platform and roll onto my knees. So much for being smooth.

Rachel screams like she's just been stabbed. I can't think about it. If I do, I'm lost. I focus on my fight, on my rage.

The Nephilim next to me takes one hand off of Rachel and pulls a knife. I'm too out of breath to breathe on him, so instead I spring up and grab his knife arm with my right hand hard enough to snap it like a twig. With the palm of my left hand I cover his mask and will my hand to heat up. He drops the knife, screaming, and tries to pry my hand off of his blistering and burning mask. My right hand free, I grab my Sedu blade and stab straight through his gut.

The moment Rachel's right arm is free, she springs backward and smashes the Nephilim holding her back against the metal railing behind them. He grunts and lets go of her.

The Nephilim holding Rachel's left arm aims his pistol at her. Before he can fire, the point of a Sedu blade bursts through his chest. He goes rigid, paralyzed. The Nephilim is lifted off of his feet by the blade in his chest and thrown off the rail.

"I've got her!" Klara, her Seduman skin hard, red, and scaly, her mouth extended into a short crocodile-like mandible, runs to Rachel. "Get L'reek before he kills Mort!"

"I'm okay," Rachel says. "Tough skin. Klara can wrap me up. Stop L'reek! I'll see to Jake!"

Klara plasters herself to the side of the platform to give me a clean run. I'll have to run to the side of the refinery, turn, then run all the way to the other side. I pull everything out of my spirit that I can, every bit of enhanced strength I have, and start running.

Across the refinery, L'reek seems panicked now that Jake took away his leverage. He left Jake lying on the platform and flew down to the level below. It looks like he's beating up Mort. I try to run faster.

Bullets pound my left arm as I race across the platform. At another intersection, more Nephilim fire at me. I keep running.

More bullets, more Nephilim chasing me, but I am finally across the refinery. I turn right and race toward L'reek. He's grabbed hold of Mort and is yelling at him and slicing him with his claws.

I scream at L'reek with all of my fury, pain, and rage. He turns to me. He looks scared. I keep running.

Only moments away.

Keep running.

L'reek extends his wings.

I hear Rachel's battle cry. I see her leap across the entire open center of the refinery. Fifty feet! I don't think I've ever seen her leap more than thirty or forty feet before!

Right before she lands on the platform above us, she spits an acid stinger. It lands in L'reek's right wing. He howls as the acid burns through the leathery membrane.

I lunge at him, grabbing him in a bear hug and throwing him down so he can't fly away. L'reek lands on the Nephilim holding Mort's left hand; the Nephilim lets go as he falls off the platform. He screams as he falls. I hear Mort fighting behind me.

L'reek opens his mouth to fire one of his energy bolts.

I breathe fire into his mouth first.

He closes his mouth fast, terror in his four eyestalks. With all four arms around me, he tries to slice my back. He shreds my trench coat but he doesn't reach my flesh. He tries to knee and shove me off of him, but I'm not budging. I reach to my belt and grab my Sedu blade. I will it to ignite with Zedek's blue flame and shove it into his chin. It barely penetrates a couple inches. It feels like his body is fighting the weapon, like something inside L'reek is pushing back.

The strain on my right arm from trying to push in my blade is enough for L'reek to gain leverage on me and throw me off. I slam against the railing of the platform. He stands and unfolds his wings.

I scream out in frustration.

He pushes down with his wings, but before his legs can leave the platform Zaebos leaps on top of him, his two rows of razor-sharp teeth clinging to L'reek's right wing. L'reek can't get off the ground with Zaebos's weight on him. L'reek growls and flings Zaebos against the railing.

I'm back on my feet. My weapons won't hurt him, but my Sedu powers still can. I wrap my hands around his neck and breathe fire on his head. He screams as his head smolders, slicing the front of my trench coat to pieces with every razor-sharp nail on his four claws. I knee him in the gut with all my Sedu strength, and when he doubles over I shove him down to the platform.

"However much this hurts...you've hurt me worse," I seethe.

I breathe fire on his head and punch the burned and charred tissue as hard as I can. It feels like I'm punching a wall, but I don't stop. L'reek tries to throw me off, but I just adjust my hold and keep punching. I think he's trying to talk to me, but I just keep punching.

My fury is beyond grief. Beyond rage. It is my sacred duty to end L'reek, here and now.

I run out of breath, but I keep punching.

I can't feel my hands or arms anymore.

I keep punching.

When my right fist goes completely through his charred skull, I pull out my hand. My fingers are raw and burning.

I choke back the pain and rise. I grab the motionless carcass that used to be L'reek and, straining under the effort, lift it over the railing. With a yell I shove him over the rail and into the vat of boiling chemicals he'd demanded I dive into.

Both my hands bleed and shake. My right fist blisters from being exposed to Rishon blood. I look around for the other Nephilim, but I see only dead ones. Klara stands about ten feet away, tears in her glowing, Seduman eyes, a quiver on her extended, crocodile-like mandible. Both her hands hold bloody Sedu blades.

"Come," a bloody and exhausted Zaebos says as he steps over the corpse of one of the Nephilim. "Let us help you up the stairs."

20

KLARA PUTS HER ARM around my back and supports me up the metal staircase to the platform above. I can barely lift my shaking arms to the rail. My hands throb like they're on fire. I didn't realize how much beating L'reek to death battered my body until I stopped to take a breath. I walk up the stairs as quickly as my exhausted legs can take me, with Klara holding me from falling backward and Zaebos by my side.

Every step, I get closer to seeing Jake's body. Every step, breathing gets harder. Every step, my lips quiver more. How long will it take his body to bleed out? A brain can survive for minutes—seven minutes, I think—once the body dies. Racing across the refinery and killing L'reek took precious minutes. I'm not sure how many. I wasn't watching the clock. But it seems like it took far too long.

I reach the top of the platform and sway backward as soon as I see his crumpled form. I emit a half moan, half cry I've never heard myself make before. My throat goes dry, my head goes light. Klara is strong in her Seduman form and keeps me from tumbling back down the stairs. We keep walking forward.

Rachel, her chest heaving, her huge, glowing red eyes pouring tears down her insect-like hardened skin, sits on her shins near Jake's head. She turns to me with a gut-wrenching look of shock and desperation.

Mort crouches over Jake. I notice that the right sleeve of his blue shirt has been torn off. When I look at Jake I can see why. Mort tied his shirt sleeve around Jake's neck to slow the bleeding. I can't tell if it worked; the blue sleeve has been completely soaked red, and blood has pooled on the metal platform.

Mort looks up at me, his large, red Seduman eyes glassy. "I had to try," he whispers.

I nod and pat Mort's shoulder and attempt a smile, but I think it just comes out like violent lip tremors.

Klara releases me and I sit down next to Mort. "I have to try, too," I inhale.

I gently caress Jake's face with my left hand. His face is still warm, but his complexion is pale. I place my right hand over his gored throat and close my eyes. I concentrate on reaching out to the cells in his body, to hearing his heartbeat, to trying to call to his body to repair itself. I imagine his cells stopping the bleeding, repairing his punctured throat, weaving new skin on his neck. I can feel those cells that are still alive trying to comply, but there's not enough. His heart hasn't stopped completely, but it doesn't beat often enough to sustain him.

Involuntarily, I let out another cry-moan. I try to hold myself together as I watch the life of my soulmate slip away. I hiccup in a loud sob so violent I nearly throw up. My hands fly to my mouth as the tears explode out of my flaming eyes. Jake doesn't deserve this.

As much angry as sad, I shut my mouth and hold my breath to stop sobbing. I close my eyes and reach out my hands again. This time I reach out to everything. To Jake, the microbes in the air, to Mort and Klara and Rachel, to all the life in the land around us. I imagine not only all the beings and their cells, but all of it as one entity, one consciousness.

"I think I can communicate with life itself, with the life force on Earth, so maybe you can hear me," I begin, steadying my voice. "I don't know why you chose me for this, but I promise you, I will strive with all my being to live up to your trust in me. I'll speak for you. I'll defend you. Whatever you ask of me. I give you my heart and my will...but I ask—I *demand*—one thing. Jake is a part of my soul, as surely as I live. And if he dies, that part of me dies with him. For me to be your warrior, I need to be whole."

"Please..." I slowly open my eyes. "Please..."

21

"MALE AND FEMALE, HE CREATED THEM," Jake mutters, slowly opening his eyes.

He gazes into my flaming eyes. A slightly dazed smile slowly awakens across his face.

I inhale and hold my breath, afraid to exhale in case he closes his eyes again.

My shaking fingers slowly reach down and touch his cheek.

Thank you, God. Thank you.

I finally exhale and start breathing again, rein in my Sedu self, and offer Jake a breaking, quivering smile as I gently caress his face and hair.

"Hi," I whisper-sob.

"Genesis, chapter one, verse twenty-seven," Mort says, his tone expressing both relief and astonishment.

"Is that what that line's from?" Jake creaks out, his voice weak as he starts to shift around. "It's sounded familiar when she said it to me."

"You saw someone?" Klara asks.

"Yeah," Jake nods, propping himself up on his elbows and staring at me with such love and joy to see me, it makes me cry even harder. I'm still in too much shock to speak, but I lean down and kiss his lips.

"Who did you see?" Rachel asks, rubbing his arm.

Jake turns to Rachel and starts to tug at the shirt sleeve around his neck. "She looked tall, muscular, and red, with flaming dark hair and the kindest flaming eyes standing over me. Kinda like Pyza, but not."

I unfasten and unwind the sleeve Mort wrapped around Jake's neck as a makeshift bandage. The hole in Jake's throat has been sealed up with a fresh layer of new pink skin. I know that I didn't do that healing. Who did?

He turns to me. "Thank for the assist," he smiles. "Even though I'd never seen her before, I know her face so well. Alex, I saw—"

Jake's eyes go wide and his expression goes blank.

"The tall, red woman smiling on the other side of the platform," Jake shakily points to the edge of the platform behind me. "I don't suppose any of you see her, do you?"

We all look toward the edge of the platform.

My jaw hits the floor.

"I see her," I gasp.

The woman in the sheer black dress looks exactly like a red, female Sedu—about seven feet tall, muscular, dark, wavy flaming hair, nasty teeth and fangs, red flaming eyes. And that face...where have I seen that face? "She does look really familiar, although I'm not sure why."

"I see her too," Klara marvels. "She just appeared out of thin air!"

"Rachel? Mort? Zaebos?" I call out.

Mort and Rachel look at each other. Rachel shrugs and shakes her head.

"I don't see her. I don't think Rachel does either. But I have no doubt that she appears before you," Mort says. "I'm guessing that rather than create a physical form, she is manifesting in the minds of those she needs to communicate with."

"Mort is correct." The red figure smiles.

"She says you're right," Klara repeats.

"Rachel?" Mort takes Rachel's hand and then motions to Zaebos. "Let's give them room to chat, shall we?"

Rachel looks up at Mort and nods. Zaebos shoots a glance toward where we're all facing with a slight snarl, clearly not pleased he's been left out of the vision. The three of them walk about fifteen feet further across the platform to give us some space.

"So...who are you?" Jake shifts until he's facing the red figure. She steps a little closer to us.

"We have been called many things," she says. "Ninsun. Durga. Matka. Danu. Terra Mater."

Klara's jaw hits the floor. Her glowing red eyes nearly pop out of her head. "Matka? Mati Syra Zemia?"

We turn to Klara.

"Friend of yours?" Jake asks.

Klara looks at Jake. I can tell she wants to answer, but all she can do is stare, wide eyed and slightly trembling.

"Matka is one of our names, yes," the red figure says to Klara. Then the apperition turns back to me. "But you can call us...Alexandra."

"You're me?" I gasp.

"This is how we see you," she says. "Our beloved champion."

"Okay," I inhale, trying to understand what is happening here.

"My mother and I used to pray to her...the Earth mother goddess...beg her..." Klara begins to tear. "I tried a few times alone, after mama died..."

"We heard you, every time." Matka smiles pensively at Klara. "We are here for our champion, Klara. We will have words and sacred duties for you as well. For now, we task you with telling your friends about this meeting once we have departed."

"Of course, Matka," Klara whispers as she wipes her eyes. "Thank you."

The red figure turns back to me. "We listen to you, too, Alex. We love you. We celebrate your victories. We buried your dead at Firebird Manor and mourned with you. We are many who speak as one—and one who speaks for many. We spring from all that lives, bind it, become it. We are all, and yet we are none."

"So...is this going to be one of those cryptic conversations where you talk in riddles and only half-answer us?"

"Ask us, Jacob Harman." She shoots him a warm but long-suffering smile. "We will answer plainly."

"How am I alive?"

"You and our champion are one soul. We need Alex as our champion, and she asked for you. You are her flesh, just as she is your resolve. So long as she remains, you shall remain, together as one whole."

"Then I have you to thank for giving my Jake back to me?" I try to keep my voice from breaking. "Thank you, thank you, thank you."

"Thank *you*, Firebird Champion," Matka smiles. "For all that you have done to rid us of this annihilation. For all that you can do. For all you will do."

"I'm your champion," I repeat. I mean, I guess I knew something was up, what with being able to tap into the life force and all. But to actually hear Mother Earth—or at least a manifestation of the Earth's life force—say it to me while appearing to us as a huge red Sedu version of me?

This is a lot to deal with. There are so many thoughts going through my head right now—about Jake, about what's happened, about what this means—just trying to calm myself down enough to listen to her is tough. But as shocked and confused as I am, I've got to admit that having Mother Earth tell me I'm her champion is pretty amazing.

"Okay, before you elaborate on that, can I ask a follow-up question?" Jake jumps in. "You say that I'll be by her side as long as she remains...does that mean that I'm going to live as long as she does?"

"Yes."

"That was nice and direct, thank you," Jake says.

She smiles.

"Do you have any idea how long I might expect that to be?" I ask. "You know, before my House rebuilt me as a full Sedu I thought I might live a couple hundred years or so. Now I have no idea."

"As a Sedu, you could be eternal. But you are our champion..." Matka trails off, looking away. "And champions die."

A chill rises up my spine as that sinks in. "So there have been others?"

"Yes," Matka's eyes begin to fill.

"They all died championing you?"

"And we loved them all," she nods, weeping.

Jake reaches for my hands. "But I'll bet they were all amazing and led amazing lives." He rubs my hand. "And hey, you'll have me, so you can't beat that, right?"

"Right," I return the smile, although it's a quivering, wet one.

Jake faces the red figure with a concerned expression. "What about aging, injury, all that? If I get hit by a bus, do I live on as long as she does as an invalid?"

"You shall always return to your prime physical health." Matka smiles, her own mouth quivering almost exactly the same way mine is.

"And if Alex is killed, I immediately drop dead."

She nods.

Jake turns to me, a warm, loving smile across his face. "I'm okay with that."

I wipe my eyes, lean down, and kiss Jake tenderly again. Then I look up at Matka. "Well, while I'm still alive, what can your current champion do for you?"

"Rid us of these scourges," she says, the warmth in her voice draining to anger. "These Nephilim and Rishonim, they destroy and leave nothing. What they take, they destroy forever. Even their corpses sting us. They break our cycle."

"Your cycle?"

"The cycle of life," she explains. "The opposite of life is not death—death is part of the cycle, necessary for life. Those monsters are our true opposite, our true nemesis—they are *lifelessness*. They destroy us utterly. We try to protect ourselves, but they are more ancient than we, more corrosive. For millennia we have needed a champion who can make war like they can, and defeat them. You can do what we cannot."

"I'll do it, I swear," I promise.

For a moment, she lights up, her smile filled with gratitude and delight. That quickly gives way to tears, like she knows I just promised to sacrifice my life for her. It's intensely unsettling. I mean, if having the love of my life wake up from near death is the good kind of unsettling, this is the bad kind.

"Well, got any words of advice for me?" I swallow.

"Yes, Firebird." She approaches me, leans down, and offers me her hand.

I'm a bit surprised; I thought she was only in our minds, but I take it. It feels as solid as any hand I've ever felt. Matka must be more than just an image, then.

"Remember..." She shakes her torso and her sheer dress falls away, revealing her muscular, red, curvy body.

The seven-foot-tall goddess takes hold of my hand like a parent or a teacher would a little girl. She slides my fingers over her hair and cheeks, making my fingers feel the texture of her hair, the curves of her cheek, her nose, every little bit of everything. It gets really weird and creepy, she makes me stick my fingers into her ears, touch her eyeballs, everything. All the while staring into my eyes, saying "remember" emphatically.

She does this for every inch of her body: every curve, every corner, every crack, every orifice, front and back, top and bottom. Needless to say, this makes me extremely uncomfortable—not just because it gets a little porntastic when she has me explore her girly bits inside and out—but she makes me feel each and every tooth in her mouth, between her fingers, her armpits, I mean *everything*. I have to keep shifting and bending and contorting to get my hand everywhere she's directing me.

"Um...Alex?" I hear Rachel from further down the platform. "Is it interpretive dance time?"

I can't help but chuckle through my discomfort, realizing what this must look like.

"I'll tell you later," I say as Matka guides my fingers between her toes and over the soles of her feet. "Remember," she keeps imploring me, begging me. "Please remember..."

Once she's had me glide my hands over and inside her entire body, she pulls away from me and smiles with the same smile, but her eyes change from red Sedu eyes burning with orange fire to green eyes, with green flames inside of her irises. Matka gently takes my face in her hands, smiles pensively, and kisses my forehead. She fades as she kisses me, until she's gone, and I'm left standing at the end of the platform, exhaling and staring at Jake with exhaustion, joy, and disbelief.

"Goodbye, Matka," Klara whispers, sitting against the railing quietly sobbing.

"She left?" Rachel asks, as she, Mort, and Zaebos return to where we are.

"Yup," Jake says as he sits up for the first time. I step over and sit down next to him, taking his hands in mine.

"So...what happened?" Rachel asks, sitting down between Klara and us.

"Well," Jake turns to Rachel. "Looks like I'm immortal now, and Alex just finished feeling up Red She-Hulk."

I can't help but laugh through my tears as I grab Jake and hold him against my chest.

22

"MATKA—that's her nickname; Mati Syra Zemia is her full name—she's the giver of life, the Earth Mother, in Ukrainian myths," Klara explains to our group once I've related to Mort, Rachel, and Zaebos everything that transpired. "I know it's pagan, but still..."

"You don't have to defend your beliefs," I smile and rub Klara's shoulder. "Not to us."

Klara returns the smile and puts her hand on mine. "Mama always taught me that when life gets hard, when I have problems I can't solve, when I have no energy left, to dig a hole in the Earth, and speak my mind. She said Matka will hear you, and if you believe, she'll comfort you. It was a nice story to tell a girl, especially when her mother was dying of cancer."

"Well, I'm in," Rachel says. "I'm already Lady Firebird's shield maiden; shield maiden to Mother Earth's champion works too."

I reach out and take Rachel's hand. "You and me forever, girlie."

"I go where you go, my lady." Zaebos bows his muzzle. "If you shall now champion life on Earth, I shall fight by your side."

"Thank you, Zaebos."

"Of course, we're all in," Mort says. "The House of Stygg is at your call, whenever you need us. And I can be of use already, now, here."

I raise my eyebrows, curious what he means.

"I recommend you all return to the House of Keroz. Jake has been through so much, and so have you, dear child. You need to rest and relax—all of you. Somewhere safe, comfortable, surrounded by family."

"I agree, my lady," Zaebos adds before I can get a word in. "This is wise."

"We need to take care of—"

"They're all dead, my lady," Zaebos says.

"When you asked me to stay in the chopper," Klara explains. "I turned to Zaebos."

"I asked Klara to guide me through this confusing construction, and as we went I dispatched every Nephilim I found...and I found them all," Zaebos says with a pleased grin.

For the first time, I realize that Zaebos's Team Firebird uniform is riddled with bullets, slices, and punctures—and nearly every tooth in his two rows of razor-sharp teeth is bloody.

"I don't doubt it." I smirk.

"Let Klara and I talk to our pilot, to the local authorities, and to General Patrick for you," Mort says. "I'm a known commodity—a wealthy defense contractor who they will listen to. Klara can inform everyone of what Matka said. I'll inform my father in Sediin about what has happened here and then return to redouble my efforts to find where these beasts are hiding. And time is so fast in Sediin, you can take your time to rest."

"I'll return to the House of Gryx as soon as I'm finished with Mort and let my family know what has transpired here."

"Okay," I agree. "Thank you, Uncle Mort. Thank you, Klara."

Mort smiles warmly at the term of endearment. Klara smiles too.

"A nap and a nibble in Sediin sounds perfect." Jake inhales deeply. "It'll also give me some time to think of what to tell my dad and Josh. I think I should probably tell them over Chinese food. Dad loves Chinese. He won't love this."

Jake holds out his hand to Mort. "Mort, if you don't mind doing me a big favor, let me give you the secret email address I've been using to leave messages for my family while they're in hiding. They know who you are already, so you can just introduce yourself, let them know I asked you to email because I'm in Sediin, and please ask them to meet us all at Yen Ching in Orange for dinner tomorrow evening. Twenty or so hours will give us nearly a month in Sediin to regain our strength."

"I'd be happy to," Mort fishes his phone out of his pocket, swipes around a little, and hands it to Jake. "I'll even make you a reservation there."

"I can already taste the mu shu chicken!" Rachel cracks.

23

Once we finally collapse in my chamber in the House of Keroz, we sleep for days. Sediin days, of course. We've been through a lot. Zogo makes sure that we've always got lots of food and water; Rachel and Vetis make trips to Earth to buy things like fresh fruit and ice cream that we can't get in Sediin. Zaebos brings his whole family—Daeba and their five puppies—to see us every Sediin day, which is great fun and wonderful therapy. Garz, Vetis, and even Pyza comes to visit us regularly and, when Jake's feeling better, accompany us on walks through the House and its grounds.

With our health and energy restored, we're overwhelmed by the need to touch and taste every inch of each other's body. We tear off each other's clothes and go at each other with more desperation than romance; we had both assumed we'd never get be with each other again. Lots of I love you's and even some tears are shed as we tumble across the soft, peach-colored sheets of my king-sized bed.

Mort was really smart about making our reservation at our favorite Chinese restaurant in Orange County, Yen Ching. He told the hostess that it was for the Gold party and that we'd need the entire banquet room. And we will: it's not just me, Jake, and Rachel coming to dinner, but Vetis and Garz are also there in their human forms, and Klara and her dad—also in his human form. I tell the receptionist who we are, so the staff is prepared for the fact that the room will be lined with Mazzikim "demons" to protect us. Zaebos has made the command decision that he's never going to let me out of the House of Keroz without a full guard. With so many people I love in one place, I'm fine with that.

An older Chinese woman shows us all to the banquet room at the back of the house-shaped restaurant. I warn her that there's going to be a few more people coming through the front door, but that I'll be introducing a lot of beings from my universe directly into the room. I don't think she quite gets what I mean, but she gives me a slight bow and very slight raising of the corners of her mouth. As soon as she leaves the room and closes the doors behind her, I open a portal. Zaebos, waiting very impatiently by the portal mirror in the House of Keroz, immediately shoves his way through, followed closely by a dozen Mazzikim, who all take positions around the room.

When the hostess escorts John and Josh Harman into the banquet room, she finally sees what I was talking about. She tries to smile nonchalantly as she departs, but she looks like she's going to need a change of pants. But she must have told the wait staff what to expect, because a Chinese man and woman come in to start giving us beverages, free appetizers, and menus, and they seem a little uncomfortable but not surprised by the inhuman company.

At first we just make idle small talk discussing the menu and which dishes we want to order, but it's pretty strained. John and Josh know that it must be something horribly serious for them to be asked by Dr. Mortimer Stygg to meet us here, rather than a direct message from Jake. Rachel tries chat with Josh; she thanks him for the Bat Mitzvah books, and he's definitely happy to see her and be in her company, but he's obviously preoccupied.

"Well, let's just get to it," Jake inhales. Starting from our arrival in Corona Del Mar, he tells his father and brother everything. The food arrives as Jake is retelling the tale. Rachel, Klara, Jake, and I fill our plates and start eating. Not John and Josh; they're near tears, unable to concentrate on anything but Jake's tale. Rachel sympathetically caresses Josh's arm and spoons out portions of stuff for him. Josh looks at his food, tries to take a bite, but just can't.

"So...yeah. That's a thing that happened," Jake tries to affect a light tone. But it's tough to quip about having sacrificed his life for me.

The misery on John Harman's face fills me with guilt. He likes me—he always has—but he always worried that this crazy life I lead will be the death of his son. And it *was*. I got his son killed. His worst fear, realized. Yeah, Jake is back, but I know what John is thinking: Jake only lives as long as I live, and as Mother Earth's champion I'm pretty much committed to dying for her.

This has got to make things tough on Josh, too. Not just because he loves his brother and would have similar fears as his dad. Fourteen-year-old Josh and thirteen-year-old Rachel are boyfriend-girlfriend lovey-dovey, and this has to turn up John's fear of Rachel getting Josh hurt. How will he feel about Josh going steady with Rachel now?

"I'm sorry, Mr. Harman. I truly am," I whisper, my eyes getting glassy.

"I know," he mumbles solemnly.

"I never would have—"

"I know," John Harman interrupts, then lowers his head. He clearly doesn't want to talk, so I stop.

The silence is occasionally broken by the sound of joyless chewing, since we're hungry. But everyone basically waits for John or Josh to speak.

Finally, John inhales and raises his head. He stares right at me, through me. "Did you have to go after the Nephilim?"

His words cut me deeper than any knife. I just stare, unable to speak. I mean, he can't expect me to not save life on Earth because it might be dangerous. Can he?

"They came after *us*," Rachel says, trying to be civil but clearly defensive. "We only first learned about them when I caught one spying on me at Tustin Middle School. We never sought them out. It was only when they tried to kill us that we took them on."

John nods with a sigh. He lowers his head again.

Josh pats Rachel's hand, a don't-worry-I-understand expression on his face. It's really sweet.

"I'm just..." Josh faces his brother with an expression deeper and sadder than his fourteen years should be capable of. "I'm glad you're back, Jake. If I went into hiding and then never saw you again...that would have been the worst."

"I'm glad too," Jake says, a slight smile on his face.

More silence.

I turn to Klara. She's sitting with her dad, the two of them pictures of sympathy for us. As upset as I am, a slight, genuine smile escapes. I am so lucky to be surrounded by such loyal and loving friends. Team Firebird 'til the end.

Jake tries to break the silence. "Dad, I know this is—"

"Do you?" John looks at his son, his face pale, his voice shaking. "Do you know what it's like to have your wife murdered and then your son killed too?"

"I'm here now, Dad," Jake softly replies.

"But for how long?"

"Forever," Garz breaks in. "I am—"

"I know who you are," John says.

"Good. Then hopefully you understand the weight my words have. This avatar of life on Earth has chosen Alex, and we are all with her. She will not fail—and she will not fall."

Garz turns to me. "You have a duty, and we all shall assist you. We shall destroy G'Suul and the Nephilim. *Utterly.* Lords Gryx, Mog, and Stygg will fight with us. Maybe others as well. The Greater Sedu shall fight with us. We shall have an army that can defeat anything."

I can see Zaebos against the wall with the other Mazzikim silently nod in agreement.

"Hear, hear!" Lord Gryx raises his daughter's glass of tea, since as a Sedu, he doesn't need to eat or drink, and doesn't have anything in front of him.

"I am a father, too," Gryx addresses John Harman. "I worry every time my Klara joins Team Firebird on a mission. But Matka has spoken, and we will all see her will done."

I smile, hoping it hides my melancholy.

"But that's not what *you* think, is it?" John looks at me accusingly. "I can read it in your face."

Everyone turns to me.

Dammit.

"I have to be honest with you all. I don't think I'm meant to walk away next time." I swallow.

"Don't get me wrong, I want to live. But 'Champions die,' Matka said.

It's like her mantra. I'm definitely going to fight; I made a promise, and even if I didn't, I feel responsible. But if I go..." I look at Jake, and the tears fall.

Jake smiles and wipes my tears. "Alex, I already died for you. I made my peace with my choice. All this...this is just bonus time. I never thought I'd get to see you again, to see my family and say a proper goodbye, to eat yummy Chinese food."

I can't help but snort out a sad chuckle.

"Seriously, though, all this is more than a dream come true. I made the choice to give up everything I had and everything I might have. To get it back again, even for a moment, is unbelievable. Even if this is all the extra time I get, right here, right now, it's enough. My life's been amazing, I love you all, and it's enough."

I turn to Jake and pat his arm with a quivering, pensive smile.

"And this is supposed to make me feel better?" Jake's dad says. "My son died. I'm happy that Jake is back, but I wish he were never part of this. Is that so hard to understand?"

"But Dad," Josh quietly joins in. "We were always part of this. Remember, Tante Toni, your great-great-great-great grandmother in Mission Viejo, she's a Seduman. The Nephilim would eventually have found out and come for her, since Sedumen have stronger spirits and are tastier meals for those Rishon things. Then they would have come for us. At least this way, Jake's helping to save all of us."

I really hope I live long enough to marry Jake, because Josh is going to be an awesome brother-in-law. I love that kid. Looking at the eyes Rachel is making to Josh, caressing his hands for sticking up for me and all of us, I doubt I'm the only one.

"Sir, if I may." Vetis turns to John Harman. "I ask, with respect, to try and understand you: what is it you wish to achieve with your outburst? Jake is already immortal, tied to Alex's spirit. This cannot be undone. I fear for my own daughter, Rachel, in this war, but I know that the course is set and nothing will stop it."

John Harman turns to me. "You could let your armies fight...sit this one out."

"No she can't, Dad," Jake says resolutely. "She's Matka's champion. This is her fight, more than anyone's. We're all going to help her win it. I love you, Dad. That's why I wanted to see you in person to tell you all this. But I wasn't asking permission. Neither is Alex or anyone here."

John Harman averts his gaze from his son, tears beginning to form.

"You fight as hard as you can, Lady Firebird," Jake takes my hand. "Give it everything you've got. And if we fall, I'm okay with it. The only thing I'm not okay with is if you hold back because of me."

Garz, clearly choked up himself, nods and pats Jake on the shoulder. He puts his hand on my arm. "Your soulmate speaks true. The way to win is to fight with both precision and abandon. And mark my words: we will win— our entire House, and the Houses of our allies, will all fight together with you to see this done. *And we will not let you fall.*"

"Not that you asked, dingbat, but I'm not okay with you dying," Rachel says. For the first time I realize she's in tears too, with Josh holding her hands, trying to console her, even though he still needs consolation himself. "I expect you up on the Bimah with me at my Bat Mitzvah. And I'm going to be at your wedding and you're going to be at mine one day, and that's that. I'm your shield maiden and I refuse to let you die."

"As do I," Zaebos adds from the side of the banquet room. "Champions may die, but firebirds do not, and so Firebird Champion shall be the first to be eternal."

"We shall call a meeting of the Sedu Council," Garz declares, then turns to John Harman. "I don't know if Alex or Jake told you about the Sedu Council. The Sedim were locked in a constant cycle of warring with each other because they had no laws or trust between them. It was Alex, Lady Firebird, after her exploits became known in Sediin, who was able to convene the first Sedu council. All the most powerful Sedim—such as our friend, Lord Gryx here—are behind the council. We all owe the current peace in Sediin to Lady Firebird. The Sedim will come. They will listen. And many will join us."

"Thanks, guys," I whisper, finally able to smile with pride. My team is the best team.

"Dad and I will head right to Lord Stygg," Rachel nods, regulating her breathing until her own tears cease. "I need to do some more aerial leaping and firing training with him anyway. He's an awesome trainer, and his Mazzikim are really cool and get along with ours. Lord Stygg even calls me Little Bug."

Rachel turns to Josh. "Which would really piss me off if anyone else called me that, but from a Spider Sedu it's endearing."

"No promises," Josh caresses her hand. Rachel pretends to narrow her eyes in anger, but she clearly enjoys his teasing.

"Speaking of sweet, this mu shu chicken is pretty amazing," Klara adds.

"It is," Jake smiles, relishing a bite like he's never eaten it before in his life. "It really is."

24

AFTER DINNER WE GO OUR SEPARATE WAYS. John and Josh Harman both took extended vacations from work and school in order to go into hiding; they decide to spend a while in a hotel in their hometown of Irvine, California, so John can go back to work and Josh can go back to school. It's a bit dangerous, but they insisted. I get it, though. Josh is keeping up with classes and John is working remotely, but they really need some semblance of normality now that everything's upside down and sideways.

Klara and Gryx return to the House of Gryx to make preparations for whatever may come.

The rest of us return to the House of Keroz. Rachel and Vetis, along with Qwyll and a few other Mazzikim, depart via The Nothingness to the House of Stygg so Rachel can continue her warrior bug training. Garz and Vetis gather some Mazzikim scouts to send word to the other Houses that we are convening an emergency meeting of the Sedu council.

Jake and I decide the best use of our time is to return to Mort's Washington, D.C., office. We want to find out how things went after we left the refinery and ask if he's making any headway in tracking down the remaining Rishon and Nephilim. However, when we return to Sediin, it's about ten at night on Wednesday in California, which means it's one o'clock Thursday morning in Washington, D.C. We might as well wait until it's eight a.m. D.C. time. Also, that will be almost thirty-six hours since Mort was in Oklahoma, so he'll have had time to recuperate in the House of Stygg and then return to Washington to get some work done.

Because time in Sediin is so much faster than on Earth, those seven Earth hours between one and eight in the morning in Washington are like a week in Sediin. It doesn't quite feel like a full week, since we never quite catch up. Days feel really short, and we never quite get used to it, like jet lag that takes a long time to get over. But it does feel like we get to take some time out of time, where we can relax, take some baths, sleep, train, and generally regain our strength.

Zogo makes sure that there's always water and dried fruit and nuts in my room, so we can always snack. He's also very careful to bang our door as loudly as he can and announce himself so he doesn't walk in on us getting frisky or anything. It's really cute. But he's got nothing to worry about. We indulged our passion before we met at Yen Ching; now I'm pretty preoccupied with my mission. Garz makes sure that Jake is always exhausted, too, from self-defense training. Jake will never be a warrior, but Garz insists that he know how to dodge and spring and defend himself, which I heartily approve of.

When it's time for us to return to Earth, Zaebos insists on coming too—and bringing at least three Mazzikim guards with us—even though we're just walking into the extremely well-protected office of a Seduman ally. I agree, but ask him to bring three Mazzikim who, like Zaebos, look like bear-sized dogs. At least then, any of Mort's employees who casually peer through the many transparent glass walls of Mort's office will see what look like huge dogs and may not think more than that. Something that looks like an ape-horse would be a bit harder to explain.

When we portal into Mort's office, he's sitting at his large black desk, staring into the middle of the room, looking extremely drawn.

"Sorry about the brightness," I wheeze as I step out of the portal and take a few strained steps so that the Mazzikim have room to enter the room.

"It's fine," Mort says, his voice taut as he holds his hand up to shield his eyes.

"Everything okay, boss?" Jake asks.

Mort says nothing as the rest of our party portals in.

Jake and I look at each other. I may not have the long, arduous recovery from portal travel I used to, but I still am straining a bit. Jake feels fine, so he walks over to Mort's desk, then around to the other side so Mort can look at him without facing the portal.

"Mort? Are you all right?"

Mort turns his head away from me, toward Jake.

"I take it dinner was a success?"

"Well, if by success you mean my dad was grateful and miserable all at once, then yes."

Mort nods. "I can imagine. Had I received similar news from any of my children or grandchildren, I would respond much the same, I'm sure."

By the time all our Mazzikim arrive, I'm feeling recovered enough to walk over to Jake.

"You seem very subdued and unfocused," I say to Mort. "Are you sure that everything is all right here? Or in the House of Stygg?"

Mort sighs, then turns to me. "Nothing is wrong here. In fact, our labs are prototyping a portable Rishon radiation detection device as we speak. But I didn't get the chance to return to my House."

"That's great, but why couldn't you return home? Is something wrong in Sediin?" Jake asks.

"I don't think so," Mort shakes his head. "No, this is about my Sedu blade."

That can't be good.

"What about it?" I swallow hard.

"At the refinery, after Jake..." Mort can't say it. I don't blame him.

"L'reek grabbed me and demanded my Sedu blade. He searched every inch of me, but he couldn't find it."

"Did you have it disguised as a pen and he missed it?" I ask.

"That's what I thought. But then I remembered I had it in dagger form when L'reek absconded with Jake and me in Broxton. I must have dropped it, either when I was grabbed or somewhere in flight."

"I'm sorry about your blade, but your father can easily make you another one," Jake says. "We can take you to the House of Keroz, and you can travel there via The Nothingness."

"Would that were my only concern. In hindsight, I think that L'reek abducted me specifically for my blade. Had he found it on me, it would have dissolved with him in the vat of chemicals you tossed him into. But he didn't find it. Now it could be anywhere between Broxton and the Wynnewood, Oklahoma, refinery we were taken to. I've been trying to track it down remotely via satellites and street cameras, but that's like finding a needle in a haystack that you're only seeing on video."

"Well, if it's hard for you to find, that means it would be hard for the Nephilim to find, too," I try to reassure Mort.

"And you don't even know they're looking," Jake adds. "I don't think there were any Nephilim survivors at the refinery, so there's nobody to report back that it wasn't still in your possession when you left."

"True. And I may have dropped it from the air at any point, and it's lost in the middle of nowhere. But my fear is that I dropped it immediately in Broxton, and remaining Nephilim there would have found it, delivered it to G'suul, and will use it to try and rescue H'ythiis and destroy my father's House at the same time."

"Yeah, maybe, but that sounds farfetched, don't you think?" Jake says.

"My lady." Zaebos directs me with his muzzle toward the portal mirror.

Two of our Ruhin run in circles in front of the portal mirror of the House of Keroz, desperately trying to wave us back to Sediin.

"Maybe not as farfetched as I'd like," Mort swallows, his voice shaking.

25

WE PORTAL INTO THE HOUSE OF KEROZ to the sounds of massive chaos.

"House of Stygg under attack!" a Ruhin with the head of a finch and the body of a dog screeches as it runs in circles, chasing its tail. "Rachel and Vetis and Qwyll and more, trapped there!"

The other Ruhin in the portal chamber, a minx-shaped being with a crocodile head, reaches a paw out to stop his partner. "Zogo is giving orders to the Ruhin who are dressing our Mazzikim warriors. He told us to have water waiting for you and to direct you to the main doors when you are recovered."

He releases his paw, and the finch-dog Ruhin keeps running in circles. The crocodile-minx Ruhin just looks at us and shrugs. I normally enjoy our wacky Ruhin, but there's nothing joyful about their news.

The Mazzikim and I recover long before Mort. I can see on his face how desperately worried he is. He turns toward our portal mirror. As a Seduman, he can think of a destination and the image in the mirror should become the image of that place. Mort closes his eyes, clearly trying to imagine a place... but we're still looking into his office.

"I'm sorry, Lord Mortimer," the crocodile-minx Ruhin says. "It seems that the attackers broke the portal mirror in your House."

Mort exhales, the strain of recovering and his disappointment weighing on him.

"Mort," I gently lay my hand on his shoulder. "We'll get there fast, don't worry."

"Let's go," a doubled over Mort squeaks out, barely able to speak.

"I can carry you, if that's all right," I offer.

Mort nods, and I pick him up. We exit the portal chamber into the great hall. Mazzikim who need weapons and armor run past us to the armory, while armored and armed Mazzikim march past us in the other direction, toward Garz standing at the door, growling orders.

"I shall be but a moment, my lady," Zaebos says, and he and his three Mazzikim join the other Mazzikim heading to the armory. Jake and I, with Mort in my arms, approach Garz by the main doors.

"The Nephilim and G'suul have invaded the House of Stygg," Garz informs us.

"They jumped through the portal mirror using my Sedu blade," Mort says, having recovered enough that the guilt and anger in his voice is obvious. He taps my arm. I place his feet on the floor. He's a bit wobbly, but okay to stand on his own.

"My sister told us of your capture and beating at the hands of L'reek." Garz gently puts a hand on Mort's shoulder. "Do not blame yourself. Clearly they intended to invade the House of Stygg to free H'ythiis one way or another."

"Thank you, Lord Garz. But the way they chose was through me, and I can't let that go."

"Then join us as we defeat them, and let that comfort you." Garz bows his head slightly.

Mort nods, then turns to Jake.

"Jake, I know how much you want to be with Alex, but I need you to return to my office. Check the status of the prototype. Make sure we're tracking their radiation signature with our satellites and sensors. When we force them back to Earth, we need to be able to chase them immediately. Especially if, God forbid, they free H'ythiis."

"But—"

"It's a good idea," I interrupt Jake and gently put my hand on his arm. "You're not going to die if you come with us, but you're not a warrior, so you're not going to do all that much. At Mort's office, you can do a lot. I always want you by my side, but I think it's more important that we each do everything we can."

Garz nods. "I applaud your courage, my soon-to-be brother. There will be occasion for you to join us on the battlefield, I am sure of it. But at this moment, you'll do the most good on Earth."

Jake huffs, but he knows we're right. He offers an almost imperceptible nod of his head, then gives me a quick kiss. "I love you, Alex. Be safe."

"I will," I promise.

"You too, Uncle Mort. You don't get a kiss, though."

"Fair enough." Mort is able to offer a faint smile. "Thank you."

"Come, I'll help." Zogo, who just ran up with a group of Mazzikim, takes Jake's hand. "The portal should still be open to where you last were."

"Thanks, Zogo," Jake says.

"Everyone make way! The future Lord Jake leaves for Earth! Get out of the way!" Zogo shouts, practically tugging Jake behind him as he bounds and bounces to the portal chamber with him. It's sweet.

As I'm turning back to Garz, I see Pyza standing in the entryway of the council chamber. She watches Garz with concern, but more than just concern.

"Garz, Pyza—"

"I see," Garz says, his affection clear.

"I wish dearly that Zedek, Kesed, and Kenuut were here," Pyza says. "Kenuut confers with Dasooj in Merkaba. In a distraught moment, Kesed ran away. Zedek thought he might have returned to The Firstlands and looks for Kesed there."

"I wish they were here too," I say. "I'm Zedek's dear one, so maybe he can hear me."

I raise my head and shout: "Zedek! We go to fight G'suul at the House of Stygg! If you find Kesed, let him know, and tell him we need you both!"

"If he can hear you, that should do it." Mort bows his head in appreciation.

"I hope so," I respond.

"Are we ready, master of the guard?" Garz asks Zaebos.

I turn and smirk. I now see why Zaebos left. He recruited another three Mazzikim into my honor guard, so it now consists of six Mazzikim and Zaebos.

"We are all armored and ready, my lord," Zaebos replies.

"Leeik?" Garz turns to his huge, powerful, and trusted Mazzik lieutenant.

"I have two dozen Mazzikim ready now, and Sento shall lead another two dozen when they are armored and ready."

Garz nods and pats Leeik on the shoulder.

"Come!" my brother bellows. "To the House of Stygg!"

26

OUR ENTOURAGE walks outside the great hall to the edge where the manifestation of ground ends and gray, endless nothing begins. We grab each other's hands, claws, or paws. Garz and the Mazzikim's eyes glow brighter for a moment, and then we're whisked away from the House of Keroz like we're being sucked into a vacuum cleaner.

There's few things I like less than traveling through The Nothingness. It hardly takes any time, but the super-fast twisting, spiraling, and swooping is nauseating as hell. I know because I've done it—and it sucks hard. Even worse: only beings from Sediin can think themselves across The Nothingness. Humans and Sedumen can't. So that means that we have to hold onto beings from this universe that can; if we let go we get stranded, and if we're left at our destination, we're stuck there. Yeah, like I said, I hate traveling The Nothingness. But that's the only way we can get to the House of Stygg, so we have no choice.

This is my first time traveling The Nothingness with the abilities of a full Sedu, however. So theoretically, I should be able to think myself across The Nothingness if I know the destination at the other end well. That won't help me get there now, since I've never been to the House of Stygg before; but hopefully, if I get stranded I can at least return to the House of Keroz. That's some comfort.

It also means that I can grab Rachel and return with her, which is even more comfort. I have no idea what condition she's in. I try not to think about it, which of course means I'm thinking about it. Dammit.

We spin and spiral until I can't tell down from up and right from left, but soon enough I see the grounds and battlements of another Sedu House in the distance below us.

Normally, when I've traveled through The Nothingness to another Sedu House, the Ruhin and Mazzikim of the House see us coming, sound their horns, and cheer in welcome. No beings are outside of this House at all. It's eerie and drives home to me just what kind of chaos we'll be jumping into. The House looms larger and larger as we spiral toward it, until finally we touch down in front of its main doors.

Previously when I reached my destination, I was so nauseated and disoriented it took me a while just to feel steady enough to walk. This time, I'm still wobbly enough that both Garz and Leeik need to help steady me on my feet, but I'm not feeling pukey.

Once we've all landed and gained our feet, Garz pulls out his huge battle ax infused with the spirit of Kesed. I draw my Sedu blade, infused with the spirit of Zedek. Mort raises a longsword that Garz created for him.

Garz lets out a loud and furious battle cry. You don't need to be a Sedu or Seduman to feel the rage burning inside every ounce of his being. We all join him in his cry and run toward the main doors.

Garz bursts open the doors, yelling as loud as an angry, eight-foot-tall barrel-chested Sedu possibly could, but the hall is so noisy and chaotic it goes unheeded.

Through the mayhem I'm able to see Lord Stygg at the other end of the hall bouncing, like he's trying to use his jumping ability, but the Nephilim keep dragging him down. He and his Mazzikim are nearly overrun by Nephilim.

"Stinger!" I shout and point into the middle of the hall, to our left. Up against a wall, Rachel growls fiercely while loading her crossbow, but the fear in her glowing red eyes reveals how she really feels. Vetis, her father, stands next to her holding three knives in his three claws. His bandoliers of throwing knives around his torso are nearly empty. They are being protected by Qwyll and two of our other Mazzikim; it looks like the other Mazzikim they brought with them are dead.

As soon as I call Stinger's name, I feel Garz's rage level, which was already high, leap to stratospheric. It feels hot, like an oven in my chest. I take that heat and let it wash over me. With my eyes burning like torches, I breathe the longest jet of fire I can and shove my way toward Rachel. I swing my fiery blade in a wide arc in front of me, cutting down two burning Nephilim. Zaebos jumps on one to my right, and Mazzikim beside me trample and tear at those Nephilim near them.

My breath runs out and I can't breathe any more fire, but I keep shoving and hacking my way toward Rachel. The Nephilim hear us and turn around. They try to stab me with blades covered in black goo. My eyes go wide—that's the VATS goo that would dissolve us. Our trench coats and leggings may be bulletproof, but they're not blade-proof.

I swing wildly in front of me with my burning blade. The Nephilim fall back, bumping into the Nephilim fighting with the Mazzikim surrounding Rachel. Good; the unexpected shove disorients the Nephilim just enough for Qwyll and his companions to gain the advantage and start beating those Nephilim into the ground. I lunge at the Nephilim in front of me, grabbing his blade and head-butting him. As his head snaps back I take the moment to skewer him on my own blade. I then swing the Nephilim to the left and slide his corpse off of my blade and onto another Nephilim.

That Nephilim quickly tosses his dead compatriot aside and springs at me, slashing down at me with his knife. I step out of the way and bump into Zaebos. The impact throws me a bit, and the Nephilim gets another swing.

I've recovered enough to breathe fire again. He steps back but not before I set his glove on fire. He screams until I chop off his head.

"Alex!" I hear Rachel scream. "Your hair!"

I quickly bat my hood away from my head, in case there's VATS goo dripping on it, careful to only touch it with the back of my gloved hand.

Vetis springs behind me and grabs a patch of hair with his upper left claw and slices the patch off with his upper right claw. He holds my hood with his prosthetic claw while his remaining claw saws away.

"Got it!" Vetis yells he slices off my hood. With his prosthetic claw he takes the hood and tosses it away, toward the center of the hall.

I look down as black, viscous goo dissolves a large handful of my no longer flaming, brown, wavy hair. That was close!

"Rachel, are you hurt? Vetis?"

"We're okay," she pants. "Great to see you, girlie! You and everyone else! Holy shit that was scary!"

"We have the advantage, my lady," Zaebos says. "But it's not over yet."

I take a moment to scan the great hall. Garz and the rest of the Mazzikim have fought their way past the wall of Nephilim and joined Lord Stygg. Nephilim bodies may be stacked from the doors to the middle of the hall and all around us, but living Nephilim still surround Lord Stygg, Mort, Garz, and our remaining warriors.

"My lord, my lady—please return to our House and heal. You have done enough. We shall continue the fight with Lord Stygg."

"Not a chance, Zaebos." Rachel pulls crossbow bolts out of the Nephilim she killed to refill her quiver. "Alex, don't agree with him."

"They attacked my daughter," Vetis growls out of his tiny, lipless mouth. "I would see them all burn."

"I shall keep them safe, my lady," Qwyll promises. "Neither G'suul nor the Nephilim shall touch them."

"Hey, wait." I swallow hard and look around. "Where *is* G'suul?"

27

A MOMENT LATER I HAVE MY ANSWER. G'suul enters the far end of the great hall from a side corridor, cradling a beaten and wounded H'ythiis in his two lower arms, while his two upper arms direct Nephilim around them, pointing them in various directions. The twelve-foot tall G'suul stands head and shoulders taller than everyone as he walks toward a room at the back of the hall. G'suul shoots blasts of blue lightening from his mouth as he advances, clearing Lord Stygg's Mazzikim out of the way.

"We've got to get them!" I yell.

Zaebos howls in agreement. My guard and I push forward, stepping over Nephilim corpses. Vetis and Rachel collect knives and crossbow bolts from the fallen Nephilim corpses as we go.

I hack through the trench coat of the Nephilim in front of me as I breathe a jet of fire on the Nephilim to my right. I kick the Nephilim off the blade in front of me into the Nephilim behind him, which creates a small opening. I dash through it, trying to catch up to G'suul.

A Nephilim to my left thrusts his blade at me, but I slip out of the way. One of my Mazzikim knocks him to the floor.

Two more Nephilim turn around. I slice one of them through his chest as I breathe fire on the other. I don't stop to finish them off. G'suul has crossed the entryway of the room he was headed to, and catching him is my priority. I won't let G'suul escape with H'ythiis. Not after everything they've done.

Two Nephilim in combat stances block the doorway. I dash toward one of them. He tries to slash at me while the other thrusts. I feint out of the way of the thrust and grab the Nephilim by the arm. I breathe fire on his compatriot while willing my hand to heat up the arm of the Nephilim I'm grasping. He screams as his arm and coat ignite. I throw him out of the way and run into the room.

The large room is empty except for a shattered portal mirror against the back wall, with the bottom half cracked but still in place. Normally, a Sedu or Seduman would need to think of a location to change the image in the portal—as far as I know, a Rishon can't do it. But G'suul has placed a shard of a Rishon portal mirror on the remaining half. A Rishon portal mirror fragment is a powerful artifact. When placed on a piece of a Sedu portal mirror, it creates an opening to the last place shown in the mirror. The bottom half of the mirror changes to what looks like the house in Broxton, Oklahoma from which Mort and Jake were kidnapped. G'suul slides H'ythiis's weak but living body through the bottom half of the mirror.

Bastard!

Two Nephilim descend on me, slashing wildly. I twist out of the way of one of the knives, but the other cuts through my own coat and slices into me. All the nerves in my abdomen feel like they're overloading as my insides begin to sizzle. I shriek and wrap my left arm across my gut as pain overtakes me from the VATS goo dissolving my organs. If I want to live through this, I'm going to have to return to my House quickly so it can heal me.

The first Nephilim punches my head. With my Sedu skin hard as concrete, it doesn't hurt me, but along with my internal agony I'm disoriented enough that a third Nephilim gets behind me and grabs me around the chest.

I breathe fire in front of me, but no Nephilim is in range. I kick backward, cracking the shin of the Nephilim behind me. He lets go just as the two Nephilim in front of me thrust blades at my gut. I dodge their blows and kick the closer one into his companion. I kick back the pain as much as I can and take a defensive stance just in time for Zaebos to leap on top of the pair of Nephilim. A gorilla-headed, cheetah-bodied Mazzik mauls the Nephilim I'd kicked to the ground.

I turn toward G'suul at the same time as he turns to me. I'm not expert at reading the expressions of an eldritch monster, but the way his two dozen eyes seem to narrow, I'm going to guess he's royally pissed.

"Dive!" I shout as his mouth tentacles begin to shift. I jump to the side as a blast of blue lightning blows a hole in the wall behind me. He races forward, each arm gashing one of my Mazzikim. He grabs me by the throat with his upper-left claw so I can't breathe fire on him and lifts me off of my feet. Then his lower-left claw wraps around my torso and pulls me closer to his face. The more I struggle, the harder it is to breathe. And as much as I try to ignore it the pain from my insides keeps getting more and more intense.

Zaebos growls as he leaps at G'suul. G'suul shoves Zaebos against the wall with his lower left claw. Zaebos falls to the floor, dazed.

"It was always going to end like this," G'suul sneers as I try to pull myself out of his grasp. His mouth tentacles retract to reveal his large mouth with rows and rows of needle-sharp teeth. He doesn't pull me any closer; instead he just holds me in place—and starts inhaling.

My eyes go wide. I feel burning worse than my organs being melted by VATS—and all I can do is squirm desperately. I feel my hair and nails and teeth and skin, as hard as they are in Sedu form, slowly being pulled apart as tiny rivulets of blood are absorbed into him like my body is being sucked through a straw. My head starts pounding. It gets harder to hold a thought. The heat of my rage slowly dims.

I know how this goes; if I don't break free, soon I'll forget who I am and what I'm doing here. G'suul holds me too tightly for me to wiggle out of his grasp, but I manage to gain a limited range of motion with my right arm.

With all my might, I thrust my Sedu blade into his upper-left shoulder. As with L'reek, my blade penetrates only inches. Through the hilt I can feel his body trying to resist, like there are spirits inside, repelling my blade. And they're winning.

But my blade is more than just sharp; it burns with Zedek's blue flame of righteousness. The heat of Zedek's fire gets to him, and he lets out a grunt of pain. He jerks his shoulder back, and the violent motion rips the blade from my hand. He then flexes his shoulder and the blade clanks to the floor.

I hear the unmistakable sound of Rachel's battle cry flying over me. She lands on G'suul's head and immediately starts spitting acid stingers into his eyes. G'suul reels and tosses me aside. My back slams into the wall so hard that I fall down flat on my chest. I don't feel the full body agony from being absorbed anymore but the internal agony from the VATS is almost too much. I try to take a breath but there's nothing to breathe in Sediin. I slowly crawl forward. G'suul grabs Rachel by her hood and with his two upper arms throws her out of the room. I prop myself up, and gritting my teeth through the pain, try to rise.

G'suul turns to me. His acid-melted eyes are already starting to heal. I see his mouth open, and before I can move he fires a blue energy bolt. It explodes onto my chest. My entire body seizes up and feels like it's melting away at the same time. The blast throws me back against the wall. I scream.

The front of my trench coat disintegrates. There's too much shredded coat and clothes for me to see for sure, but it feels like there's a massive crater in my chest. Just when I thought that I couldn't hurt more than I already did. My whole body shakes and spasms. I can't focus my eyes. I double over on the ground.

I need to move, but just raising my head takes everything I have left.

"Alex!" I hear Rachel shout.

G'suul faces me, another blue energy bolt forming in his mouth.

I try to push myself to the side.

G'suul fires.

"R—"

28

BLACKNESS.

My pain is gone—but so is everything.

One moment I was in the House of Stygg, trying to evade G'suul's line of sight. He spit another bolt at me. Every inch of my being erupted in agony. Did I scream? I think I screamed. I'm not sure. Everything flashed white and then...

Only this blackness.

I'm aware of nothing around me. I can't move my head to see anything. Do I have a head? I have no body awareness. Maybe no body? I only experience thoughts and darkness.

Oh God—is this what death is?

I didn't get a chance to say goodbye to Jake. I assumed if I died he would drop dead too and our souls would be united. Jake, if you have any consciousness or awareness of my thoughts, I love you. I'm sorry we weren't together. I'm sorry that we didn't get to have a life together. I'm sorry...I'm sorry for everything.

Matka, I let you down, and it breaks my heart. Not that I have a heart anymore. You were relying on me as a champion, and I charged headfirst at a being far more powerful than me and got myself killed. My blade couldn't even penetrate G'suul at all—I'm thinking he had spirits inside his body fighting against me. Some champion I turned out to be.

Is this it? Just thinking to myself, forever? Talking to myself for eternity? How long have I been like this? Minutes? Hours? Years? Centuries? If this is all I will experience forever, I'm definitely going to lose it.

Have I already lost it?

Make it stop!

Wait—what if all of these thoughts I'm having are just the very instant before I'm dead and gone forever? Then these thoughts will end, and I'll truly be gone. How long have I got left? God, maybe I don't want this to stop, after all. Then again, maybe being gone forever is better than eternity as an isolated consciousness.

But am I an isolated consciousness? I'm only aware of my thoughts, but is there another consciousness out there, aware of me? Something I can reach out to?

Help! Is there anything aware of me?

Yes.

Okay, that was a yes. But am I making up my own dialogue? Or is something external to my thoughts actually communicating with me?

I am external to you, little firebird.

Okay, you really must be external, because I wouldn't have called myself "little firebird"—Dad always said that the spirit of the House of Keroz was his spirit. So...Dad, is that you?

Yes—and no. Keroz was a Sedu with a vast spirit, and by focusing on his power rune, he caused some of his spirit to manifest itself as this House and its grounds. So you are not communicating with the manifestation of Keroz that walked Sediin and Earth, fell in love with your mother, and trained you. But the Keroz that walked and I were one whole, and connected, so I know you. And more.

More?

Yes, Alexandra. The Keroz you knew was vaster than the other Sedu. Not just from rumam and victories, but from his honesty. When that part of me was destroyed, I was not as diminished as I expected to be upon his death. That is why I had enough spirit left to heal you into a true Sedu.

Wow. That's amazing to hear about my dad—you—sorry, it's still confusing. It's just so good to be communicating with something that isn't me. Thanks for making me a full Sedu. I'm sorry I couldn't do you proud.

You do, little firebird.

That's kind of you, but come on, all I did was end up dead.

You are not dead. When Sedim are killed in this universe, their spirit snaps back to their House. If you were dead, you would be either destroyed forever, ended completely, or floating in Gehenna now. No, child, you are alive. In fact, you are the Life of the House of Keroz.

What does that mean, I'm the "Life" of the House of Keroz?

It means that our House is unlike all the other Sedu Houses. Where they can only manifest the imitation of life, you, as a living being made Sedu, can do more. You have a Sedu spirit but are truly alive, Alex, a material being, even now. Where other spirit beings that lose their forms can manifest approximations of bodies out of spirit, you can create true material life from spirit.

We are all connected, Alex. The living energy that calls to you in the material realm as Matka, the spirits of this realm, all of it. It's why humans have rumam in our universe. And it's why you can sense both life on Earth and the spirits of our House.

That sounds incredibly hopeful, but intimidating at the same time. Zedek once called me "something new in all of creation"—is that what you mean? Do I have some greater responsibility or duty?

That is for the fullness of time. For now, you must return to your friends, your House, your Earth, and save them.

Good call. One thing at a time. So how do I do that? Can I create a body the way that beings from Sediin can?

You can do even better, little firebird. Concentrate on forming a body out of the spirit of the House. Concentrate on every detail of your body, internal and external, and you will again walk as a living being, not simply a spirit with a form.

How? When you—the part of you that walked around as Keroz—trained me, I was taught to focus on a warmth that felt like it emanated from the center of my chest. I have no chest, no center, no warmth. What do I do?

Think.

Okay. Here goes...

I imagine myself: five-foot-nine, porcelain white skin, brown hair, blue-eyes. I concentrate on forming a picture of the shape of my face, my Jewy nose, my muscular arms, my sorta perky boobs.

As I concentrate, the blackness around me begins to fade into a slightly reddish color. It must be working! I'm perceiving things! The reddish color becomes more pronounced, until I can see what looks like a blurry, out-of-focus room.

I continue concentrating on my body, expecting the room to continue coming into focus.

Only it doesn't.

Okay, what's happening? Why am I not forming a full body, spirit of the House?

You need to focus on every aspect of that body before it can manifest. Be specific about everything, inside and out.

Every aspect, huh? Okay, I try to remember everything I'd see if I were staring into a mirror. The room gets a little clearer, but not much. I try to remember more details about my appearance, and that helps, too, but everything is still a very unclear blur.

This is so hard! I mean, I know I have blue eyes, but I've never really stared into them and memorized the patterns of color streaks in my irises. Or what my eyelashes look like. The pores in my skin. The creases in the crick of my elbow. I mean, how am I supposed to remember every little hair? Nobody can remember...

Wait...

Remember!

Everything Matka did makes sense now. Matka appeared to me as a female Sedu with my face and said it's how she thought of me. Then she meticulously guided me over every inch. I figured she was trying to teach me some kind of lesson; now I realize that she wanted to make sure I could re-create that body if I ever needed to.

I recall not just the color and shape of how Matka appeared to me, but the texture of absolutely everything about her. The feel of running my fingers through her thick hair, her eyeballs, her nostrils, her hard, leathery skin, every curve and cavity she made me explore.

I don't stop there. I remember her smell. I think about the bones and organs inside. I imagine a pumping heart, lungs, diaphragm, stomach, liver, ovaries, uterus, every organ I can. I think about blood vessels, nerves, lymph nodes, every system I know about.

As my thoughts form the body, the red glowing walls of the spirit chamber come into sharp focus. Finally, the room looks as clear as ever. I look down and see a tall, muscular, naked, fully formed red female body.

I focus on creating a mirror out of the spirit of the House, and in no time, I feel spirit swirl around me, and an eight-foot-tall mirror appears against the side wall between two runes.

I look at the body in the mirror. Yup, it's the same one I saw when Matka came to me: a seven-foot-tall, red Sedu female, muscular with modest boobs for her size and pronounced curves, burning eyes, burning dark hair, and nasty, pointy teeth and fangs. I did it! I have a body again!

Now I will myself to rein in my Sedu self, the way I always had before when I wanted to return to my usual form.

Nothing happens.

I concentrate harder, focusing on how it would feel when my hair and eyes would stop flaming, my teeth would revert to their non-pointy shape, my skin would return to normal.

Still nothing.

I try a few more times, but nothing works. I'm still looking at a seven-foot-tall, red, muscular female Sedu with my facial features in the mirror.

I think about blinking, and the image in the mirror blinks. I concentrate on moving the arms, and they move. I stare at the large, red woman in the mirror. I still can't quite believe it. I'm...her? That's me, staring back at me? Does being able to make a "real" body mean that I can't change form any-more, that this is it? What does it mean for who I am now?

I wish my mom were here. She'd know what to say at a moment like this. Mom was my guardian angel. She reassured me when I thought I was an evil demon, terrified of my abilities. And in death, it turned out she had been a Nistar, one of thirty-six pure, righteous souls on Earth that are not capable of doing any living thing any harm, which gives them more power than the rest of the human spirits in this universe. Normally, spirits can't move between Merkaba, the place of blessed spirits, and Sediin. But the Nistar can, and my mom comes here every now and again to check on me and help out.

But she's not here now. I'm on my own. And I can't just stay here in this room, staring at this naked body in the mirror, wondering what the hell to do now. I have a job to do.

I imagine a solid black, sleeveless dress with my firebird symbol on the front. It appears on the ground next to me. I pick it up and slip into it.

If you can still hear my thoughts, spirit of Keroz, thank you for guiding me.

It has been my joy, little firebird. Now go—Life needs you, Life of Keroz.

I take one last look at the figure in the mirror, open the thick door, and walk out of the spirit chamber.

29

AT THE BACK OF THE GREAT HALL, the spirit chamber is not exactly hidden, but out of the way in a hallway behind and underneath the stairs to the second floor. As I approach the great hall, the chaos and panic becomes louder and louder. I turn the corner of the hallway.

"...saw G'suul kill her, before I died and reformed here," one Mazzik says. "I'm telling you, our lady Seduman is gone."

"No!" Zogo howls. "She is Sedu! She'll be back!"

"I can't believe she's dead!" a high-pitched voice, probably a Ruhin, wails. "She's not!"

"As powerful as she is, she's not a spirit," another says.

"But I thought she was now?" a small, weak voice asks.

I round the staircase, so I'm in full view of everyone in the great hall. Ruhin and Mazzikim are all shuffling around anxiously, looking to each other, unsure of themselves.

"Don't you understand?" Zogo insists, briskly pacing. "She..."

He turns toward me. His jaw drops.

Zogo falls to his knees, his eyes bursting with tears.

In the steadiest voice he can muster, he yells, "All hail Firebird Alex, Sedu Lady of the House of Keroz!"

I try to make this new face smile. I feel the corners of the mouth move.

Mazzikim and Ruhin turn to me. Many take their knees. Others just stare in awe.

"Please, join me." I hold a hand out to Zogo.

He runs over to me and wraps both arms around one of my legs. "My lady..." he sobs into my thigh. "My lady..."

"I fear I'm no longer the most beautiful female Sedu." Pyza smiles, walking toward me from a hallway off the far side of the great hall.

"Why would you say that?"

"We tried to create approximations of females," Pyza says, taking my hand. "What we tried to copy, you *are*."

"Am I?" I ask, almost pleading.

"You are Sedu, but you still live." Pyza smiles. "Here—" she holds out her wrist and flips it so that the underside faces me. "Tell me what you feel."

I put my thumb where her veins would be if she were a human woman.

"Just my wrist, correct?"

I nod.

"But you..." Pyza holds up my hand and turns it around, then puts her own thumb on the underside of my wrist. "You have a pulse. Tell me, Alex; are you hungry?"

I think about it for a moment. "Yeah...my stomach is growling."

"Sedim don't need to eat, as you well know." Pyza releases my wrist.

"But this body...it's not me."

"It is you," Pyza assures me. "It is true flesh, true blood, and contains the life that your mother bore on Earth."

"You're taller." Zogo lifts his beak away from my leg. "But you've always been big to me."

"Thanks, Zogo." I smile a bit more successfully.

Blinding light bursts forth from the portal chamber, and the sounds of footsteps clattering on the floor soon follow. Garz and Zaebos, straining with every step due to still recovering from portal travel, trudge in as fast as they can. When they see me, they each light up with relief. I walk over to them.

Zaebos rears up and puts his paws around me, rubbing his muzzle on my stomach. "My lady," he snuffles.

Garz puts his arm around my head, leans down, and kisses my flaming hair.

"I returned with our war party as fast as we could, after..." Garz chokes on his sentence, unable to finish it. "I believed that you would snap back to the House of Keroz, as would I. I thought I'd need to enter the spirit chamber and guide you to create a body. I see that you have managed better than I could ever have helped you. Your body—this is the form the avatar of Life wore for you?"

"Quite a change, huh?"

"Yes, but no." Zaebos pulls his muzzle off my belly. "This is how we always saw you. To us, you have always been a Sedu Lady. We saw you as one of us completely, our—our Lady Firebird. All is as it should be, to us."

Garz adds, "I can only imagine your shock. But trust Zaebos, who would never speak anything but truth to you: your body matches the spirit that you've always had. Your body is new, but you are as much yourself as ever."

"Am I?" I whisper, still pleading.

"You will always be your mother's daughter. Your spirit will always be human, just as it always will be Sedu."

I nod, wanting to believe what my brother and Zaebos are saying, but not quite feeling it.

Garz steps to the side so that a tearful Rachel, who was standing behind him, can approach me.

"This is yours," she says, her smile quivering as she reaches up and hands me my blessed Sedu blade. "You left this at the House of Stygg."

"Thanks, girlie." I take my blade from her hands.

"Just when I get a little taller, you have to go and get huge. And red."

Rachel looks down and says almost in a whisper, "I thought you were dead."

"Sorry." I pull her close.

"I'm not." She throws her arms around me. "I'm glad you're back."

"I am too," I sniff. "But it's..."

"It is," Rachel agrees before I can even finish. "It's gonna take some getting used to." Rachel shrugs. "But it's still your voice, your face, the way you move. And you're still my girl, even if you're a crazy badass huge red Sedu."

"Thanks, girlie." I kneel down so that I'm a little shorter than Rachel and hug her tightly, but not so tightly that I squish her.

"I'll always love you," I promise.

"Me too," she sniffles.

The main doors burst open as Zedek flies into the main hall with Kesed on his back. Mazzikim and Ruhin scatter to the sides of the hall as Zedek flaps his wings forward to stop himself and drops to the ground in front of us. Rachel and I end our embrace and I stand up.

Zedek bows his purple, bearded dragon–like head low. "I have let you down once again, dear one. You called to me to join you at the House of Stygg, yet I was too far away to help."

"It's my fault! My fault! Mine! Mine! Mine!" A tearful, nearly hysterical Kesed leaps off Zedek's back and runs over to me. "When Zedek found me in The Firstlands I asked him to search with me. I thought if I could retrace their steps...and I got distracted...thought I felt something.... I'm sorry! I should have—"

"I'm okay." I put my arms around Kesed's leg. He's still far taller than me, but now that I'm seven feet tall, I come up to the middle of his thigh instead of below his knees. "Both of you—I'm okay."

"It will never happen again," Zedek says. "You have my word."

"Zedek, if Kesed ever needs you, really, it's fine. I don't expect—"

Loud footsteps hurry in from the main doors. The crowd of Mazzikim and Ruhin again parts, and I see Kenuut coming through. Both Zedek and Kesed slip to the side of the hall to give Kenuut a clear path to me.

He clearly looks worried about me, which is nice because he wears the face of my father. In a way, Kenuut and I have something in common. Kenuut has the memories of my father in a brand-new twenty-foot-tall body, and I am also in a brand-new, taller body.

"Daasooj told me what happened to you. Words cannot express my joy that you still live, daughter of Keroz."

"You know, it was that part of your spirit, the spirit of Keroz, that remains alive in this house that guided me back. So once again, Dad saved me."

Kenuut beams. "Even though my duty is as the Greater Sedu of Honesty, I will always do everything I can for you."

"How about taking me to the edge of Merkaba? I've been thinking about how to bring down G'suul. Our weapons can't hurt him; he heals too quickly and spirits inside of him repel even Greater Sedu–blessed weapons. But I think I've come up with an answer. For it to work, I'll need to ask Daasooj for help."

"Of course." He holds out his huge hand. "It would be my honor, little firebird."

30

"LET ME FLY YOU THERE," Zedek offers.

Beings travel to the edge Merkaba the same way they travel to anywhere else in these spirit realms: they imagine themselves at their destination, and their bodies twist and swirl through The Nothingness. While travel from one House to another in Sediin feels like it only takes moments, travel to the edge of Merkaba seems like a much longer journey—which means even more spiraling and nausea. But flying on Zedek is smooth and nausea-free.

"Are you sure that's wise?" Kenuut says. "After your last visit?"

Zedek exhales with a thoughtful expression. Last time Zedek and I traveled to Merkaba, in order to save my life, he absorbed the spirit of the Kaayot—huge spirit guardians of Merkaba—which was killing me. Destroying a Kaayot didn't sit well with the Reebaal, who was the leader of the Kaayot. When we defeated Reebaal, Daasooj took over as leader. Daasooj acknowledged that Reebaal was in the wrong, and he and Kenuut ended the hostilities between Kaayot and Sedim, but there's no guarantee that Daasooj will be all that friendly to Zedek.

"Kenuut, do you believe that my presence would hinder Alex's mission?"

"Daasooj is reasonable; he will understand that you are bringing Alex so that traveling will be less unsettling for her living body. But your presence will serve as a reminder that might not be pleasant."

"Hey, Zedek—it's okay." I pat his scaly purple neck. "You don't need to feel guilty for not being at the House of Stygg."

"Dear one, I didn't offer—"

"Oh, I know," I interrupt. "I just want you to know, you don't owe me anything. Kenuut makes sense. I'm a Sedu now, and traveling The Nothingness doesn't make me as nauseated. I'll be okay."

"Remember, since Sedim are forever denied entry to Merkaba, travel there will be painful for you. It will be easier if you can hold onto me."

"She can hold onto me," Kenuut says. "Zedek, I deeply appreciate your desire—"

"But I should remain. I understand." Zedek lowers his muzzle and sighs.

Kesed gently puts his hands around Zedek's reptilian head and lifts it up. Kesed kisses Zedek's cheek. He then cradles Zedek's head against his chest. "Zedek will be fine. Go with our blessing, and the best of luck."

"Thanks," I say, then turn to the assemblage. "I'll be back soon, I promise. No fighting or danger this time—Daasooj will either help or we'll leave in peace."

"You better be." Rachel chides, her cheeks finally dry.

I take my leave of my House, and Kenuut and I walk out the two main doors. Everyone outside stares at me with the same dumbstruck look as the Ruhin and Mazzikim inside. It's really unnerving.

"Wrap yourself completely around me," Kenuut says. "It will be easier."

"Okay." Even though I'm seven feet tall now, compared to Kenuut's twenty-foot frame I'm still a pipsqueak. I wrap my legs around his knees and arms around his waist, clinging to his side like a child.

His eyes glow white for a moment, and then we're lifted off our feet and spiral upward or downward, or right or left; I can't tell. This continues long enough for me to completely lose all sense of time and place. But after a while, the gray of The Nothingness lightens from gray to gray-white, and my entire body, every inch, feels pressure, like I'm being squeezed in a mechanical press or something. After a short while, that pressure combines with a feeling like my whole body is being stuck by prickly little thorns. I try to shift and squirm as we twist and whirl, but nothing makes it go away.

"This pain will not recede, little firebird. It is the cost of being a Sedu and seeking Daasooj near Merkaba."

"Lucky me," I wheeze. I close my eyes and hope we get there soon.

After an indeterminate amount of time, we abruptly stop. The sensation of being squeezed and poked, unfortunately, doesn't.

"Daasooj," Kenuut projects into the empty grayish white. "I bring a Sedu who wishes to ask you for assistance."

Out of nowhere, in the distance in front of us a tiny pinpoint of light enlarges to a nearly blinding sphere larger than both Kenuut and me. In that light, the outline of a smile appears.

"I am aware of you, Alexandra." The smile speaks in the hushed tone of a whisper, but it echoes through me louder than a shout. "Not just for the rebellion of Reebaal. I see what you have become. Kenuut still has the memories of Keroz and beams like a father, even though he is more than spirit now. What do you need from Merkaba, Champion?"

"Greetings, Daasooj," I begin. "Please forgive me if there's some kind of formal procedure I should be following. I'm new...well, to everything. To being a Sedu, a champion, all of it."

"There is nothing to forgive," Daasooj says. "Worry not."

"Thank you. It's the champion of life on Earth part that brings me to you. I need to cleanse the Earth of G'suul and the Nephilim. He is lifelessness, and I must defeat him to preserve life. When I faced him, I felt his soul, or those souls he has absorbed and destroyed, rebuffing my blade. I believe that what my blade needs is its own soul—the soul of a fallen champion. I would never force a spirit to join me against its will, so what I ask of you is that you let me talk with such a soul and ask for its help."

The outline of eyes and eyebrows appears above the outline of the mouth. The eyes widen and eyebrows raise. "You would ask the guardian of spirits to give up a spirit so that you can make war on one little world out of all that is?"

When Daasooj puts it like that, I sure feel small.

"No—I would ask you to let me plead with a warrior spirit from my world. If it wants to fight with me for our world of its own choice, that you respect its wishes."

Daasooj laughs. "Well argued, Champion. I shall agree to this. In fact, I believe that Shoshana has already found one for you!"

"Mom?"

A small sphere of light, the size of a basketball, appears behind Daasooj, and comes toward me. A warm, pleased smile washes over Kenuut's face as the light approaches.

"I'm here, little firebird," the sphere—my mom—says.

"How did you know?" I ask Daasooj.

"I anticipated your request when I sensed you traveling here with Kenuut," Daasooj explains. "I had always intended to agree, so I tasked your mother's Nistar spirit with finding a suitable champion."

"Is the spirit with you?" I ask my mom's spirit.

"Yes. I'm sorry you can't see spirits that aren't Nistar. But I can make sure you can speak with her."

"It's a her?"

Yes, I'm a her, I hear a disembodied voice emanating from around my mom's sphere.

"Great. Awesome. Sorry," I stumble out. "I suppose as a female champion myself, I should have expected that. My name is Alexandra Gold. Alex. Firebird Alex. Lady Firebird."

You have many names.

"Well, I'm also nervous and winging it," I admit. "May I ask your name?"

Boudicca. Queen of the Iceni, and defender of Lady Britannia against the scourge of the Romans. I led a hundred-thousand against that filthy empire. I was the champion of Life, of my people, for a short while.

"That sounds pretty amazing. I'm here to ask you if, as a spirit, you would like another chance to be a champion."

I am interested. I am bored to the point of madness here. As much as being one with my ancestors pleases me, my spirit yearns to feel useful, not simply coddled.

"In my own way, I can identify," I say, remembering how I worried I'd go insane when I first became aware in the blackness.

"I would ask your spirit to enter my Sedu blade. I will wield you in combat against a Rishon, an eldritch spirit that threatens to destroy all that lives on Earth. Their bodies are filled with devoured spirits that repulse the blade of any attacker—"

And your blade needs the soul of a champion to fight back.

"Yes."

How?

"I can bind your spirit to Lady Firebird's Sedu blade," Kenuut says.

Could my spirit be wielded by an enemy?

"Good question. Well, my Sedu blade is locked to me; nobody else can use it. So while I am alive, there is no danger of anyone else wielding my blade. I never asked if that remains true if I'm killed. Daasooj, if I die, can you take her spirit back into Merkaba?"

"I can take Boudicca's spirit back anytime she wishes," Daasooj agrees. "And if you are curious, your blade remains locked to you even in death."

"So there you go. If I die, you can ask to return; you're not stuck in my blade any longer than you want to be there."

I agree to this. Bind me to the blade.

"Thank you, Boudicca."

My mom's sphere drifts closer to me, until we're almost touching. Then Kenuut leans down and starts breathing on my blade. I can't see anything happening, but then all of a sudden I feel a jolt from the pommel of my blade, like it gave me a nasty electric shock.

"It is done," Kenuut says.

"How do you feel?" I ask Boudicca.

I haven't felt anything since I died. I still don't. I look forward to feeling these souls in battle—to feel something again.

"You now hold a contradiction in your hands," Daasooj notes. "You wield an instrument of death that is infused with life."

"It makes sense to me—I am a warrior, a champion, but I fight for life."

"You know, in a way you are working for Merkaba as well," Daasooj smiles. "When the Rishon devour spirits and when they poison life on your little world, they take away souls that might have ended up here."

"I am honored that I can be of service not just to life, but to the Kaayot, and to deserving spirits here." I bow. "I shall succeed in the name of Merkaba, as well as Matka."

Daasooj laughs. It's a hearty laugh, and I'm grateful for his warmth, but his voice is so powerful that each chuckle feels like a punch to the gut. "You know, Sedu who are destroyed are denied entry into Merkaba, but I'll make an exception for you, Champion. Merkaba will be a better place with your spirit among us."

"I...am humbled and thrilled. But I also should ask—insist, really—that Jacob Harman be admitted, because his soul is tied to mine. And Rachel Silver is my soul sister; an eternity without her would be unthinkable."

Daasooj's smile now turns to a playful smirk. "Matka chose well; you are fearless and true. Jake is part of your spirit and shall share your fate. Your dear Stinger has her own path to follow, but it too will lead to Merkaba."

"Thank you, Daasooj."

"This, however, is where the line is to be drawn today. I shall not be talked into letting in the entire House of Keroz."

"I understand," I chuckle. "You've already done more than I came here for, and I am thrilled beyond words. You have made Merkaba closer to my perception of Heaven, and I promise to do right by you all here."

"That is all I would ask of you. I have enjoyed our interaction. I wish you much success, Alexandra." And with that, the huge sphere of light that is Daasooj blinks out.

"I, too, wish you nothing but success," my mom says. "All my hopes and my love goes with you, little firebird."

"I love you too. I wished you were with me when I became this...this new thing."

"Hush, Alex. You are as you've always been. You are more than the shape of your body. You are still my daughter. You are still the same soul. And you are still beautiful, inside and out."

"Thanks, Mom," I say, not quite convinced. "Okay, Kenuut, I think we're done here."

31

THE RUHIN AND MAZZIKIM maintaining the grounds of the House of Keroz cheer as they see Kenuut and I spiraling toward the House of Keroz, thrusting their fists or whatever appendage they might have to welcome us. Kenuut helps me off of his side, smiles, and pats me on the back, encouraging me to walk in front of him. The assemblage parts for us as one of the Ruhin by the massive main doors blows the large horn. The doors are opened for us, and we walk inside.

Mazzikim and Ruhin line the walls, all at attention, smiling and proud. If I didn't feel like I feel, I'd probably be thrilled. At the far end of the hall at the base of the staircase, Garz, Zogo, Pyza, Zaebos, and my guard beam. Rachel and Vetis aren't there, which is odd. Zedek and Kesed also stand at the entryway to their wing of the House. Zedek smiles warmly. Kesed bounces like a schoolgirl.

I can feel the ambivalence in your spirit, Boudicca says. *They welcome you as their queen. Be the leader they need. Save your doubts for when you are alone.*

Thanks for the advice, I think to Boudicca.

I walk to the middle of the great hall. Standing as tall as I can, I slowly scan everyone, trying to put on as proud a face as I can, like I'm sizing them up.

"Our journey was a success," I say, projecting my voice. "My Sedu blade, already blessed by Zedek, has been infused with the spirit of a queen of Earth."

I pause for dramatic effect before yelling, "Now it can destroy G'suul and H'ythiis!" I unsheathe the blade and hold it above my head, willing it to ignite. Normally its flames would be blue, the color of Zedek's flames. But now they are bluish-green.

The Ruhin and Mazzikim let out a deafening roar. I'm glad that I've made them feel strong and unified.

Garz and Zaebos and Zogo all approach me in the center of the hall. Garz looks nearly giddy.

"In the three days you were gone—"

"*Three days?*"

"Only three hours on Earth," Garz reminds me. "And that is why Rachel and Vetis are not here—they are on Earth and shall return soon."

"It didn't feel that long." I shrug.

"Time moves differently in Merkaba," Kenuut explains. "It races in Sedi-in compared to Earth, but slows to nearly imperceptible in Merkaba."

"Gotcha," I say.

"In that time, we held a council meeting," Garz continues. "Our most powerful allies—the Houses of Gryx, Mog, and Stygg—shall themselves fight with us. Less powerful allies shall ready war parties to accompany us while the Sedim and most of their households remain in Sediin, alert for any sign of a breech by the Nephilim or Ruhin to our realm. And those who refuse to fight have still pledged themselves to keep the peace, and not use this as an opportunity to attack vulnerable Houses."

"This is welcome news, son of Keroz," Kenuut nods. "As the Greater Sedu of Honesty, I shall remain in Sediin and police this pledge to ensure the honesty of the remaining Sedim."

"Thank you, Kenuut," Garz says. "This gives me much greater peace of mind."

Kenuut bows to Garz.

"The Greater Sedim can only remain on Earth for two hours, so Ruhin shall fetch Zedek and Kesed when the battle is engaged," Garz explains to me.

"Wait, Ruhin? I thought they weren't vast enough of spirit to ever travel to Earth?"

"This is correct. However, gemstones of Azziz will wrap them in the spirit of the great, long-dead Sedu, so they can travel with us and stay as long as necessary," Zaebos explains. "We and our allies are bringing everyone we can spare: Mazzikim warriors to engage the Nephilim, Ruhin to burn their bodies to spare your Earth Mother—"

"And the Sedim and Greater Sedim to kill the Rishonim," Garz finishes Zaebos's sentence. "All the armies shall gather in our great hall and the grounds outside as soon as we are ready with gemstones of Azziz for all of them."

I nod, then close my eyes and swallow hard. This is war. Real war. I mean, I knew it would be, but now it sinks in. And I'm...what am I now? Just a big red war machine?

Don't worry, Garz says directly to my mind. *I can sense you are overwhelmed by all this. It's normal to feel this way. I have been leading battle parties for millennia. All you need to do is give them hope. I know you can do this, little firebird. You give me hope.*

I look up. *Thank you, Garz.*

"We Sedim—myself, Pyza, and Vetis when he returns—are all going transfer the spirit of Azziz into gemstones," Garz speaks aloud. "We will need many, many gemstones to be infused. If you wish to help us, I can show you how."

"Yeah, of course I'll help. But right now, I'm really hungry. And I need a bath. Is that okay?"

"Of course," Garz says, gently patting my shoulder. "Take your time."

There is no rush—we'll be at this for days' worth of time in Sediin."

Zogo, who had been silent this entire time, attaches himself to my leg with a huge smile. "The kitchen staff and I will bring a feast of snacks to your chamber, my lady. And extra water for your bath, now that you're taller."

"That sounds wonderful, thanks."

Zogo hugs my leg again for good measure and runs off toward the kitchen, waving his arms and shouting orders.

"He has missed his lady." Zaebos says. "We all did."

"Go, dear sister. Take care of yourself, eat, and bathe. When you feel ready, join us."

I nod to my brother and pat his arm.

"Why don't you spend some time with Daeba and your puppies?" I say to Zaebos. "I'm not leaving the House, and I won't do anything without telling you."

"Thank you, my lady." Zaebos bows his muzzle.

"Come, Mazzikim," Garz says. "Let us organize."

I climb the stairs, listening to the loud footsteps of the huge, thunderous, muscular red legs carrying me. I feel tired, hungry, and dirty. I walk down the hall and shove open my door. I can't help but snort out a chuckle and shake my head.

While I was away with Kenuut, Garz increased the dimensions of my room. That goes for the dresser, table, and bed as well—all are larger and longer. There have always been a couple of large chairs in the room, because Garz is eight feet tall. He's added a couple more larger chairs, I'm guessing so that I have a choice of being a little tall in a human-sized chair or a little short in a Sedu-sized chair.

I put my hand on my Sedu blade and will it to the size of a dagger. "Boudicca, I usually leave my blade as a dagger on my dresser. Is that okay? You mentioned being bored in Merkaba. Is there a way I can keep you engaged? Do you need anything? I've never had a soul in my blade before. Is it...lonely?"

Thank you for asking, champion. Being a spirit is quite an experience. I have no bounds, and yet for the first time, I am bound in this sword. If I am to fight other spirits, I would like to explore my connection to this blade more deeply. I enjoy our conversations, but I think I shall enjoy focusing on the task at hand as well. Besides, I can communicate with the spirit of your House, so I am not alone.

"I'm glad. Say hi to Keroz for me. If you need me, just reach out your spirit, and I'll be aware of it."

Enjoy your rest, Firebird, Boudicca says, and I place my blade on top of my dresser, as I have a thousand times before. I inhale deeply and walk over to the round table at the other side of the room.

I pat the seat of one of the tall chairs. It feels soft and padded, as does the seat back. I sit down and exhale deeply. As I scan the room, I realize that seated in this chair I'm basically at the same height I used to be when I was standing. It's an odd sensation.

Zogo pushes open the door, and half a dozen Ruhin trot in. Two bipedal Ruhin with the heads of different kinds of monkey push a food-filled cart that is larger than they are. The other four are four-legged Ruhin, hauling between them vats of water.

"Put the food on the table next to our lady," he instructs. "Put the water in the tub."

Zogo smiles and practically skips over to the table along with the two Ruhin wheeling the cart filled with food.

"I didn't know how hungry you were. I wanted to make sure you had enough, so..."

Zogo beams with pride as the Ruhin place multiple loaves of bread, baskets of still ripe apples and oranges, full wheels of cheese, bowls of nuts, a plate of cookies, some knives and forks, and pitchers of water on the table for me.

"Thanks, Zogo." I try to give him as genuine a smile as I can. "I don't know how much I need to eat anymore, either. I appreciate the spread."

"There's enough water to fill your new tub as well," he says, his smile fading into a look of sympathy. I guess I'm not as good at hiding my melancholy as I'd hoped.

"Figures Garz would create a new tub for me, too."

Zogo nods. The Ruhin are done unloading everything, so he motions for them all to leave, until he is the only one left. For a moment, Zogo stands awkwardly, like he has something to say but isn't sure how to say it.

Finally, he speaks. "My lady, I...you...did you want to eat alone? If not, I'd be happy to stay."

"Thank you for the offer, Zogo. I think I may bathe first, before I eat. I just...I need to think. Lot of change for me to deal with, you know?"

Zogo nods. "Very well, my lady. As ever, you need only pull the rope and I'll return."

"Thanks, Zogo. I really appreciate all you do for me, I want you to know that."

"It's my pleasure, my lady." Zogo bows. He turns to leave, but after only a step, he turns back to me.

"In the House of Es, where I was Vetis's servant before we came to the House of Keroz, Vetis's parents and Mazzikim used to kill me all the time. Every time I came back, I always felt somehow...*unoriginal*, like maybe the real me didn't come back. But after a while, I'd get used to the new form, and I'd feel like I was fully me. Then they'd kill me again, and I'd go through it all over."

"I understand what you're telling me, Zogo. I'll be okay. I just need time.

And I'm sorry you went through that."

Zogo shrugs. "It made me what I am. Which may not be much, but it's the real me, regardless of my body."

"I wouldn't want you any other way." I give him a smile that I know is more successful, because he smiles back. "Thanks for telling me that, Zogo. It helps."

He nods, clearly proud of himself, and takes his leave. I look at the food. Will taste the same to me in this body? I grab the loaf of bread and tear off a chunk. I slice off some cheese and place it on the bread. I put it in my mouth and start chewing. It tastes like I expect French bread with sharp cheese to taste. I close my eyes and sigh with relief.

The bread and cheese is good, but I chew with no enthusiasm. I'm still hungry, but I do think I want that bath now. I walk over to my bed, take off the outfit I created in the spirit chamber, and push through the beads covering the entryway to my bathroom.

Garz made it larger, just like my main chamber. The sink basin is larger, the toilet is larger, and the iron claw-foot tub now looks huge. But the Ruhin brought a goodly amount of water, so it's nice and full. I grab my bubble bath from under the sink, pour some in the tub, and then dunk my arm in. I will my hand to heat up and start warming the water. Thankfully, I can still feel the pleasant warmth of the heated water on this new skin. I continue heating the water and stirring it until it's just the right temperature and has a good amount of bubble foam, then lower myself into the bath.

It feels nice, rubbing the soapy water over this huge, red form. I run these new fingers over my new arms, my new neck, my new legs, my new breasts, my new hair. This is me now. I have to get used to it. Everyone else seems to know it's me, so why can't I be okay with it?

Because they didn't spend a lifetime watching themselves growing into the body they always assumed would be the only body they'd ever have. I went through puberty in that body. I held my mother's hand as her cancer ate her alive in that body. I felt Jake touch me in that body.

This body has not lived through any of that. It may be mine, but it's not me. It's just...not.

At first the tears come slowly, quietly, as I wrap these long red arms around each other. These arms...my arms. I wrap my arms around myself. The arms I had for my whole life are gone forever. Destroyed.

The tears come faster.

32

"WANT COMPANY?" Jake pushes through the curtain of beads into my bathroom.

Instinctively, I shrink into the bubbles, my arms across my chest. A silly reaction to my fiancé, I know. I guess I'm embarrassed for him to see me like this.

"C'mon, I've already seen you naked, Alex," Jake smiles.

"That's true," I sniff, regulating my breathing to slow my tears. "You saw me feeling up this body at the refinery."

"That's not what I meant, Alex," he says, taking off his shirt. "When I first saw that body in my dreams, I knew it was you. Yeah, your body was tall and red, but I knew it was you."

"I guess...I've had dreams where someone doesn't look like I know they look, but I still know it's supposed to be that person."

"Stop trying to avoid what I'm saying." He shakes his head as he unties his shoes. "I've seen *you*. I've touched *you*. I love touching you."

"But this body—"

"Alex, if someone gains weight, loses weight, loses their hair or a limb, whatever, do they stop being themselves?"

"You know this is different. I've lost a lot more than a limb. I've had a full body replacement."

"So? You went through complete cellular regeneration. But it's you. After I closed my eyes and impaled myself on L'reek's claw, once the pain started to recede, I saw my dad, Josh, and you, and just repeated to you all that I love you."

"I love you too," I sniffle.

"Thanks, but really, I'm just trying to finish my story here." Jake cracks a wide ear-to-ear smile as he takes off his jeans.

"It was in that darkness, as everything faded away, even my thoughts, suddenly a red Sedu woman appeared to me. And my first thought wasn't 'Who is that?' but 'Wow, Alex is a full Sedu in heaven.'"

"Really?"

"Really really," Jake says, slipping his underwear to the floor. "My point is, I immediately knew it was you. Big and red and all hulked out, but you. So yeah, when Rachel and Vetis came into my office and told me what happened to you, the part about how you were blasted to bits really hurt me because I thought about how much it hurt you. But the rest didn't bother me. And I really, really want to get in that bath with you." Jake stands stark naked with a wide grin.

"Okay." I can't help but shoot him a warm but sad half-grin as I wipe away my tears. "But I'm not feeling sexy right now. I'm not sure what I'm feeling."

"I can only imagine," Jake says as he climbs in and sits down at the other end of the long, large tub, his skinny legs looking like twigs next to my huge ones. "But I'm here, and I love you. More than anything."

"Thanks." I shoot him more of a full smile. "When I was killed, did you feel anything?"

"Yeah," he nods. "I was reading the latest results of our prototyping trials on my screen when suddenly I felt weak and confused. I wondered for a second if I was having a stroke or something, but then I remembered that wasn't possible. That's when I realized that what I felt was probably related to what was happening to you."

"Did you get scared that you—"

Jake shakes his head. "Remember, I would have dropped dead immediately. But I figured you had gone through something massively traumatic and were in pain. I wanted to return to Sediin to find out what had happened, but I felt...weird. Kinda lightheaded and unsure of myself. So I stayed in my office, lying on the couch, hoping I'd get over my vertigo or whatever it was. That's how Rachel found me when she came through and told me what was up. That got me off my ass. They helped me through the portal, Zogo walked me to your chamber, and by the time I pushed open the door I felt like myself again."

"I'm glad you're here. I'm just...I'm sorry I'm like this." My eyes get hot again.

"I'm not," Jake smiles. "I love you, big and red or short and white. You're you. And you're still hot, by the way."

"Now much more literally," I quip.

Suddenly, excitement erupts across Jake's entire face. "Marry me!"

"Of course I'll still marry you. I'm glad you still want—"

"No, I mean *now*. Marry me here, now."

"In the tub?"

"We can dry off and get dressed if you'd like," Jake laughs. "But I mean in the House of Keroz, right now."

"Why now?"

"Why wait? I love you. I want to marry you. I see everyone gearing up for the big battle. So this might be our last chance."

"So if we die, at least we will have been married?"

"Basically. I want to announce before man and God—well, at least Sediin—that I love you and want to be your husband. I'm sure one of the Sedim or Greater Sedim can marry us. If we live we can have another wedding on

Earth and invite our people. And have a wedding night. And a honeymoon."

I just inhale and exhale, looking at Jacob Harman across from me in the tub. The boy who from the moment we first met, never judged me. Who always accepted me exactly as I am and encouraged me to be the best I can be. There's nobody else I could imagine taking this crazy, messed up journey with. I almost can't believe he still wants to take it with me.

"Okay?" he asks.

"Okay." I smile.

"Okay!" Jake exhales excitedly, but with some nerves, too.

"You really are my foundation, you know, Jake?"

"And your flesh, Matka said that too," Jake quips.

Suddenly, his eyes go serious and far away, like he's looking inward. "Matka said that I'm your flesh…"

Jake scoots closer and props himself up on the sides of the tub and leans forward. Now that I'm a foot taller than he is, he has to pretty much stand all the way over me. Jake then bends his head to mine and kisses my lips.

I surrender completely to his kiss, cradling the back of his head in my soaking left hand, getting bubbles all over his dry hair. As we kiss I can feel myself changing, getting shorter, softer. He presses his body closer to mine and kisses me harder. When he lifts his head away from mine, he smiles and wipes a tear from my eye. "And that's what she meant."

I look down, and I've got my Seduman body back. I look like the same girl I'd been since puberty. I gasp and run my hands over my shoulders, chest, arms, and legs just to be sure they're real.

"That was one hell of a kiss! How did you do that?"

"I don't know," Jake shrugs as he leans back and plops back into his seat across the tub. Now that I'm back to being five-foot-nine, our feet barely touch. "But somehow, it just jumped into my mind that when I touch you, I can help you access your old form again."

"This is still a brand-new body," I say, twisting my arms and looking at my thighs and the sides of my breasts for the stretch marks and imperfections I remember were there, but that aren't now. "It's as new as the Sedu body."

"But it's also you," Jake says pointedly. "You are more than whatever form you have. You've always been changing. You've always had multiple forms."

"Well, which form do you want to marry me in? Do you want to marry me big and red or in the body you fell for?"

"You still don't get it, do you?" Jake mocks frustration with me, splashes some bubbles at me. I shoot him a smile and splash him back, sitting up and scooting forward.

"I fell for *you*, Alex," he says, caressing my arms gently. "It's you either way. I want to marry you as a Sedu. I want to marry you as a Seduman."

"I love you so much, Jacob Harman." I lean toward him, and he leans toward me, and we kiss again. I wrap my arms around his back.

"I love you too, Alexandra Gold. Which is good, because my soul is tied to yours forever, and that would be a bummer if I couldn't stand you."

"Good point," I chuckle.

"So, shall we get out of the tub and tell the others?"

"Not quite yet," I maneuver my legs around his sides and run my hands across his back. "You've made me feel sexy again...."

33

Zogo stands on the edge of the stairs facing Jake and me. He's unable to keep from bouncing in his excitement, which of course rubs off on us.

"Are you ready my lady? My lord?"

I turn to Jake, a huge smile on my face. He returns the smile. We both share the same look of devotion.

Jake and I turn around toward Zaebos. He stands at attention directly behind us with two of his trusted hairless bear-dog-like Mazzikim.

"Your guard is ready, my lady." Zaebos bows his head to me, then turns to Jake with his head still bowed. "My lord."

"Can you just call me Jake?"

"No." Zaebos raises his head, an impish grin across his muzzle. "My lord *Jacob.*"

Jake runs his fingers through the rust-colored fur of Zaebos's head.

"We are." I nod to Zogo.

Zogo turns around and slides the bullhorn I'd created for him over his beak. "Sedim, Mazzikim, and Ruhin: I present to you Lady Firebird and Lord Jake Harman!"

The bullhorn has the desired effect. The great hall is loud as can be as preparations for war are being made. While Zogo is larger than most Ruhin, he's still only a three-foot-tall bipedal, shell-less turtle. Even with a bullhorn amplifying his reedy voice, it's not all that loud, but it's loud enough—and unusual enough, since bullhorns are basically unknown in Sediin—that everyone stops to listen.

Zogo lowers the bullhorn and starts down the stairs. He loves every second of this—feeling both important and in the thick of everything. After he's a few steps down, Jake and I start down the stairs, arm in arm. I'm back in my seven-foot-tall Sedu form. We're both dressed unconventionally, but still in our versions of formal attire.

Wearing a white dress didn't feel right to me. Maybe I will for my human wedding, if I have one, because it's kind of expected. But I've never really been one to wear white. As a lonely, self-loathing teenager who thought she was a half-demon, I gravitated toward black clothes. Even though I've left my goth days behind, now that I feel less human than ever, I thought a callback to my human past was in order. So I created for myself a sleeveless, knee-length silk and lace black dress. I accessorized it with a gray belt embroidered with the symbols of the House of Keroz from our spirit chamber, tall black boots, and a silver necklace with a large silver pendant of my firebird symbol.

Not to be outdone, Jake asked me to create for him a full-on Dracula-style tux. Thankfully, he'd showed them to me online when we'd talked about future wedding stuff, and I've seen Bela Lugosi's old *Dracula* movie enough times to call it up from memory. Jake sports the black trousers, formal jacket with tails, white shirt, everything but the bow tie. He's a laid back California boy, after all, so he's a tieless vampire. He wanted a top hat, too. I made him a pretty tall top hat that adds about six inches, making him appear about six-foot-six to my seven-foot height. He's still obviously shorter than me, but we look much more even this way. Of course, Jake's so scrawny that he looks like a strong breeze could blow him over, but I think he's handsome as hell.

Zaebos wanted for himself and the other two Mazzikim of my guard fresh, bullet- and goo-free Team Firebird uniforms. Only Garz has intimate enough knowledge of the fabrics involved to create those, so instead I made them white leathery canine-style coats with my symbol on the sides. Where Zogo practically bounces down the stairs in his excitement, and Jake and I step together, overjoyed and slightly anxious, my guard carry themselves with pride and precision, lending a sense of pomp and circumstance to what otherwise feels like awkward nerds playing at being nobles.

The assembled crowd stares in awed silence, their mouths, beaks, muzzles, or mandibles agape as we descend the stairs. By the time we're halfway down, Garz, Pyza, Vetis, and Rachel enter the great hall from the council chamber. Garz and Vetis beam joy and pride in equal measure. So does Rachel, but her smile quivers and her eyes redden. Pyza looks happy for me and almost a little wistful.

From the hallway on the side of the stairs that leads to the wing of the Greater Sedim, Zedek, Kesed, and Kenuut all approach. They stop at the edge of the hallway and immediately understand what is happening. Kesed embraces Zedek's neck and weeps into it for joy. Kenuut grins with approval.

I stop walking about four steps from the bottom. Jake pulls his foot back and stops with me. We both glance backwards to see that Zaebos and our guard have stopped as well. We smile at each other, warmly, nervously. I then turn back toward the great hall. I'm not used to this huge space, with all of its scores of beings milling about and walking through it, being so silent.

"So...who officiates weddings in Sediin?" I exhale with far more butterflies in my stomach than I thought I'd have.

"The head of any Sedu House," Garz answers, his voice uncharacteristically tender. "Or any Greater Sedu."

"It would be my great honor to marry you," Zedek offers. "Unless Garz—"

"Zedek, there is nothing I would wish for more than to have my sister soul-mated by the Greater Sedu of Righteousness himself. Besides"—a wry grin creeps across Garz's reptilian lips—"it has been so many millennia since a female Sedu wed a male Sedu, you may be the only one who remembers the rituals."

"I remember." Zedek tips his head, the same grin across his muzzle.

Kesed starts bawling even louder.

"Okay then," I inhale. "Garz, please send some Mazzikim to fetch Klara from the House of Gryx. Let's get this—"

"How long have we got?" Rachel interrupts. "I'll get Josh."

Vetis puts his two left claws on his daughter's back, a puzzled expression on his face.

Everyone else looks to me for an answer.

I turn to Jake. He shrugs and shakes his head.

"Rachel, this is our Sediin wedding. The plan is that if we survive this, we'll have an Earth wedding too," Jake says. "With a Rabbi and chupah and everything. Josh can—"

"You will survive this," Rachel cuts him off. "Josh and I will be at that wedding, too, with your dad. But Alex has her family here; don't you want someone from your family here, too?"

Jake looks at me again. I raise my eyebrows to indicate that I didn't expect this reaction from Rachel, but it's up to him.

"It would be cool, sure."

"I'll just get him and come right back," Rachel promises. "What's the hotel Josh and your dad are staying at in Irvine? I can portal really close, I'm sure, and just get him. He should be doing homework, right?"

"Rachel..." Jake exhales, shaking his head.

"Alex, please. I want... Please," Rachel's eyes get glassier.

"Okay," I smile. "Go get him."

Jake nods and walks the rest of the way down the staircase. "They're staying at the Candlewood Suites by the Irvine Spectrum. I'll—"

"I know it; I've been there with Rabbi Norm," Rachel cuts him off. "Back in a sec. And I'll need a dress!"

Rachel leaps over the heads of the Mazzikim and Ruhin, landing inside the portal chamber.

Garz almost, but not quite, represses a tight-lipped smirk.

"Alex?" Jake looks puzzled as I walk down to where he is.

"One of Rachel's biggest fears is that being a Seduman—being a hero—means that she can't have the normal things that humans take for granted. Friends, boyfriends, husband, kids, all that."

"Okay, I get that," Jake nods. "But why does she need Josh there? She planning to propose to him when she turns fourteen?"

"Hey, at nineteen I'm still a teenager too, you twenty-one-year-old cradle-robber," I offer a wry half-grin and swat Jake on the arm as he laughs and puts an arm around me.

"I think I understand." Vetis approaches us. "She wants this to be at least partially a human experience, which means sharing this with a human contemporary. Her best friend Emma Kelley is in hiding, and that leaves your brother. Maybe she'll marry Josh one day, maybe not. I think it's less about him and more about her having a friend at the wedding."

"I'm with Vetis on this," I add. "Rachel and Josh are totally hot for each other, but this is more for her than him."

"And to think she tried to pass this off as being all for me. Cheeky girl." Jake shakes his head, trying to pretend he's upset, but he can't hide his smile.

"I have sent two Mazzikim to the House of Gryx to inform them of your nuptials," Garz announces.

"Should we get Erin and her mom here? Erin is a Seduman, and since she designed our Team Firebird uniforms, she's a member of Team Firebird, too, even if a support member."

"Her mom's been really helpful to us too," Jake adds.

"They're hiding from the Nephilim in Australia, but we know exactly where they are, since we brought them there," I point out.

"No, no." Vetis shakes his head nervously, like we just challenged him to ask a girl to the senior prom. And in a way, we did, since Millie Cavendish has a total crush on Vetis—and he returns the affection, too, but is really shy about it. "Remember, Erin and Millie do not like to travel to Sediin. They would come out of love and obligation, but they'd prefer attending a wedding on Earth."

"Good point," I agree. "So you're off the hook, Vetis."

He nods, but that doesn't quite hide the look of relief on his dragon-fly-like face.

"Come." Garz holds out his arms to usher us off the stairs. He guides Vetis, Jake, and I into the council chamber. The Greater Sedim remain in their hallway. The assemblage backs up to the middle of the great hall, freeing up the space from the stairs to the entryway to the council chamber. Garz and Zedek confer for a moment, with Zedek telling Garz what I assume is how he wants to conduct the wedding.

Garz's eyes glow brightly as he creates a low and wide stepped platform that reaches from the second step just past the entryway to the council chamber. It's large enough to hold probably a dozen humanoid-sized and Greater Sedu–sized beings. In the middle of the stage, a high canopy that looks like a traditional Jewish chupah, adorned with the spirit runes of the House of Keroz, covers an area large enough for two human-sized beings and one gigantic dragon-sized being.

"Let us gather, my friends," Garz says.

Zedek nods and steps onto the platform. He walks to the center of it, his back legs going up a few of the stairs so that he can get his long dragon-like neck and head under the canopy and still leave room for us.

Garz stands to the left side of the canopy. Zaebos and the two guards, who never left the stairs, now step onto the platform and take their places behind Garz.

Garz holds his arm out toward Pyza. Pyza's eyes widen and she turns to me, her expression clearly asking permission.

"Pyza, I would be honored to have you stand by Garz's side and be part of this ceremony. You're more than a guest. You're my friend—our friend—and a treasured part of our lives."

"Thank you," she whispers, clearly moved.

"Besides, it'll be nice not to be the only red, seven-foot-tall lady up here." I wink.

Pyza nods with a slight grin and steps onto the platform to join Garz.

"In Sediin, there's no father marching the bride or anything. We all take our position and then begin at the proper time," Vetis explains. "Are we ready to take our places?"

I turn to Jake.

"Absolutely," he answers. "Although my nervous stomach is telling me that having bread and cheese before the wedding might not have been the smartest move."

"Aww," I offer my husband-to-be-with-the-porcelain-gut a compassionate expression, and Vetis, Jake, and I walk onto the platform. Vetis stands on right side of the canopy. Jake and I stand in front of the canopy, me on the left, Jake on the right. One of the advantages of the ceremony being administered by a twenty-foot-long dragon is that even though I'm seven feet tall, his head still towers above me, and all the collected Mazzikim and Ruhin can see us.

I see that Daeba and her puppies are standing at the edge of the council chamber. "If they can't see, you can let them stand on the platform steps; it's fine."

Daeba bows her muzzle.

I see Qwyll, Pelegor, and Leeik in the front row, in front of the other Mazzikim. "C'mon, get up here." I smile.

They turn to each other in surprise, then back to us.

"Pelegor, you are my steed. Qwyll, you have flown me and are the mentor and friend of Rachel, my soul sister and shield maiden. And Leeik, you have counseled and taught me. Please stand with Zaebos."

They bow, and together they ascend the steps of the platform, taking their place with my honored Mazzikim next to Garz.

"Lord Gryx arrives!" Two Ruhin shout from the main doors just before they swing open. Lord Gryx and Klara stride in with two of their Mazzikim. I'm guessing the Mazzikim that Garz sent must have given them some kind of heads up about what I was wearing, because Klara is wearing a very cute, satiny, long-sleeved tight black dress with a high neckline.

Our Mazzikim and Ruhin all bow and clear a path for them to the platform. Klara rushes forward, her expression one of concern, shock, and excitement all at once.

"So it's true—you were killed and came back in the shape Matka wore for you," Klara marvels as she approaches the platform.

"Long story. I'll tell you all of it later. I'm sorry if my new form—"

"You're beautiful." She smiles with the hint of a quiver on her lips. Her red, glassy eyes threaten to burst. "Nice dress, too."

"I wish Erin had been around here to design one for me, but thanks." I return the smile. "So is yours. Please join us up here."

"What?" Her eyes go wide.

"You're Team Firebird," Jake says. "You can stand behind me, with Vetis and eventually Rachel and my brother."

Gryx nods and gently encourages his daughter forward.

"Thanks," she sniffles as she climbs the two steps onto the platform and stands next to Vetis.

"So when is—"

Klara's words are interrupted by a blinding flash from the portal room.

Garz looks over at Jake and Klara, then turns to the portal chamber. His eyes glow for a moment and then return to normal.

Jake looks at me, unsure what Garz just did.

"Shut up and put it on! *Now!*" We hear Rachel wheeze.

"Ah," Jake says.

"Rachel will be recovering. I should help her dress." We all agree, and Qwyll takes a few steps away from us so that he has room to unfurl his albatross-like wings. He flies to the portal chamber.

We all stand in silence, waiting.

"Just take your pants off," we hear Rachel grunt, more recovered. "Do think the Ruhin care about your junk?"

We all giggle a bit and wait some more. After a moment, Josh walks out of the portal room in a tux that looks almost identical to Jake's, but without the hat. Rachel shakes, clearly still feeling the effects of crossing the portal, but makes a show of trying to walk herself to the platform, wearing a very nice black dress. Qwyll stands right behind her, so if she stumbles he can immediately grab her.

"Nice tux," Jake says to his little brother as he reaches the platform.

"Yeah, whatever." Josh shakes his head. Then he looks up at me. "Oh my God!"

"Shut up!" Rachel glowers at him. "I told you about Alex and said not to freak!"

"Sorry," he says sheepishly as he and Qwyll help Rachel up the platform.

I smile and shake my head to indicate it's completely fine. Hell, I freaked too. I totally get it.

Rachel smiles at Klara, who squeezes Rachel's hand. Qwyll returns to his place beside Zaebos, Pelegor, and Leeik.

"So I guess we're bridesmaids," Rachel says. For the first time I realize that Garz created the same dress for Rachel that Gryx created for his daughter. Rachel takes Josh's hand. Klara stands on Josh's left.

Jake and I look around. We're all here. We're all in place. You could hear a pin drop. I look at Jake and smile, my eyes beginning to tear. He smiles back, his eyes just as red.

I turn to Zedek. "Showtime."

34

ZEDEK RAISES HIS HEAD. "We are here to witness the binding of two spirits into one: that of Alexandra Gold, Lady Firebird of the House of Keroz,
chosen champion of Mati Syra Zemia, avatar of the life force of Earth; and
Jacob Harman, immortal human. Before the binding, have you words for
each other?"

Oh, geez. Vows totally slipped my mind. I flash Jake a quick look, be-
seeching him to go first.

Jake inhales quickly, takes my hands, and gazes up into my eyes. "Only
that I adore you, in every universe, every shape, every way. I'm grateful for
every moment with you, and whenever, wherever you need me, I'll always be
there."

I offer him a quivering smile as tears stream down my huge red cheeks. "I
love you, Jacob Harman. With every ounce of my soul, with every beat of my
heart. I have duties to my House, to life on Earth, but always know you are
my center."

We both turn to Zedek. He lowers his head so he's at our level. "Matka
already bound your spirits on Earth. Now shall I, in Sediin."

Zedek slowly exhales. Instead of blue flames shooting out of his mouth, a
sort of blue glow floats out of his mouth and surrounds us. It feels warm and
tingly, then it's gone. An excited hush comes over the crowd.

"Lord Garz," Zedek bows his head and steps backward up a few steps so
that there is room for my brother to stand in front of him.

Jake looks at me with a questioning expression, but I have no idea what's
happening.

"Jacob Harman, please face me," Garz says solemnly.

I drop Jake's hands and he turns to Garz, gazing reverently up at him.

Garz's eyes begin to glow, and he leans over Jake. He inhales, like when
G'suul tried to absorb my soul, but far more slowly. Cuts and cracks begin to
appear in Jake's face. His eyes go wide and although Jake doesn't flinch, he's
terrified. I am, too, for an instant before I realize there's no way that Garz is
going to end my wedding by murdering my new husband.

After another second, Garz exhales just as slowly onto Jake. The cracks
and cuts disappear, and Jake breathes a huge, but quiet, sigh of relief. "There,"
Garz pronounces. "I have now taken some of your spirit and joined it with
the spirit of the House of Keroz, as well as given you some of the spirit of our
House. You can now heal in this House and direct our portal mirror with
your thoughts, the way that Sedumen and the beings of this House can."

"That's going to come in handy, with you being immortal and all," I whisper.

"Yeah, thanks Garz, I'm honored and thrilled." Jake swallows. "I just wish I knew it was coming."

"My apologies," Garz smiles. "I didn't mean to frighten you. A being from Sediin who remembered the ancient wedding rituals would have expected it. I forgot you would not have."

"No worries. I just need to change my pants, but other than that I'm good."

I smile sympathetically and rub Jake's arm. Garz good-naturedly pats Jake's other arm and returns to his place behind me at the side of the canopy.

Zedek returns to his position. Jake and I take each other's hands again.

Zedek raises his head so that his deep, rich voice might project even more strongly throughout our great hall—maybe even through all of Sediin.

"You have been accepted as one by the spirit of this great Sedu House. These spirits are now bound, throughout time, in any form, and in all realms, as one. May your union be a source of strength for both of you. All our hopes that you grow ever more bonded as you journey together, now and forever. As your kind do, you may now kiss."

I smile down at Jake, my soulmate, my husband. Jake leans up for a kiss. I can't help but think of all the times I had to lean up to kiss him. We press our lips together tenderly. We've been through so much, together and apart. We've almost died and returned. We've kissed and kissed and kissed. We've done much more than kiss. But this feels different.

As soon as we kiss, Zedek and Garz crane their necks and breathe fire toward the ceiling. At the same time, all the Ruhin and Mazzikim in the hall raise their paws, fists, and claws with a deafening cheer. It startles both Jake and I and we jump; even so, we can't help but giggle at the intensity, almost absurdity, of it. It's odd, but it's beautiful too.

I look over Jake's shoulder. Rachel offers me a quivering, wet smile and tries to share our giggle, with Josh holding her hand. Klara has both hands on her chest, smiling and softly crying for us.

"I'm so glad each and every one of you is here," I tell everyone on the platform.

"Wouldn't have missed it for the world," Rachel says.

"Me neither," Klara adds.

"I'm glad you were here too, nerd." Jake winks at his brother.

"At least it was short." Josh shrugs, but as much as he may try to be disaffected and cool, his glassy eyes tell the real story.

"Don't be a goober," Rachel says. "Admit it, this is crazy amazing stuff right here. I mean, who has a dragon breathe on them and a full-on demon cheer as part of their wedding?"

"Good point," Josh agrees. He rubs his fingers over Rachel's hand. She's satisfied.

Garz walks to the edge of the platform to address the crowd. "I could not be more proud of this union. Now let us prepare for war—that they may live to enjoy it."

Once again, the roar is deafening.

35

IT'S KINDA EXCITING, stepping off that platform into the crowd of Mazzikim and Nephilim. They treat both Jake and I like royalty. Jake especially is taken by it. They'd always been nice to him, but never like this. They're accepting him as my true partner. It's great to see and even better to feel.

We both hoped that getting married would make us feel more connected. Not to each other; we already couldn't feel more connected. But Jake wanted to feel more connected to the House of Keroz, and I wanted to feel more connected to my new body. It worked on both counts. I can see that Jake really feels comfortable with my Mazzikim and Ruhin. I'm still not used to being seven feet tall and red, but at least I feel like it's *me* that is seven feet tall and red, not some other body that I'm inhabiting instead of my own.

What I didn't count on is how joyous this would make all the beings of our House. It's wonderful to see. I'm so used to the Mazzikim being all business as they go about scouting Sediin, collecting rumam, or training, and the Ruhin being unwittingly wacky but otherwise preoccupied with maintaining the House and pleasing everyone else. There are Happenings—a sort of impromptu talent show—occasionally, which breaks the routine. But I'm sure that a wedding is even more precious of an event for them, as they're so rare in Sediin.

And they're enjoying every second: cheering, dancing, attempting to sing—which is a little painful, as none of them can get even close to a recognizable pitch—and otherwise making merry. The Mazzikim bounce away with song and dance to the armory to prepare for war, and the Ruhin to the walls to help maintain the House with their spirits.

"I'm glad that we could make them so happy," Jake says, reading my expression.

"You really are my soulmate, you know." I smile. I bend down and kiss him again. As soon as I do, more cheers erupt from every corner. When we end our kiss, we both can't help but laugh a warm, grateful laugh.

"Let us to the council chamber," Garz instructs. "I shall join you in a moment. First, I shall command scouts to every House in Sediin, to inform them of your marriage and let them know of our plans."

I turn around to find my guard. The two hairless bear-dogs are right behind Rachel, Josh, and Klara, but Zaebos is next to Daeba and their puppies.

"Garz wants us in the council chamber," I tell my friends. "Shall we?"

We step into the council chamber. After a moment, Zaebos runs in. "Forgive me, my—"

"You don't need forgiveness for wanting to talk to your mate and pups, Zaebos." I shake my head good-naturedly.

Zaebos bows his muzzle right as Garz joins us in the chamber.

"Our scouts will travel far and wide throughout Sediin," Garz declares. "Every corner shall know that you, Jake, are to be treated as a Seduman Lord and that we prepare to fight with Earth's champion."

"Thanks, Garz," I say.

"So is everyone going?" Rachel asks.

"Nearly," Gryx responds. "Every Sedu House tries to leave at least one Sedu or Seduman behind. There are many reasons for this. It keeps the Ruhin and remaining Mazzikim calmer. It leaves a leader behind in case one of the Sedu Houses that is not allied decides to try and take advantage. And if there is ever a need for coordination outside the battlefield, there will be an authority in the House."

"Lorek will stay," Klara says, knowing that her Sedu uncle is a bookish Sedu who doesn't do much fighting.

"He will." Gryx pats his daughter on the back. "And Lord Mog will fight with us, leaving his Seduman son Agyei to run his House."

"I hadn't even thought about Agyei." Rachel lowers her head.

"Yeah..." Neither had I. Agyei had been the most powerful Seduman on Earth, born of a Sedu and a Seduman instead of a Sedu and a human. He protected his village of Dajibo-Ondo in Nigeria. He is deeply loving. His wife, Tinuke, in fact, is a Nistar like my mother was. And they had a beautiful Sedu daughter, Efi. The Nephilim captured Tinuke and Efi, and before we could rescue them, H'ythiis absorbed Efi, the way G'suul tried to absorb me.

"I can't imagine what it's like to lose a child," I say. "I'm sure it would break me."

"They will never be the same," Garz says, a deep weight and knowing in his voice. And boy, he'd know. He saw his mother and his wife—who was carrying his unborn child—raped and murdered while he was chained and forced to watch. "And yet, life will continue. They will learn to walk again, and then run. Perhaps even find joy, as I have today."

I nod. It makes me happy to think that after all the misery and pain my brother has been through, I could give him a moment of peace. I wish we could offer that to Agyei and Tinuke.

"Who will stay behind at the House of Keroz?" Vetis asks nervously. I understand his nerves. He's amazing with throwing knives, he can spit acid stingers and jump even farther than Rachel, but that doesn't change the fact we're going up against giants, and he's a five-foot-nine spindly insect, not a stout warrior. His daughter is my shield maiden and a more robust warrior. Garz is the greatest warrior in all of Sediin, nearly strength personified. And me, well, this is my deal; I have to be there. Vetis clearly wants to be with his daughter and not stay home. But he's the obvious choice.

"Dad...it'll be okay, I promise," Rachel says, clearly thinking what we all are.

"Maybe, now that Jake is one of us..." Vetis suggests, almost pleading.

"If I can I will, but even though I can't fight, I may need to be there. Mort has been working on a prototype mobile radiation detector that has a range of around a mile radius—including underground. That's how we can show up where they will be, hopefully before they know we're onto them. But I might have to operate it myself, on site."

"This would be of great value," Garz notes.

"Vetis, I'll return to Earth and review the state of the prototype, and if it's something I could teach you to use, I'll let you know."

"Thank you," Vetis exhales, his gratitude obvious. "That is all I can ask."

"I...I can remain here," Pyza quietly adds from the side of the room. "I can represent the Sedim of the House. If you would allow it."

Vetis looks at Garz.

Garz slowly approaches Pyza. "I ask only one thing."

Pyza gazes expectantly into his eyes.

"Please stay, even after the war has been won." He gently takes her hands in his.

She nods, a bashful smile on her lips as she caresses his fingers with her own.

"Looks like you're off the hook, Vetis." I grin, happy for my brother. Both my brothers, in fact.

"Josh, I'm about to leave for Washington, D.C., but before I do I'll drop you off in Irvine and say hi to dad."

Josh nods, seeming kind of uncomfortable. He turns to me with an odd expression. Odd enough that Rachel, who still standing next to him, shoots him a puzzled look.

"Josh, is everything okay?" I ask.

"Yeah. I mean...yeah. It's just..."

"It's just what, Josh?" I prod.

"So...is this you forever, now? When you walk around Earth, is that what you're gonna look like? Not that there's anything wrong with you, and welcome to the family and all that, but it kinda makes it tough to go unnoticed, you know?"

"Yes, it does." I smile. I hold my hand out to Jake. He understands. He takes my hand, closes his eyes, and concentrates. I close my eyes and join him in concentration. I can feel my body shifting and changing. By the time I open my eyes, I look like I used to. Well, except I look amazingly dorky in a dress that is now insanely too large on me. The skirt now spills to the floor, and the straps of both dress and bra are too broad for my shoulders and flop down my arms, my way-huge bra now flopping over in the dress and barely covering anything.

Josh casts a side glance nervously at Rachel, then makes a very obvious play of staring only into my eyes, so that Rachel sees he's not trying to look at my far-smaller-but-semi-exposed boobs. Rachel pretends she doesn't notice, but I can see the corners of her mouth twitch as she represses a grin.

I imagine myself a pair of blue jeans and a T-shirt. Jake sees what I want to do and holds up my dress as a sort of screen for me to put on my clothes.

"Jake and I were pronounced of one flesh," I explain, sliding my jeans over my legs under my dress. "Jake's part of us is still human. So with his help, I can access my old form again. But Josh, it's not that this is me and my Sedu form is not. I can return to my Sedu form at will, but I can only access this one with Jake's help. So really, the Sedu form is more me now."

I pull my arms into the now tent-like dress, grab the T-shirt, and slip it on. Jake lifts the dress over my head now that I've changed, folds the dress, and walks it to the table.

"Do you understand?" I ask.

All the Sedim, Mazzikim, and Sedumen nod. Josh, however, still looks half-confused. Well, he looks confused when he's not vacillating between trying to see my nipples through my black T-shirt and looking back at my eyes slightly guiltily. Guess I should have materialized a bra.

Josh raises his eyes to my eyes and inhales. "I think so. I mean, I understand the bit about both of you need to concentrate to change you back into a Seduman. But why did you want to get married in Sedu form?"

"Because she *is* Sedu," Garz says. "This was a wedding before the spirits of this universe. Alex wanted them to feel connected to her—and perhaps to feel more connected to them. Besides, being married as a Sedu shows everyone that Jake accepts her as a Sedu, as partner and equal and soulmate. It makes them feel more connected to your brother as well."

"Yup, that pretty much covers it," I agree. "I'm new to my Sedu form, Josh. I totally get that you have to get used to it, too. But slowly, with everyone's help and acceptance, I'm learning to realize that my Sedu form is me—truly me."

"See?" Rachel says, elbowing Josh.

We all can't help but grin, imagining what conversation they must have had.

"I get it," Josh nods. "And really, I didn't mean to make you feel uncomfortable or anything. I know that you and Jake really love each other, and that's awesome. It's just this is crazy to me—in a good way, but still crazy."

"Oh, and, uh, sorry." He averts his gaze and shuffles a bit nervously. "I didn't mean to stare at my sister-in-law changing and stuff."

"You don't have to apologize, brother-in-law," I say.

"And there's nothing wrong with her being a full Sedu," Rachel adds.

"Got anything you need to tell me, Rachel?" Josh quips.

"Not yet," she shoots back, eyebrows raised.

Josh whispers in her ear.

"You better," Rachel says, clearly trying hard to keep from tearing up.

"So..." Josh looks at his brother.

"Okay, yeah," Jake nods.

He takes my hands and kisses me gently but passionately. "I shall return in a while, Mrs. Harman."

"You do that, Mr. Gold," I smirk, half my mouth curved up in a wry grin.

He kisses me again, bids his farewells to all of us, and pats his brother on the shoulder to guide him out of the council chamber.

Garz watches Jake walk his brother toward our portal for a moment. I can feel his emotions: deep affection, pride, and resolve. I get a bit glassy-eyed. I'm so glad that Garz loves Jake. I'm just as glad that for at least a moment Garz has a release from the general rage that seems to be the go-to emotion of our House.

"Come, let us prepare gemstones. We shall need hundreds." Garz turns to us and waves his arm at the long, rectangular table in the center of the room.

"Yeah, sounds good," I exhale. I turn to Rachel. She puts her arm around mine and we walk over to the long, rectangular table in the center of the room. Vetis, Pyza, and Garz join us at the table. Garz's eyes glow, and soon hundreds of bracers, gauntlets, and collars, from large to tiny, appear on the table. Enough, I imagine, for all the Mazzikim and Ruhin in our House and then some.

"Okay, so how do I do this? Do I need to be in Sedu form?" I ask as I take a seat. Rachel knows she can't do this, so she stands behind my chair and massages my shoulders.

"On Earth, you might need to revert to Sedu form to access your Sedu abilities, but in Sediin you are Sedu regardless of form. Here." Garz hands me a glowing gemstone of Azziz from the pouch on his belt. "Feel the spirit within. Concentrate. It will feel like a life force that isn't part of our House, unlike all the others you feel."

I roll the gemstone of Azziz around my fingers. I focus on the glow inside of it, of feeling that glow in my chest.

"I can feel it," I say. "It's weird, though. It's warm, like a spirit, but also sharp, like there's something unpleasant about it, something that doesn't like me and is trying to cut me."

"Excellent, my sister. That is exactly what it feels like. Azziz was an evil, corrupt Sedu, and even now these slight traces of his spirit are unpleasant. Focus on moving that energy from where you feel it into one of the other gems on the table. If you succeed, you'll feel two life forces with the same energy and that same sharpness, one in each gem."

I grab one of the gemstones out of the huge pile in the middle of the table. I reach out to the spirit that I feel in my chest and then picture the glow moving across gemstones. As I focus on the picture in my mind, the radiance from the gemstone of Azziz gets brighter, until after a while I've got two glowing gemstones in my hands.

"Whoa, cool!" Rachel exclaims.

"That is how it is done," Garz says, taking a seat next to me at the table. "This is tedious and painstaking, and after a while you'll tire. But with all of us working together, we can get it done far quicker than if I were working alone."

"Absolutely. I'll keep at it until we have enough." I place the newly created gemstone of Azziz in a new pile and grab more gems.

"Is there anything I can do, Uncle Garz?" Rachel asks.

"There is, young Stinger," Garz says. "If you wish to assist, you can take these gems and hand them to everyone in our House who shall accompany us to Earth. You will need to affix the gemstones to whatever type of armament best suits the being in question—some will need arm braces, others leg braces, still others necklaces, depending on their physical attributes."

"I can do that," she says.

"And bring Qwyll," Zaebos adds. While we were talking amongst ourselves, he managed to find a spot behind my chair to curl in a ball and lie down, both out of the way and by my side. "Have him carry bracers and necklaces in a sack on his belt. That way you can carry more, and he can help you affix them to the beings."

"Yeah, that sounds smart," Rachel agrees.

"We will keep a skeleton crew of Mazzikim and Ruhin to protect and maintain the House, but most will choose to go, which means you'll be handing gems to over one hundred spirits," Garz says. "Other Houses that fight with us will send Mazzikim to collect gemstones for their Houses; you won't be responsible for dressing them."

"Got it. I'll go get Qwyll." Rachel turns to go.

"Hey, one thing." I put my hand on Rachel's hand; she turns back to me and leans down to my ear. "What did Josh whisper before he left?"

Rachel inhales to speak, but stops herself when eyes start misting up. She shakes her head and turns to go again.

"Hey." I get out of my chair and hold her tight.

"It's okay, just whisper it to me."

She leans up to my ear and whispers, "He said that...he said that he'd still want to be with me even if I went 'full bug.'"

"I'll bet he would." I smile, rubbing her arms and kissing her hair.

"Okay," Rachel exhales as she collects herself. "Time to find Qwyll."

36

DAYS IN SEDIIN GO SO FAST, I barely can keep track of how many cycles of light and dark come and go while I'm in the council chamber creating new gemstones of Azziz. At some point, Klara and Gryx take their leave of us and return to the House of Gryx. Zaebos asks me if I'd mind if he spends time with his family. Of course I don't mind! Rachel and Qwyll continually run in to grab gemstones and armaments to equip more of our Mazzikim and Ruhin. Every so often, Zogo and the kitchen Ruhin come in with plates of snacks and even cooked dishes like chow mein and pasta. When food comes, Rachel stays and eats with me.

I revert to my Sedu form. I really only took my Seduman form for Josh's sake. I'm in Sediin, acting as a Sedu, in my Sedu House. Besides, as much as I'm glad I can go back to Earth and look like my old self, that's not my old body, either. I have to just get used to the reality that I'm big and red and buffed out like all of the Sedim. I'm still not one-hundred percent with my new body, and sometimes I can see on Rachel's face that she's still getting used to it too. But I want to get to the point that I always feel like myself, and not like I'm wearing someone else's skin.

With four Sedim creating new gemstones more or less constantly, it seems like after a few days we've created over a hundred. And after only a couple days after that, Rachel and Qwyll proudly report that every Ruhin and Sedu in our House who will be accompanying us to Earth is wearing a gemstone.

"Excellent work, Rachel!" Vetis says. Rachel hugs her dad.

"Rachel, I'm going to have to be making these for a while longer," I begin, "but there's nothing you need to do—these will now be for our allies who fight with us, and they'll pick up the gemstones they need."

"It will not be a long while," Garz interrupts. "Our allies will create their own bracers, leggings, and necklaces, so we can create more gemstones of Azziz faster."

"Don't you want to hang out with Josh a bit?" I finish my thought. "I'm sure Mr. Harman will welcome you. Get Jake to find the Kelleys in hiding, and let your foster parents and sisters know how you feel about them and what we'll be doing. And please, coordinate with Jake and get back to me with any information."

"Are you sure?" Rachel asks. Her tone says she's willing to stay, but her face lights up at the suggestion of hanging out with Josh.

"Totally sure," I insist. "When we're done creating gemstones, I want to sleep and rest here, where time is faster. And then I think I'm going to spend a whole lot of quality time with Garz, learning to fight in this form."

Garz nods his head without stopping what he's doing.

"And I think Garz would have insisted, even if I hadn't suggested it," I crack.

Garz keeps nodding.

"Yeah, Uncle Garz. You train her until she can survive anything. She's going to be at my Bat Mitzvah whether she likes it or not."

Garz, still not stopping, can't suppress the wry grin that crosses his lips.

"So..." I get out of my seat and walk over to Rachel. "You're really okay with me as a red, seven-foot-tall Sedu? Really really?"

"I really am." She puts her arms around me and hugs my abdomen tight. "We're more than just our skins. We're spirit beings, too. This is your spirit, same as it ever was. Honestly, I thought it would take me a long time to get used to you like this...but the truth is, even though these days in Sediin are only hours on Earth, I already see you as Alex, not Alex-turned-into-a big-red-Sedu. Although it figures that just when I finally get taller, you get crazy tall."

I can't help but snort out a chuckle. "Thanks, girlie. Sorry I'm so tall."

"You can make it up to me by taking out those lifeless soul suckers once and for all." Rachel turns to Garz. "Give her hell—I don't care what Matka said about the other champions, Alex doesn't have my permission to die."

"Nor mine." Garz rises from his seat and puts his hand on her shoulder. "And trust me—I will."

37

"TRAIN WELL." Vetis bows slightly as he begs his leave to oversee the distribution of the gemstones of Azziz to our allied Houses.

"Thanks, Vetis."

He leaves the council chamber and heads toward the main doors to greet incoming Mazzikim.

"Come." Garz holds out his arm out to invite me to walk with him. He guides me down the hallway just to the left of the council chamber that leads to the large, open space that serves as my main training area. As soon as it comes into view, I see that Garz made everything bigger—not just more space, but the punching bags are larger, the track around the perimeter of the training area is wider, and even the huge collection of dulled weapons on the wall is Sedu-sized, rather than human-sized. I grin as soon as I realize that Leeik and Zaebos are already there, waiting for me, along with a dozen very large and intimidating bipedal Mazzikim.

"Close your eyes," Garz instructs. "Take the spirit of the House in, let it flow through you."

I close my eyes and open myself to the sensation I had when I was a disembodied spirit, joined with the House. Inside my chest, I feel what begins as a tiny dot of warmth and quickly becomes almost searing, without actually burning me.

"I feel it."

"Good! What do you feel?"

"At first, it felt like heat. Now I think I can feel Dad. And you. Everyone in the whole house, if I concentrate."

"Excellent, my sister. Now reach into that spirit."

"I am," I nod. "It feels strong, determined—and angry, like an unquenchable rage."

"Correct," Garz nods. "The spirit of Keroz is in many ways defined by fury. It has fueled us, healed us, given us strength when we waver. And you're right—the spirit of Keroz is angry—seething with anger."

"Where does that anger come from?"

"Many things. The dishonesty of other Sedim. The losses we have suffered. Right now, our spirit rages at the Nephilim, and what the Rishon have done to you."

Can't really argue with any of that. It all enrages me too.

"You feel this all the time?"

"Yes, but I have learned to let it flow through me and not consume me,"

Garz explains. "You are a being of compassion and embody the living force of the spirit of Keroz, but it is anger that shaped that spirit."

"What does that mean for me, Garz?"

"It means that in your daily life, be yourself, Alex. Be the avatar of love and compassion. Be Life's champion. But in combat, tap into the rage within the spirit of Keroz. Let it flow through you like an energy. Anger for what happened to our father. For what the Nephilim did to Rachel. To you. To Wyatt, to Firebird Manor. Let that rage inform your own rage. Let it sharpen your senses, but dull your pain. Let it give you strength and take away your fatigue. Your training and your mind propel your body, but let the fury of our House be the fuel that powers it."

I imagine that warmth, that rage, coursing through me, tensing and untensing every muscle. I feel hyperaware of everything around me. Far from this rage making me lose control, I've never felt this controlled before, like a bomb right before it goes off. I feel supercharged.

"I feel alive." I open my eyes, flames shooting out of them.

"Good!" Garz growls, his lips pulled back in an impish grin. Then he lunges.

I spring back and to the left, but I'm ungainly on my legs, and he grabs me as soon as my feet leave the ground and throws me over his shoulder. I land on my butt, hard. Garz lands next to me on his stomach and rolls away.

When Garz first trained me as a Seduman, he was not only harsh, but terrifying. I crawled away from his sparring in tears as he berated me. Now, however, he props himself up on one elbow. "Do you agree, Lady Firebird, that you have much to learn?" he chuckles.

How things have changed between us!

"I do." I smile back. "I need to be as fluid with my new body as I was with my old."

"Excellent!" Garz leaps to his feet and holds a hand out to help me up. I think he's just showing off how nimble he is with his eight-foot-tall Sedu body. But that's okay; he's the most badass warrior in all of Sediin. I'm grateful to have him as my teacher.

"With your Sedu body, I am unsure if you'll need sleep anymore, although you may still need rest. I assume that you will need sustenance, as yours is a living body, not a spirit form. So let us know when you need to break for food and drink, or if you tire. For otherwise, I would train you nonstop, until you are the fiercest Sedu warrior besides me."

"Will do, Garz. Let's get started."

Garz claps and the Mazzikim all spread out around the edges of the training area. Garz starts with the very basics, as he did when I first arrived as an untrained Seduman: with balance, basic stands, body awareness, and stuff like that. But it's good, I know I need it. It takes time, but with Garz's help—sometimes with Leeik and Zaebos to help out by giving me targets to aim at—I can again smoothly execute the martial arts and krav maga moves I'd learned before and strike with precision in my new body.

That's when Leeik throws Mazzik after Mazzik at me—sometimes my balance or technique is off and I'm not as good as I used to be, so a coordinated attack of a few of our Mazzikim succeeds in bringing me down. Whenever I'm laid out on my ass, Garz helps me up, and we go over in detail what did wrong and how to improve. Zogo usually takes those opportunities to run up with some water and food. Sometimes I do need to take a break to relax; when I do, Zaebos curls up next to me. It's really sweet. And when I'm refreshed, I get right back up, and it's back to training.

After a while, I not only reach my previous level of proficiency, but I feel like I'm even better, stronger, more balanced. That's when Garz starts training me with weapons. We spar with blades of all sizes, axes, pole arms. As he did before, when training with weapons, only Garz spars with me. He says it's because I need to learn to fight with opponents taller and stronger than me, since that's what G'suul and H'ythiis will be. I don't doubt that's true, but I also am certain another reason is because he knows exactly how to pull his swings and slashes so that as hard as he fights, he never gives me more than a scratch.

Days pass, but I never leave the training area, so I've lost track of how many. Garz is free to train me nonstop because Vetis is taking care of our House. The days blur, but it also means I get better, faster.

Occasionally, Vetis runs in to throw me some words of encouragement, which is sweet, and to tell Garz various bits of news. We hoped that when the Sedim were fully aware of what happened to Lord Stygg, the outrage of an invasion into Sediin would be enough that even Houses that aren't allied with us yet would want to fight. But no; selfishness and fear outweigh any indignation they might feel. Our allies and Lord Stygg's allies will all fight, but the Sedim who aren't our allies are going to sit this one out. They have excuses, but what it comes down to is they're scared.

The only non-allied Sedu who contributes anything is Lord Bexx; he is a selfish and cowardly fire-based Sedu, kinda like a scrawny version of Garz. He's the Sedu father of Tante Toni, Jake's great-great-great-great-great grandmother, and in honor of our mating, two Mazzikim from his house will join our Mazzikim. Not exactly a huge force, but it's two more than any other non-ally, so that's something, I guess.

Garz, Vetis, and our Mazzikim aren't surprised. They expect that sort of behavior. But even if I shouldn't, I can't help but be pissed off. This is an existential threat to all the Sedim. The Rishonim and Nephilim can cross portals and destroy all the Sedim. And if they kill all life on Earth, that means no more of the human rumam that the beings here rely on to maintain their forms and Houses, and all of Sediin will crumble.

I let my frustration over their behavior mix with the underlying anger I'm already tapped into. It spurs me on even more. I train harder. I get better. I get faster. I get to the point that I can spar to a draw with Garz using my blade or any number of Sedu weapons. A dozen Mazzikim can rush me at once, and I can fend them off. Not only can I tap into the rage of the spirit of Keroz for strength and focus, but I even enjoy it a bit, although I'm not sure that's a good thing. But when fighting, it disconnects me a little from my empathy, which in battle is a good thing. Don't get me wrong: I never lose my sense of loss and concern for all living things, but I learn to let that compassion fuel my righteous sense of anger, and that anger pushes me to greater feats of strength.

Perhaps the best result of all my training is that I finally feel completely at one and comfortable in my big, red Sedu skin. I am Alexandra Gold, Lady Firebird of the House of Keroz, and I am a seven-foot-tall, red, muscular Sedu warrior. I can still access my previous form with Jake's help, but this is who I am.

"Make way! Mistress Stinger to see our Lords and Lady!" I hear Zogo shouting as he approaches the training area. Sure enough, a moment later he and Rachel round the corner and run in.

"Alex, Uncle Garz, I have news," Rachel says, hunched over with her hands on her knees. She clearly ran in before she'd fully recovered from the portal.

"Shoot," I say.

"Okay, so Mort's been busy. He's been gathering...hold on, I wrote it down." Rachel digs into the back pocket of her jeans and pulls out a crumpled piece of paper.

"Thermobaric hand bombs," Rachel continues. "Which he said is a fuel-air bomb one of his weapons-contracting companies had been working on, and Mazzikim can drop them through portals or something like that? I'm not sure what that means, but he sounded pretty proud of himself."

"He should be," Garz says. "This is brilliant. Please tell Mort that if he can, our allies who are only sending a few Mazzikim could use these from their own Houses and be of great help."

"Okay," Rachel nods, again glancing at her notes. "There's more, too. Jake's been using a subterranean radiation mapping satellite to track a huge amount of that special Nephilim radiation under the Gila National Forest in New Mexico. They could compare different satellite images to figure out that the radiation is moving slowly toward the Arizona border."

"New Mexico?"

"Yeah. Seems like they're heading straight west from where they portaled from the House of Stygg back to Broxton, Oklahoma," Rachel shrugs.

"Well, that's shitty." I frown. "Can we get a precise enough reading to intercept them?"

"That's the good news; Jake thinks so." Rachel crinkles up and shoves her notes back in her pocket. "That prototype handheld radiation detection thingie—Jake had a name for it, which he told me and I was too much of a doofus to write down—it's kinda complicated, sorry. Anyway, it's usable now. Kinda. Jake says that it's really basic, has no real interface, and that he has to operate it by direct coding or something, so he'll need to come with us."

"Okay," I sigh. I hate having him that close to the fighting when he's not a trained warrior. He's immortal, but that doesn't mean he can't be torn to shreds, and that can't be pleasant. "So where do we go to intercept them? We've been to Tucson, Arizona; is that good?"

"Mort has been to Phoenix, about two hours from San Carlos Reservation in the Arizona desert, which is even better," Rachel says. "Jake figures at the rate they're moving and the rate he guesstimates a Sedu army can travel, if we go to the reservation and try to head them off, we'll end up meeting them in the open desert or meadows, away from populated areas."

"Does Mort have some super-secret digging tool for intercepting them underground?"

"Yeah—lots of Mazzikim with lots of shovels."

"Oh geez...I hope there's a lot of Mazzikim that have arms." I curl my mouth downward.

"Hey, it's all we got on short notice, so it will have to do."

"Good point," I agree with Rachel.

"Garz, please make a huge pile of shovels that we can put in bags and strap across four-legged Mazzikim."

"It shall be done," Garz says.

"So is Mort taking us to Phoenix?" I ask Rachel.

"Mort's taking Jake to Phoenix via portals from the House of Stygg right now, and then Jake will be brought here. He should be here within a day of Sediin time."

"Okay, cool, that works," I nod.

"So have all you guys been nonstop training the entire two Sediin months I've been away?" Rachel turns to both Garz and me.

"Two months?" I blurt out. I knew we'd been here a while, but didn't realize it was quite that long.

"We have," Garz confirms. "And your Lady is ready to face G'Suul and all his Nephilim—and destroy them."

38

So many Mazzikim and Ruhin fill the great hall that Garz has to temporarily extend the front grounds of the House of Keroz to accommodate them. It's a crazy motley assembly of beings with all kinds of appearances—bipedal and quadrupedal, winged and non-winged, clawed and fingered, mandibled and jawed, all in bulletproof tunics with the logo of their respective Houses. Those with opposable thumbs or claws carry daggers, swords, or axes in their belts, depending on their size. Those with wings and arms have bows and arrows. They squawk, growl, bark, and whistle amongst each other, antsy but excited.

Lord Mog stands with his five dozen or so Mazzikim warriors. Lord Gryx stands toward the back of the hall with nearly eight dozen. And Lord Stygg, who has lost so much to H'ythiis and G'suul, has matched our nine dozen Mazzikim warriors. We have other, weaker allies I've only met in passing who all sent a few Mazzikim to join our House's forces as they promised, and Lord Bexx's two Mazzikim. Zaebos told me that there are well over four hundred Mazzikim in the main hall, with nearly half that number of Ruhin. It's the most bizarre and fierce-looking collection of "demons" I've ever seen.

Garz reformed the staircase into a stage six feet high so that we're above even the tallest Mazzikim. Garz positions himself in the middle of the stage and out front, wearing a black tunic, leggings, and boots, with the symbol of the House of Keroz in red on his chest. He stands taller than all of us on stage. A few paces behind him, I'm to his right in my full Sedu glory. Garz created a special Team Firebird uniform that's not only protective but clingy and stretchy, so I can transform between human and Sedu sizes. I'm even wearing makeup. No, I didn't glam up to stand in front of the Mazzikim. I was thinking about Boudicca, and the way that she used to put on war paint to psych herself up as well as hopefully terrify her enemies. Well, I'm not an Iceni queen like she was, but I did do dark and brooding as a goth girl. So I painted my lips and nails black. No point in eyeshadow since I have flaming eyes. And I'm sure my lipstick will burn off as soon as I breathe fire. But hopefully it will make me look more menacing while it lasts.

Zaebos stands to my left. To my right is Team Firebird: Rachel, Jake, and Klara, all in Team Firebird dark red trench coats, fingerless gloves, black pants, and boots. Rachel is in full Stinger mode; Klara looks every bit Gryx's daughter with her reptilian red skin, glowing eyes, and mandible extended out a couple inches and filled with alligator teeth. My honor guard stands at attention behind us, along with Pelegor and Qwyll. The right side of the stage is filled out by Vetis and a row of extremely tall, bipedal Mazzikim, fronted by

Leeik. At the very back of the stage, Zedek sits on his hind legs, with Kesed seated next to him on a large throne that I created out of the spirit of the House.

Garz paces the stage, a ghoulish smile on his face. As he starts to nod, the Mazzikim match his smile and nod, reveling in the approval of the most powerful Sedu in all of Sediin.

"So...when do we start?" Rachel leans toward me.

"Soon...I think?"

As if on cue, I notice Garz catch Lord Mog's eye, and the two of them breathe fire above everyone's heads. I guess that's the Sedu signal for "your attention, please" in rowdy gatherings of Mazzikim warriors.

"All of you have my gratitude for volunteering to fight with us." Garz steps forward to the edge of the stage. "And make no mistake, this is a fight not just to preserve Earth and our rumam, but for the soul of Sediin, from those who would invade our Houses and lay waste to us."

The Mazzikim nod, growl, and rumble their agreement.

"Fighting on Earth will be new to many. So let its champion say a few words to you." Garz turns to me and holds out his arm to invite me forward as he steps back.

I knew he'd ask me to speak. I thought about what to say. I know that they're eager to listen. But that doesn't make me any less nervous. I bow my head to Garz and approach the front of the stage. Showtime.

"I know you have your own reasons for fighting," I begin. "But I want you all to know that I am grateful. I also know many of you will be seeing Earth for the first time, especially you Ruhin, who cannot cross the portal without these gemstones. Believe me, the beauty you will find will be almost overwhelming. Even at night, the sounds, the feeling of wind against your skin, the smell of the grass, the stars in the waking sky..."

I can feel my red, flaming eyes getting glassy and wet. I can't help it, I just love my world so much. No offense to the House of Keroz, but Sediin is at best an imitation of a medieval world. Earth is the real thing. Its sun and stars, its animals and plants, its deserts and forests...unmatchable.

"You will all agree it is worth saving, trust me."

I stop myself, because if I keep talking, my voice might break. I feel kinda dumb, since most of the beings in the crowd have never seen Earth, so they aren't really sure what I'm talking about.

I turn to Garz. *Help*...I think to him.

Garz walks up to me. He pats me on the arm and then turns to the assembled army, pulling back his lips to show his sharp teeth and fangs as he smiles. I return to my position with Team Firebird.

"What Lady Firebird says of the beauty to be found on Earth is true. Treat all the animal and plant life with respect, as she would."

The Mazzikim all nod.

"And when you face the Nephilim, treat them as I would: *Burn them! Burn them all!*" Garz yells and then shoots a jet of flame above their heads.

"Burn them all! Burn them all!" the Mazzikim shout, thrusting their arms and hands and claws and paws in the air. They're so loud the walls shake.

"They have hurt our Houses and gone unpunished. No longer!" Garz shoves his fist in the air, eliciting even more cheers. "They shall face the wrath of Sediin!"

I can feel Garz's pride in this force, his pride in Sediin, and his joy in firing them up. But I dunno...I feel a bit nervous.

Are they out of control? I think to Garz.

See for yourself, he answers. *Demand their attention.*

Again I approach the front of the stage. Surprisingly, it takes only what I think is a few seconds for the crowd to quiet down. Okay, I got their attention, now I need something to say. I don't want it to just be sappy, it needs to keep their fire going. That's not my thing, I'm not really the fiery type of orator, but I have to try.

"I am tied to the natural life on Earth, and I am tied to the life on Sediin. I need you to not only kill the Nephilim—but to not die yourselves. We burn them, but we return."

The Mazzikim bob their heads, seemingly happy I'm looking out for their well-being.

"We will return!" I shout, throwing my own fist in the air. The Mazzikim raise fists, arms, and claws and cheer me on.

Well done, Garz thinks to me. *Well done, indeed.*

Garz smiles and walks up to me, resting a hand on my shoulder. "Each Sedu House shall create multiple portal mirrors and new Sedu blades tied to each new portal. Ruhin shall go with every Mazzikim. They shall carry torches lit with Sedu fire, and Sedu blades from different portals from their House. Mazzikim, as you defeat the Nephilim, leave the carcasses for the Ruhin to burn, so their filth cannot poison the earth. And Ruhin, if you see Mazzikim injured, immediately open a portal. Anyone wounded shall portal back to their House to recover. With each House having multiple portal mirrors, multiple Mazzikim will be able to be sent home at once—we will destroy the Nephilim and live to tell tales of it forever!"

The Ruhin agree enthusiastically—their voices aren't nearly as loud as the Mazzikim, but they give it their best try. I get it. They never get to visit Earth; this is a special joy for them. The Mazzikim also—they love the fight, but they also are happy to hear that their leaders don't think of them as expendable.

You showed compassion as well as leadership in war. They will take inspira-

tion from you and follow you, Garz thinks to me. *Trust me.*

Nah, they follow you, I answer. *They tolerate me.*

Do not underestimate yourself, sister. Yes, I am their war leader—but they are prepared to follow you as well. They wouldn't cheer you otherwise.

Okay, well, let me give some leadership a try.

"How long do you all need to prepare?" I ask the gathered Houses.

On cue they stop their cheering and all start conferring amongst themselves and their Sedu Lords.

"Damn, girl," I hear Rachel say behind me.

I can't help but smirk a bit.

You see, Garz thinks to me, nodding.

Thanks, Garz.

Various lieutenants confer with their Lords and warriors and start shouting out numbers of hours. It's hard to make out anything, but Garz seems in his element.

"Six? Six hours?" Garz looks to Gryx and Mog, as well as the larger warriors that are Mazzikim lieutenants. They all cheer.

"It shall be done. Make any preparations you need, in any of your Houses. Be sure to travel to the House of Stygg first, where Mortimer Stygg, Lord Stygg's Seduman son, has delivered Earth weapons we can throw through our portal to the Earth below. In six hours, we gather at this portal, in the House of Keroz."

The assembled crowd of warriors all cheer again. I step back to my team. Zaebos is beaming. I can tell he's proud of me, which is awesome, and I also know how much he wants the Rishon and Nephilim killed. I turn to my team. Like me, they seem somewhere between thrilled and terrified. They know how dangerous this is going to be. They know that some of us won't be coming back to Sediin, no matter how much Garz and I want everyone to. I know that I very likely won't be coming back either, given what Matka said.

I turn to Zedek and Kesed behind me. Zedek stares ahead blankly. Kesed makes eye contact with me and cries.

39

TEAM AFTER TEAM of Mazzikim and Ruhin cross the portal into a small valley in the Arizona desert. They shuffle, crawl, or glide out of the way of the portal opening, and then another team crosses as soon as there's room. All the Sedu lords— Garz and Vetis, Gryx, Stygg, and Mog—take position in a very large semicircle around the portal, so as the Mazzikim cross over, each can join his liege. The nearly pitch-black three a.m. sky forty miles outside of Phoenix is alive with blinding flashes every time new beings shove their way through the portal mirror.

Next to Garz and Vetis, Leeik stands at attention. Rachel, Zogo, and I sit atop Pelegor. Thankfully, Pelegor is big and strong enough that he can easily handle a seven-foot-tall Sedu woman and the five-foot-three Seduman behind me on his back—and three-foot-tall Zogo in front of me weighs next to nothing.

Jake sits next to us on the back of a Mazzik with the body of a horse and the tail, neck, and head of a rattlesnake. His name is Kydriss, a good friend of Pelegor. Jake needed a steed, and Pelegor vouched for his buddy. I've never met Kydriss before now, and his voice is a bit intimidating because it always sounds like he's hissing—yeah, I know, he's got a snake head, go figure. But he's been very helpful to Jake, and they seem to be bonding, which is cool. Zaebos has assigned my guard to all of Team Firebird and swelled its ranks, so that we are being protected by a dozen Mazzikim, all of which resemble Zaebos—dog-bears with two rows of shark teeth in their muzzles—but only Zaebos has rust-colored fur; the rest are hairless.

All the beings from Sediin wear gemstones of Azziz somewhere on their bodies—on chokers, armlets, anklets, whatever works best for their particular body form. The gemstones allow them to stay on Earth as long as they need to. Otherwise, they'd be limited to two hours before their bodies would start disintegrating. That's why Zedek and Kesed aren't with us. They're still limited to two hours. We'll open a portal for them as soon as the battle begins, but not before.

Since this is my first time on Earth in my Sedu body, I was a little concerned that I might need a gemstone myself. I was relieved to discover that I don't; I feel as comfortable here as in Sediin. Pyza, Garz, and everyone tried to tell me that I was still a being of flesh and bone; my spirit wasn't created in the spirit universe. It's nice to see proof of that.

When I squint and try to peer through the portal, I can just make out Klara on the other side. I'm glad she's remaining in Sediin. When I suggested she remain in Sediin she halfheartedly replied that she felt she should be with us. I appreciate Klara being willing to come, even if the idea terrifies her. We're a team, and she didn't want to abandon us. But she's not a warrior, and this is war. Her father, and Gryx's Mazzikim, are training her to fight, but she's not there yet. Right now, her main assets are her paralyzing saliva and her quick thinking as a field nurse. Since all the beings that are fighting will heal any and all wounds in Sediin, there's no real need for "nursing." It's better that she remains in Sediin and helps by reaching through the portal and pulling the wounded back to our House. I think she's relieved, but of course she's worried for us.

There's another reason I wanted her back in Sediin. I think...I think this is it for me. I am trained and determined with a huge army to ensure I get to the Rishonim. I have no doubt that I have the ability to defeat them. But I don't think that I'm meant to walk away this time. Matka knew it. Jake knows it. I'm glad that Klara's safe, so when I'm gone she can help Rachel pick up the pieces so Team Firebird can carry on. I know she has it in her.

I just wish Rachel were staying in the House of Keroz, safe with Klara. But there's no way in hell she would.

"Pretty cool that we're portaling to Earth outside a city named after a mythical firebird, isn't it?" Rachel grins.

"I'm not sure if it's fitting or ironic," I quip. "But I think Jake found a good spot for us."

"Huh?" Jake looks up from his prototype machine that looks to me like a Star Trek tricorder, but mostly screen.

"We're just chatting," I smile. "Didn't mean to distract."

"No, it's cool," Jake says, peering down again. "This is just a wacky combination of a responsive touchscreen for the maps and a mechanical keyboard for typing Linux command line instructions. There's just an EPROM here, there wasn't enough time to..."

Jake looks up with a wry grin. "You have no idea what I'm saying, do you?"

"You're saying that we're going to save life on Earth because you and Mort know what you're doing. That's what matters."

"Seriously, Jake, you're awesome," Rachel adds. "I couldn't work a thingy like that if I tried."

"Does this mean I shouldn't tell you about the problems I'm having?"

At that, the Sedim and Mazzikim all turn to Jake.

"No, please do," Garz says.

"It relies on satellite communication. Does that make sense?"

Rachel, Garz, Vetis, and I all nod. The Mazzikim look clueless.

"It means that this box"—he holds it out so everyone standing where we are can see it—"has to be able to listen to a machine in the sky to tell us if the

Nephilim are near us under the ground."

"And it cannot hear the machine in the ssssky?" Jake's steed Kydriss hisses.

"Exactly." Jake strokes Kydriss's reptilian neck. "I'm hoping it's temporary. But for now, it's just giving me connection errors."

"Do what you can," Garz says. "We know you can make this work."

"I will," Jake says, looking down again. "I'll try everything."

I rub Jake's shoulder affectionately as I turn to the portal, averting my gaze so that I'm not blinded.

"Thanks, love," Jake says, still looking at his device. "I'll get something happening with this."

It seems like nearly all the Mazzikim and Ruhin have arrived. At least, it looks like the numbers of beings surrounding us and the other Sedu Lords is about what I remember from our great hall. After the flashes from the portal subsides, I gaze into it and see Klara standing there with her thumb up.

I turn to Garz. "I think that's everyone."

Garz nods, motioning to our Ruhin. They all gather around him and hold up their unlit torches. He breathes fire to light them all. Then those Ruhin back off, other Ruhin step forward and hold up their torches. As soon as Lord Mog sees Garz lighting the torches, he does the same with his own Ruhin. When all of our and Lord Mog's Ruhin have lit torches, Garz moves toward Lord Gryx and Lord Mog joins Lord Stygg, because those two don't breathe fire, but acid.

When all the torches are lit, Garz holds up his fist. Leeik bows to him. Lieutenant Mazzikim for all our Sedu allies do the same. After each Sedu hears from his lieutenants, he raises his fist. Finally, all are silent, looking to Garz.

"Okay, the reservation is sort of northeast—that way." Jake holds out his arm and points diagonally to our left.

Garz puts his hand on Leeik's shoulder.

"Criers!" Leeik calls out.

On cue, all of our Mazzikim with canine-like heads lift up their muzzles and howl, about two dozen in all. It is a fearsome sound, like an angry wolf pack, but also unnatural, like a pack of angry werewolves. Garz holds his arm up toward the direction Jake pointed.

"We go," Garz instructs.

All the Mazzikim and Ruhin turn to the direction Garz pointed. We gallop, march, and fly toward San Carlos Reservation, the House of Keroz out front.

"Are we there yet?" Rachel cracks.

"It's gonna be hours," Jake says. "Unless we're ambushed before I can get this hunk of junk working, that is."

40

A SIGN on the right shoulder of the two-lane highway we've been following welcomes us to the San Carlos Indian Reservation. It's after four-thirty in the morning—getting lighter, but still pretty dark. We stay off the road just in case some people want to drive in or out. Nobody comes by, which really isn't surprising, considering the hour.

I direct our Ruhin and Mazzikim to spread the word that everyone should be as quiet as possible. Of course, hundreds of creatures of all shapes and sizes, some carrying bags of shovels, others carrying weapons, make a lot of noise, even if they're being careful. Still, we haven't seen anyone yet, and I want to keep it that way.

"Okay, cool—got something!" Jake whispers and leans between Kydriss and Pelegor to show Rachel and me his detector thingy. "See those sort of scattered green dots? That's them."

Garz and Vetis walk over and take a look. Jake twists his hand so they can get a better view.

"They're just at the opposite edge of the reservation, almost directly east of us."

"Is there a dot or other color that represents us?" I ask.

"No," Jake shakes his head. "Remember, this is a prototype. It's not user-friendly or feature-complete. It's really more proof of concept than anything."

"Well, it's definitely proving to be awesome, so no complaints from me," I reach out and rub his shoulder a little.

"So we're heading the right direction?" Rachel asks.

"Yeah. We just need to alter our course slightly." Jake holds his right arm forward but slightly to the right.

Garz nods to Jake and holds up his fist. Nearly instantly, the other Sedim hold up their fists. Garz then points his arm in the direction that Jake did. The Sedim lower their fists, and we all correct our course slightly to match Jake's direction.

We continue without talking for a while. Jake keeps his head buried in his detector, occasionally mumbling, "Okay, good" or "Damn, lost the— okay, cool."

"We still on track?" I ask.

"Yeah. My satellite connection is pretty rough, so at any moment I—"

An eagle-winged Mazzikim with an owl head on a chimpanzee body lands right in front of Garz and says something to him in a language I don't understand. Garz answers him, and the Mazzikim bows and launches himself back into the sky.

"Humans are gathering about a mile ahead of us," Garz explains. "Xynn says that they don't seem to be carrying weapons or in a hostile formation. I told Xynn to continue to monitor them."

"Should we go around them?" Rachel asks.

"I don't think we can; there are too many of us." I shake my head. "Let's just tell them why we're here and ask them to stay inside and safe."

"Okay, cool," Rachel says.

Garz nods.

"I think you might want to talk to them in your Earth form," Jake suggests.

"Is that what we're calling the appearance that I grew up with? My Earth form?"

"What do you want to call it? Red She-Hulk is your 'real' form now." He offers me a thin, wry grin.

"What do you think, girlie?" I spin my head to look at Rachel.

"We can call it your human form," Rachel suggests. "You're a Sedu now, but you're also a real human, not just pretending."

"I like that," I lean backward and kiss Rachel on top of her head. "Anyway, yeah, you're right, Jake; I should meet them in my human form."

Jake guides Kydriss a little closer to Pelegor and takes my hand. He closes his eyes, and I close my eyes. We concentrate on my human form, and before I know it I can feel myself shrinking in my saddle, my stretchy uniform clinging to my contracting body . I open my eyes when I can tell I've stopped changing.

Garz turns around and gives me an approving nod. "Why not ride in front, so you, Rachel, Zogo, and Pelegor are the first of us they will see."

"Good idea," I answer, and Pelegor canters out in front of Garz.

"You're still wearing black lipstick, you know," Rachel pats my back and whispers to me.

"I'm going to guess the tribespeople won't mind."

We're moving slowly, but it doesn't take us that long to advance a mile. We see the headlights of cars and older trucks before we see people. Xynn flies back and forth, reporting what he sees, which is about a dozen tall but stocky-looking men. I'm surprised. I guess I was expecting either nobody or a crowd of hundreds, not just a few.

The people are clearly Native American. Even in the slowly brightening darkness, they seem worse for the wear: their skin seems lined and ruddy, their hair straight and black, their clothes shabby and old. I know that the United States has treated the Native peoples like shit; are they here because they think we're here to screw them over, like the government has done so many times and keeps doing?

When our forces are only yards away, one of them steps out of the road and walks out until he stands directly in Pelegor's path.

I instruct Garz to stop our warriors, and I gallop up to the man in the road. His people all stare, wide-eyed, at the collection of bizarre beings in front of them. But the guy in front of me doesn't flinch as we ride up to him.

"Greetings," he says, making eye contact but also glancing around me, trying to make out the odd creatures surrounding me. "My name is Terral Miles. Most people call me Terry."

"Hi, Terry. I'm Lady Firebird. Or Firebird Alex. Whichever you prefer to call me. Sitting behind me is Stinger."

Rachel smiles and waves at Terry.

"And our little helper is Zogo."

Zogo very shyly looks up with a sheepish grin on his beak and holds up a hand to wave.

"And my brave steed is named Pelegor."

Pelegor bows his head.

Terry inhales and raises his eyebrows. I don't blame him. No doubt a three-foot bipedal turtle without a shell and two teenage girls riding a silver-haired eagle-horse-cheetah isn't what he thought he'd be seeing when he woke up this morning.

"I run the San Carlos Spiritual Center, over in the center of the res," Terry says, pointing behind him and left. "I'm the Apache shaman as well. In fact, I was expecting you and all your warriors."

"Expecting us?" That doesn't make me feel warm and fuzzy. I mean, I know we're loud, but still...

"Yes. The Earth-Daughter came to me in a dream last night. She said that tonight, the Watchers-Who-Poison-the-Earth will carve their way through her belly, under the reservation, bleeding out the soul of our land."

"Terry, I don't know Apache mythology, but your Earth-Daughter sounds a lot like Matka, or Mother Earth, whom I saw, too."

"She told me that, also," Terry says. "Earth-Daughter said that she met with the Firebird and her family, and you are her Champion."

"Hey—uh, excuse me, Mr. Miles, Terry, Apache shaman, sir." Jake swallows as Kydriss canters up to us. "I'm sorry to interrupt. I'm the official navigator here—"

"And the other half of the Firebird, I know." Terry bows his head.

Both Jake and I look at each other. Damn, Matka really meant this whole two parts of a whole thing.

"So here's my question." Jake turns back to Terry. "I've got this device here—"

"You can say 'phone' or 'tablet,' you know," Terry admonishes. "We're poor, but we live in the same century you do, we have Wi-Fi and Internet and all that."

"Of course. I'm sorry, sir. I didn't mean to imply you didn't. But this isn't a phone or tablet." Jake urges Kydriss a few steps closer to Terry and shows it to him. "I called it a device because it's a one-of-a-kind prototype that can detect the specific radiation footprint of the Nephilim and Rishonim, even underground."

"Oh—sorry about that."

"It's cool, no need to apologize. But look here." Jake points to scattered green dots on the screen. "This tells me they're due east, maybe four miles out, off the road over here," Jake points at the screen, then off in the distance. "Those weird coordinates and numbers under the screen tells me they're underground, maybe a hundred feet or so. Anything sacred there?"

Terry exhales, his face drawn. There is a pensiveness carved into the deep lines on his face. He looks up. "In days past, our ancestors were buried one mile due east."

Goddammit.

"We'll hurry," I promise. "We'll cut them off before they dig through the graves. We'll save as much of the grounds as we can. And Team Firebird will return to try to nurse back to health that land that is bled dry. You have my word."

"Thank you, Champion," Terry bows. "The Earth-Daughter loves you, and I see why. You and your otherworldly army may go straight through our cemetery."

"Are you sure? If it's a holy—"

"Every place is holy," Terry says. "All the land is sacred. The Nephilim, the Watchers, they defile it, and the Earth-Daughter cries to me in my dreams. To help her, I know that I must help her champion."

"I appreciate that. I don't know anything about how your people communicate with your ancestors, but—"

"You needn't worry; our ancestors are in the warm embrace of Earth-Daughter, and they would want you intercept her enemies as soon as possible," Terry nods. "Is there anything that we can do to help you?"

"Actually, yeah," I nod slowly, thinking. "I don't want any of your people caught in the crossfire. Can you call everyone who might find themselves east of here and tell them to stay inside until they get the all-clear from you?"

"We can," Terry confirms. "We'll do that now."

"Perfect. I want as few people hurt as possible. When this is over, we will cement the relationship between the Native peoples of the San Carlos Reservation and the House of Keroz."

Terry nods and holds out his hand in farewell. He and his companions return to their cars. We return to Garz.

"I heard everything," Garz says. "You acquitted yourself well, like a true leader."

"Thanks, Garz." I pat his arm. Jake leans over and shows Garz his detector. Garz nods and relays the plan to the rest of our forces.

"Don't think I didn't notice you said Team Firebird instead of I or we," Rachel says.

"Really?" I play dumb. Of course I knew what I said. And she knows I knew what I said.

"You said it because you think you're going to die," Rachel says matter-of-factly.

I don't respond.

"I'm not going to let you," she declares.

"We aren't going to let you," Pelegor adds.

Zogo turns around, nodding emphatically.

I don't have a death wish. I'm married now and want to have life with my husband, maybe even a family if I still can. I want to help make two worlds better. But Matka's words keep spinning in my head. Yeah, I'm a Sedu champion, not a human champion. And the other champions didn't have the soul of a previous champion in their blade. But then again, none of them faced Rishonim.

"Don't worry, I want to live."

"I know," Rachel says, this time patting my back. "But if you keep up this morbid thinking, I'm going to give you a really complicated prayer to read at my Bat Mitzvah."

"Okay, deal," I laugh.

I return to my Sedu form. We slow as we reach the edge of an old cemetery, bounded only by low hills on the north and south sides. I close my eyes, inhale slowly, and try to reach out to the living earth, the life force in the ground and around me. After I make contact, I slowly exhale and open my eyes.

"Everything okay?" Rachel asks.

"Yeah. I know that Terry said it was cool, but I still wanted to ask permission of the life force here before our crew goes tromping over sacred ground."

"And?"

"I feel a sense of serenity. I'm pretty sure that means it's okay."

"Good. Trying to get hundreds of warriors and Ruhin to move around this place would be a nightmare," Garz adds.

We cross the cemetery and keep heading east on the wide, flat plain between the low hills. We march in silence until after a half hour or so, when Jake breaks the silence.

"Ah, shit. Not now, Jesus..." Jake huffs. "And you were doing so well."

Garz holds up his fist to stop everyone.

We all turn to see Jake frantically typing, swiping, and slapping his tricorder-like contraption.

"It just kicked out again." He looks up and frowns. "After being online for a good few hours. Dammit. Okay, I'm gonna reboot it, relink to the satellite, and hopefully it'll come back. Of all the times..."

"Where were the green specs when you last saw them?" I ask.

"The green dots were pretty near, and we were coming at them head on, but I don't know how near—and I think that their depth was decreasing, like they were getting closer to the surface."

"Perhaps they feel the vibrations of our forces, and know we're coming. So much for surprise," Garz frowns. "No matter; if we were coming at them head on, let us continue. But we shall prepare."

"I'll work on getting this up and running again while we're on the move," Jake pledges.

Garz nods to Jake, then turns to Leeik. He says something to him that I don't hear, and then Leeik cries out to his Mazzikim in a language I don't understand. Our warriors shift around—all our flying Mazzikim and Ruhin come to the front and rear of our group. All the Ruhin holding torches draw their Sedu blades in their other hand.

Garz waits until all the other groups have also shifted their flying troops to their front and back, then raises his arm once more, his open hand pointing forward. Everyone starts moving again.

I turn to Garz and inhale to speak, but Garz anticipates my question.

"Our flying Mazzikim can take to the air if the Nephilim open up the ground in front of us or behind us, as well as grab hold of Mazzikim so they don't get pulled in. The Ruhin are at the ready to fly, burn, and open portals as needed."

"Excellent."

We continue on for a while. Jake gets his device to crackle to life long enough for him to give our direction the thumbs up and tell us that it seems like they're only fifty feet underground, but then it craps out again before he can get a more precise reading. I start getting antsy. Rachel picks up on it.

"Maybe you can ask?" Rachel taps my back.

"To really spread out my thoughts and try to feel things miles away, I'll need to be closer to the ground."

Garz has been listening; he nods to me, then raises his fist to stop everyone. When we've come to a halt, I get off Pelegor, walk a few steps forward, then kneel. I hold out my hands, spread my fingers, and close my eyes. "Matka, Earth-Daughter, your army is here. But our enemy is unseen. If you can warn us, please help."

I open my eyes, rise, and turn around. All the Sedim have congregated around Garz to confer about the best course of action. I remount Pelegor and ask him to approach the Sedim. I want to see if I can help. Jake and Kydriss follow.

"It's...it's so beautiful," I hear Zogo say, looking straight ahead.

"It really is," Rachel agrees.

It's 5:45 a.m. and the sun is slowly waking up. I put my hand on Zogo's leg. Rachel puts a hand on my other shoulder.

"I see now...why you all love this place so," Zogo whispers, tears in his eyes as the glowing fireball creeps over the horizon, lightening the sky. I scan the Mazzikim Ruhin, and they're nearly all transfixed by its beauty.

"I hardly ever get to see sunrises," I smile to Zogo.

"They really are—"

Coyotes howl.

My eyes go wide. I inhale to speak.

The ground gives way.

41

THE INSTANT the ground starts shaking and crumbling, the flying Ruhin and Mazzikim launch themselves into the early morning sky. The airborne Mazzikim pick up as many of their fellow nonflying Mazzikim as they can; between the Mazzikim in the front and back of our forces, that's most of them. The winged Ruhin also grab their fellow wingless Ruhin and fly straight up, as high as they can. I'm not sure why, but they clearly have a plan, because that's what they all do.

Pelegor's legs start to slip. I put one arm around Zogo, my other hand on Rachel's leg, and try to keep us steady.

I turn toward Jake and Kydriss just in time to see Kydriss falling over. Thankfully, Jake's training kicks in and he springs off his mount's back just before he goes down. Good for you, Jake!

I feel Lord Stygg's two spider-like, thin, hairy left arms wrap around me. I see his two right arms wrap around Garz. I grab Zogo tightly as Lord Stygg shoves off the ground just as it begins to crack beneath us. I try to look around and I'm thankful to see Vetis jumping alongside us. Slightly behind, I see Rachel in the air, too.

Lord Stygg lands on bended knees about twenty feet from where we were. I loosen my grip on a terrified Zogo.

"The hills!" Lord Stygg yells.

I retighten my grip on Zogo, who's even more terrified now.

Lord Stygg launches himself—with Garz, Zogo, and I in tow—again.

After another twenty-five-foot leap, we land on the side of one of the low hills beside where our forces had been. I put Zogo down and he grabs my left calf for dear life and hyperventilates into it. A moment later, Vetis and Rachel land. I inhale sharply as a horrible thought punches my brain. My eyes dart around the lightening sky. I breathe a sigh of relief as I see Qwyll carrying Pelegor and Zaebos in his arms and legs, and another large, raven-headed, lizard-bodied Mazzik with gorilla-like arms and legs and vulture-like wings carrying Kydriss and Jake. Both land next to us.

I turn toward the huge trenches that appeared under our feet. I don't see too many Mazzikim or Ruhin on the ground. I'm guessing some fell in the trenches, but most are airborne. I reach out with my mind to tell the coyotes to scatter, but I can't feel them anymore.

A loud explosion rocks us all, and one of the trenches fills with flame. Then we hear another explosion, and another trench goes up in flames.

"Holy shit!" Rachel points into the morning sky.

My jaw drops as huge, thick Mazzikim arms shoot out of a dozen portals carved into the sky, throwing rocket-shaped bombs at lightning speed into the trenches.

"Mort was right!" Jake exclaims.

"Those are his bombs?"

"Yeah, they're handheld thermobaric bombs Mort's munitions company based on the Russian Bumble Bee," Jake explains. "Normally they're fired out of a single-use rocket launcher. A Mazzik throwing one straight down from a portal in the sky aims toward a trench, and just before impact the bomb sprays out fuel and then ignites it. Perfect for lighting up entire trenches like that."

Garz raises his arm and waves the flying Mazzikim out of the way of the remaining trenches, giving the Mazzikim bombers even cleaner targets. Time being so fast in Sediin, not only is the velocity of the rockets super fast but they can be thrown one right after another in rapid succession.

"Eat that, bastards!" Rachel yells.

"This has to be taking out tons of them!"

My relief doesn't last as a sharp jolt stabs into my abdomen and shakes me around. I double over. Zogo backs away, shaking, his eyes darting to the Sedu and Mazzikim.

"What is it?" Rachel holds my sides to steady me. "Did you get hit?"

"I'm fine," I grunt, shoving my arm into my gut as counter pressure to the pain. I look toward the trenches. It seems new trenches keep popping up, and Nephilim keep streaming out. When those trenches are bombed, even newer trenches open up.

And they keep coming. Like roaches.

"Time for reinforcements," Garz says, his tone determined and grim as he waves the Mazzikim to engage the Nephilim. As our warriors fly toward the trenches, the portals in the sky slow their dropping bombs, only aiming for those trenches without Mazzikim nearby. Which is good, these rockets have a huge radius.

"There must be thousands of them," I swallow.

"But our warriors are stronger," Garz says. "Rachel, let them see our full might."

Rachel nods, draws her Sedu blade, flexes her legs, and inhales. Her face taut and muscles straining, with a fierce yell she leaps straight up, maybe thirty feet with her blade pointing out, a tear in the sky trailing from her blade's sharp tip. I've seen her jump a hundred times, and she never fails to blow me away.

As she reaches her maximum height, she doesn't twist and assume the landing position I'm familiar with. She must have put everything into the height and opening a portal, and now she's simply dropping. I shudder, eyes wide, but quickly recover. I dart to where I think she'll land so I can catch her.

I shouldn't have worried; Qwyll flies up and grabs her in his powerful chimpanzee-like arms when she's still maybe ten feet off the ground. "I will never let you fall, my mistress."

Finally, something to smile about.

He lands with her gently, and a grateful, sweaty, and panting Stinger gives him a quick hug and a peck on the cheek. I sigh with relief and put my hand on her shoulder.

"Stinger, that was—"

I wince and grab my stomach.

"Again?" Rachel walks closer.

"When the ground first opened...those coyotes that warned us..."

"The Nephilim killed them all? Is that what you're feeling?"

A dozen knives poke me in the gut. Or it feels that way, as I grip my side and concentrate on not shrieking.

"What is it?" Rachel cries, holding onto my red shoulders. "What's happening?"

"I..." I barely open my mouth before I feel a dozen more knives. What the hell?

I look beyond the hills at the chaos. The fissures keep opening in the ground. I can't imagine how many were blown apart or burned to death by our bombardment, and yet they keep coming out of the earth. It's sickening.

Those Mazzikim and Ruhin that were set down on solid ground by our fliers suddenly find themselves desperate to escape the crumbling Earth. Lord Mog and Lord Gryx are stuck with them. The Sedim are trying to shout orders and fight the Nephilim as they rise from the cracks in the earth. Ruhin open portals to drag in wounded Mazzikim, to reduce our casualty count.

H'ythiis and G'suul fly out from one of the cracks, firing energy blasts at the confused mass. I watch two pulses slam into two of the Mazzikim who are dressed House of Keroz tunics. One of them is hit in the chest; his armor holds but he's knocked off his feet. The other was blasted in the face, and his head explodes. I feel another sharp sting.

"It's...our Mazzikim...I feel them..."

"It is as she said," Garz grits his fangs. "She is connected to the life force of this realm and the spirits of ours. Alex feels those Mazzikim and Ruhin who fall into the Earth."

That must be it. I'm feeling our forces being murdered by Nephilim. Wracked with pain, I suck air through my fangs, close my eyes, and reach out with my mind.

The coyotes are all dead. I can feel no life at all in this dirt—no worms, moles, nothing. All gone. And I can feel our Mazzikim and Ruhin being snuffed out, one by one. And I can feel Matka, terrified at all the losses, the lives and spirits being snuffed out.

"Those worthless bastards!" I seethe.

"Yes," Garz says, putting his hand on my shoulder. "Feel our spirit. Listen to it."

Eyes still closed, I reach inward. I've never felt this much rage and anger burning me from the inside.

I suck air into my lungs—my Sedu yet human lungs—and open my eyes. I can tell by the heat radiating from them, they've never flamed this fiercely.

My dad's rage. Garz's rage. My rage. I feared that it arose from hate—a hate that if I didn't control it would make me a monster. Now I know the source isn't hatred, but it is the injustices we suffer, the loss, the shattered lives from which our fury rises. This rage doesn't control me, it feeds me.

I let it fill me like blood.

I feel invigorated.

Focused.

Aware.

Alive.

I don't feel the knives and stings anymore.

"You understand now," Garz says, an expression on his face that in another situation might have continued into a smile.

"I understand," I hiss.

I rise and draw my Sedu blade, the only blade in any universe blessed by Righteousness and infused with the soul of a Champion. I will it to the length of a long, curved sword and call out its blue-green flames, which burn as brightly as the burnt orange flames radiating off my hair and eyes.

I turn to my companions. All of them nod.

Are you ready, Boudicca? I think to my blade.

I am, Champion. Let's end this.

I turn to Garz. He reaches out his hand to me. We lock fists and raise them into the air.

I raise my blade.

He raises his axe.

We turn to our forces and yell together, so loudly it echoes through the hills:

"Kill them all!"

42

Blinding light from the portal flashes through the sky as Zedek roars and flies out, breathing out jets of blue flames. On his back rides Kesed, crazed and screaming like a banshee, swinging his aquamarine glowing axe above his head, his third eye glowing bright red.

All of our forces let up a massive cheer. Righteousness to burn down the unrighteous. Mercy to cut down the merciless. I can feel a surge of confidence sweep through our Mazzikim and Ruhin. God may not be on the battlefield, but God's Greater Sedu and Greater Rishon and Mother Earth's champions are. That's gotta count for something.

Mazzikim charge into the amassing Nephilim. Our numbers may have been cut in half, but our warriors are more powerful than they are. The Nephilim have machine guns, but our Mazzikim's tunics can handle all but the most explosive of bullets. Ruhin follow behind with torches alight with Sedu fire, to roast any Nephilim carcasses.

Zedek chases after H'ythiis, beating his huge wings to match her height, course, and speed. She tries to ditch him by flying up and diving down, looping backwards and feinting right and left, but Zedek is too nimble. After a short dogfight in the sky, Zedek overtakes her, and Kesed, with a shout even louder than Garz's and my battle cries, springs off Zedek and crashes onto H'ythiis. Kesed's twenty-foot frame engulfs the twelve-foot Rishon. Kesed pins H'ythiis's neck between his body and axe as the two giants plummet toward the broken ground. Zedek dives after them.

Garz turns to Qwyll. "Fly me to H'ythiis. I shall assist the Greater Sedim in bringing her down."

Qwyll bows.

"Go get her, brother. I have a date with G'suul."

"We do," Rachel corrects me.

I gently cradle her head against the side of my red, seven-foot-tall body.

Kesed lands hard on H'ythiis as they slam into the ground from hundreds of feet up. That's gotta hurt. The two struggle for Kesed's axe.

Garz puts his hand on Lord Stygg's upper-right shoulder. "I leave my most precious treasures in your hands."

Lord Stygg tips his spider-like head. "I shall see Alex and Rachel to G'suul; I swear it."

"I'll jump with Zogo," Vetis says.

"Be careful!" I call after Garz. "Remember, if you die, it just might kill me too!"

Garz tightens his grip on his axe and offers me an impish grin, his eyes burning like suns as Qwyll grabs him. "When the Greater Sedim dispatch H'ythiis, we shall help you bring down G'suul."

"We're holding you to that!" Rachel shouts as Garz and Qwyll fly toward the battling giants.

"I know I'm not a warrior," Jake speaks up. "But I also can't die. I want to be there."

We turn to Lord Stygg.

"Come; I have two arms for Alex, one for Rachel, and another for you, Jake."

"Kydriss, run after us," Jake pats his steed's head. Kydriss bows.

"Lord Stygg, I can jump," Rachel protests.

"Not as far as Vetis and I. Not yet."

Rachel huffs but doesn't argue.

"Zaebos, climb on my back," Pelegor says, lying down on the dirt. "I shall ride under Lord Stygg as he leaps."

"Thank you, my friend." Zaebos scrambles onto Pelegor's back.

Zogo leaps into Vetis's arms.

Kesed, Zedek, and H'ythiis are right in the thick of the fighting, in the middle of a huge swath of Nephilim and Mazzikim. G'suul had flown past the battlefield after strafing our Mazzikim with energy blasts. He spins back toward the battle, probably to try to save his mate.

"We can head him off there," Lord Stygg points with his upper right claw between G'suul and the main battle.

"Shouldn't we join the battle directly?" I ask. "I don't want to look like I'm avoiding the fight."

"You are part of the battle," Lord Stygg wraps his arms around me, Rachel, and Jake. "You are a beacon of hope. Hold up your flaming blade. Our warriors will see you and know you go to face G'suul. Better that you face G'suul with all your strength than already depleted from fighting."

I nod. Vetis and Lord Stygg leap some thirty feet toward G'suul. I hold up my flaming blade. As I fly by the edge of our warriors, I can hear them cheer. I hope Lord Stygg's right, and seeing me leaping into battle inspires them.

Lord Stygg and Vetis land, flex their legs, and immediately leap again. We can see G'suul maybe some two hundred feet ahead of us, but between our leaping and his flying, we're closing fast. G'suul seems to be paying no heed to us, aiming directly for H'ythiis.

"Do you think we'll—"

Before I can finish my sentence, G'suul flips his head toward us in mid-flight and lets fly two energy blasts. Lord Stygg is pounded so hard we fly backward. He desperately tries to keep his arms wrapped around us. He's only half successful. One of his arms around me comes loose. He lets go of Jake entirely—I hear him scream as he falls. Instinctively I drop my blade and grab onto Lord Stygg's spidery head. Normally, my arachnophobia would have me shaking and vomiting by now. With all this adrenaline and rage, I'm just pissed off that I dropped Boudicca.

Lord Stygg keeps hold of Rachel. Despite our spiraling downward, she manages to get off two crossbow bolts at G'suul. One flies wide, but it looks like the other hit a wing. Her crossbow bolts are laced with Klara's neurotoxin; that should hinder his flying, at least.

Spiraling down fast—

I let go of Lord Stygg and put both arms around Rachel to shield her from the impact.

We slam into the ground.

43

My huge, muscular arms feel like they've been pounded by wrecking balls. But they didn't splatter, and Rachel's in one piece, her crossbow pressed tightly between our chests.

"You okay?" I wince as I roll over and release her.

"Uh huh," she pants. "You?"

"When my arms stop throbbing, I will be."

I look around for Jake but I don't see him. Dammit. Well, I know he can't die, but still, I wish I knew what shape he was in.

"Lord Stygg?" Rachel calls.

The eight-foot-tall, four-armed Sedu lies maybe fifteen feet away from us. He raises one of his claws, and it quickly flops back to the ground.

"Can you move?" I ask.

"I..." he gasps through the pain.

"Well, *he's* moving," Rachel seethes, springing to her feet. I turn to where she's pointing her crossbow and see G'suul lumbering toward us on his two thick legs, all of his razor-sharp claws at the end of his four brawny arms reaching out. His two dozen eyes all burn with vengefulness. One wing seems droopy, like it got damaged in his fall.

I reach past my pain and take in the rage of the House of Keroz. I let it steel me as I spring to my feet. This is it. This is the moment. I don't have my blade, but I can still burn him and punch through him like I did L'reek. G'suul is more powerful than any single Sedu, but I can't let that stop me. I can't let Matka down. I can't let the world down. I dig deep, flaming out my hair and eyes and hardening my skin to the limits of my red Sedu body.

Rachel plugs him with two crossbow bolts. They barely sink an inch into his hide. Klara's paralyzing agent slows him, but not enough. At twelve feet tall G'suul is upon Rachel in only a few paces and swats her away, pummeling her onto her back about ten feet away with claw marks carved into her insect-plated skin.

He opens his mouth to blast Rachel, but I've trained for this; I'm lighter and faster. I launch into a flying kick as high as I possibly can. I'm five feet shorter than G'suul—my head only comes up to his rib cage—but my boot still connects with his chest. The impact knocks him off balance so that his blast misses Rachel.

I land to his right. G'suul grabs at me with his two right arms, but I pivot away before his claws connect. I breathe the longest jet of fire I can on his left arms. He cries out from the burn. Rather than recoiling, he twists and leans into my flames and slashes down at me with all four of his claws. I spring back but not fast enough. His lower-right claw catches me and cuts deep. Even with my skin as hard as concrete, his four nails rip through my uniform and into flesh and bone. It knocks me to the ground.

I can feel my blood gushing out. Putting my arms across my chest, I concentrate on connecting with the cells in my own body, visualizing them closing up the opened blood vessels and patching the torn skin. The bleeding slows but doesn't stop. G'suul's mouth tentacles spread apart as he prepares to spit an energy blast at me.

I push myself off the ground. My bleeding worsens.

Rachel leaps onto G'suul's large head with a high-pitched yell of fury. She grips his neck with her legs and plunges two Sedu blades into the top of his head. Or tries to, anyway. They barely scratch the surface. Thinking quickly, Rachel immediately spits an acid stinger into one of his two dozen eyes.

G'suul flinches with pain as his eye sizzles. Before Rachel can spit a second one, G'suul grabs her and tosses her to the ground, hard. She grunts as her back slams into the hard earth.

He leans down to blast her.

"Get away from her!" I draw two spare Sedu blade daggers from my belt and lunge with all my might, stabbing G'suul in the gut. Rachel scurries out of the way.

The blades barely sink an inch into his thick skin, but the momentum of my seven-foot frame coupled with my two piercing daggers knocks him back a few paces. I let the daggers fall and sucker punch him in the gut with both fists, one after the other. He winces and falls back another step before swiping at me with all four arms. I duck under his arms and then punch up between his legs as I rise. He grimaces as I punch him with both fists again, followed immediately by another sweep kick to the groin. He takes another step back, but this time he leans forward and grabs my shoulder with his lower-right claw. I spring out of his grasp, but awkwardly enough that I stumble backward and land on my butt.

Rachel fires two more crossbow bolts at G'suul's side, but he swats them out of the air. He turns his head and fires off a blast at her. She tries to leap away, but I can see that he still managed to graze her leg and she tumbles out of the sky.

"Bastard!" I yell.

G'suul growls as he stands still for a moment and puts his two upper arms over his acid-burned eye.

I tell my cells to keep healing, but I am getting weaker by the minute.

Rachel and I slowly prop ourselves up, when we hear two high-pitched screams from the center of the battle. We turn to see Kesed holding H'ythiis's severed head. But something's wrong. Kesed isn't standing victorious. He's on his knees. Zedek holds Kesed with his two front legs. I can make out Garz and Leeik and other Mazzikim fighting off Nephilim.

Then Kesed drops H'ythiis's head and pitches forward.

"No!" Rachel screams. "Oh God—no!"

Zedek raises his long neck and howls into the morning sky. He drops Kesed's body. He seems to say something to Garz, who throws him a Sedu blade. Zedek then flies up, slicing a portal in the air, and flies through it.

"Mercy can't be dead." I swallow, my eyes hot and wet. "He can't be."

I turn back to G'suul as he removes his hands from his eye, which is now completely healed. G'suul has regained all his strength. He launches himself at me, still unable to fly, but his leap is still faster than a being his size should be capable of. His upper claws slash down at me while his lower claws try to grab me. I'm able to twist away from him but he still manages to slice my throat. Not enough to kill me, thanks to my Sedu skin, but enough that now I have another fast-bleeding wound.

I feel woozy.

I'm seeing double.

I drop to my knees.

G'suul spreads his mouth tentacles. I twist out of the way G'suul's blast, but I'm not fast enough. My left side explodes. I roll on the dirt and look at my wound. My trench coat, skin, and a few ribs all seem to be seared off and missing from my body. The wound is cauterized and doesn't bleed, but it hurts so badly I scream and shake all over, every nerve in my gaping side throbbing.

I concentrate on my nerves not sending messages of pain to my brain. I try to tell my cells to heal my blood vessels and slashes. But I can't concentrate for long.

I try to keep rolling away, but now that G'suul has his speed back, he is upon me in only a few strides. He reaches down with his upper-left arm and grabs my throat, sinking his claws into my skin. My hands instinctively grab onto his upper-left claw, trying to pry it off. It won't budge. I can't breathe fire with his claw this tight around my neck. I will my hands to heat up, hoping to burn his claw off me. He howls in pain and squeezes tighter. I will my hands hotter.

He shoves his lower-left claw through my armored trench coat, through my rock-hard skin, and into my stomach. I gasp as my gut implodes with agony. I can feel what little blood I have left pooling around the claw inside of me. I grab his lower-left claw, but I have no strength to pull it out and no will to heat my hands anymore. Just remaining conscious takes everything I have left. My entire body shakes uncontrollably. I try to scream, but only a hiss comes out.

G'suul's upper-right claw grabs my hair and pulls back my head so I'm looking into his eyes. His lower-right claw steadies my torso from the shakes.

G'suul lifts me to his mouth. "Are you happy with the carnage and death you've caused?" he spits, hate dripping from every word. "Had you simply stayed hidden and let us feed off the humans, all of this could have been avoided."

I look around for some kind of way out of this. I see that Nephilim and Mazzikim have seen us and the fight is coming our way, but they're all still too far away to help me now. But behind G'suul, coming fast, I see what I hope is my salvation.

"Someone..." I wheeze, desperately stalling for time. "Would...have—"

"And they would have failed, like you," G'suul growls, lifting me up higher. "The strength of the House of Keroz has failed."

"You're mistaken. I'm the *life* of the House of Keroz," I gasp, attempting a menacing smile. "Meet its strength..."

44

Garz leaps onto G'suul's back with a cry that echoes throughout the flatlands. He wraps his legs around the giant Rishon. He slams his fists down on G'suul's back with all the force he can muster. I feel the shockwave from his blows through G'suul's claws. G'suul shrieks as both his left shoulders shatter, his left wing crushed.

My body slides off the claw that impaled me as his useless left arms fall to his side. I gasp for air and crawl away with one arm against the hole in my belly. I can't see clearly or catch my breath. I try to concentrate on healing, but I can't hold a thought.

With his lower arms G'suul grabs at Garz's legs. With another yell as loud as his first, Garz pounds the back of G'suul's neck. G'suul arches forward with a wheeze that almost sounds panicked.

I look into my brother's eyes. I've seen him in battle many times but I've never seen him like this. Garz is frantic, his fighting desperate. When he meets my gaze, I understand why. He's drawing on every ounce of the strength and spirit of our House to end G'suul before G'suul ends me. With weapons useless against G'suul, Garz himself is the weapon—the first weapon that has G'suul scared.

G'suul has good reason to be scared—if God has fists, they are the fists of Garz.

G'suul succeeds in wrenching Garz off of his back. He throws my brother at least ten feet away, firing off a flurry of energy bolts at him. I can't see clearly, but it looks like at least a couple of them hit my brother.

"*Garz!*" I wheeze.

I try to push myself up from the dirt. I manage to rise to my knees before pain and blood loss stop me.

I close my eyes.

Matka. Earth-Daughter. I will fight for you. I will die for you. But I need whatever aid you can give me. Please.

I feel my skin tingle as the hole in my gut slowly begins to repair itself. I open my eyes. G'suul's eyes are all blinking, as if he's fighting off gnats or other nuisances. He starts waving his upper-right arm in front of his face.

I inhale deeply and try to muster the strength to stand.

G'suul shifts his mouth tentacles to blast me. He opens his mouth, inhales—and three throwing knives fly inside.

G'suul grimaces as his tentacles reach into his mouth and remove the knives. He shakes his head spastically—Vetis's blades must have had some of

Klara's toxin on them. G'suul's mouth tentacles toss the knives toward me but miss wildly. He sends one blast after another behind and to the right of me. I turn my head—nearly all of them miss, but one explodes directly on Vetis's armored chest. I turn back to face the evil Rishon, my eyes red and hot from more than just fire.

"My brother!"

"My...mate!" G'suul says, his speech slurred from toxin as he blasts the ground next to me.

"My...offspring!" G'suul fires another energy bolt past me. It seems the toxin has also affected his aim, thankfully.

"Tell others what you wish," he seethes, "but you are petty and cruel and—"

"Aaaaaaaaaaah!" Zogo shrieks as he sticks G'suul's shin with his little knife again and again and again.

With a slightly annoyed expression, G'suul flicks his leg and tosses Zogo into the air.

I rise to my feet.

"You should never have come here," I grimace. "You never had a right to—"

"I don't ask permission." G'suul continues toward me. "I take what is—"

Dozens of crackling noises erupt from behind me. G'suul stops, turns sideways, and covers his head and arms at the barrage of gunshots. Two bullets pierce his legs. I can see from the large hole and seeping black goo that these are the VATS bullets that the Nephilim use against us.

I swing my head to the side to see Pelegor charging G'suul, with Jake holding one of the Nephilim's machine guns on Pelegor's back. Zaebos sits on Pelegor's back with his rear legs squeezing Pelegor's side as tightly as they can, and his front legs and paws holding Jake. That's when I realize the horrible shape that Jake is in. It looks like he has some bullet holes in him. The one leg of his I can see looks flattened like a pancake, and his torso and neck are twisted in unnatural positions. Jake's one functioning arm holds the machine gun, with the barrel of the weapon propped up on Pelegor's eagle-like head. I can't see his other arm.

Pelegor stops charging as they reach me.

"Got something for ya," Jake gasps, his voice gurgling like his throat his filled with blood. His eyes point to his crushed leg. I look closer—between Pelegor's saddle and Jake's leg, he has my Sedu blade.

"Take it!"

I reach out, grasping the hilt and pulling the sword from under him.

"Jake, thank—"

Pelegor flips his body sideways, knocking me back on my ass, as G'suul starts firing blasts at us. Thanks to Pelegor I'm not hit. Pelegor is hit so many times that his armor nearly disintegrates and he falls on his side, twitching and throwing Jake and Zaebos. I see Jake's trench coat burst open from a direct hit as he rolls on the ground. Zaebos tries to rise but is blasted down.

You are weak, Firebird. I feel it, Boudicca says. *Reach into my spirit. Use it to heal yourself. Leave me only enough to fight the souls that G'suul has devoured.*

Are you sure, Boudicca? I think to her.

I knew always this was a one-way journey. Champions die. Win this battle, Firebird. For both of us.

Champions die, I nod, close my eyes, and reach out with my mind, trying to feel the life force in my blade. It radiates a warmth, wholeness, and power. I imagine that warmth and power transferring into me. I inhale as a newfound energy floods me. Every move, every breath still shoots pain through me, but I no longer feel like I'll pass out. I stop the transfer—I don't want to take too much of Boudicca's spirit. I'll need it if I can get close enough to G'suul.

I rise.

G'suul turns from Pelegor, Jake, and Zaebos, to me.

I hold my Sedu blade in front of me and will it to ignite with blue-green flames.

G'suul's tentacles move out of the way so that he can blast me.

With as much energy as I can muster, I spring forward.

G'suul inhales.

I land inches from G'suul and shove my blade into his midsection. I can feel the spirits that G'suul has absorbed fighting back as I force my blade deeper. G'suul's body tries to reject Boudicca, as they have every weapon. But Boudicca is a warrior spirit, a champion. She pushes through G'suul's stolen souls, and I impale the Rishon up to the hilt.

I crane my head up and breathe fire. He's too tall for me to toast his face, but I put some nasty burns on his chest.

He swallows his breath and punches me in the face with his upper-right fist while his lower-right arm tries to wrest my blade away. His punches are whoppers, like I'm being smacked in the head by a train. My vision flashes black and comes back grainy. But I don't let go.

"For Matka!" I wheeze and pull up on my blade, enlarging the wound. Blue goo slowly oozes out of him as he shrieks in pain.

He kicks out, but I shift so he misses me. He swings at my face again, but I duck. No matter how deeply his claws dig into my hands and arms, I don't release my blade, instead twisting it, making the hole larger and larger. The goo flows faster.

G'suul lets go of my hand and both his right arms shove me. Hard. I go flying, blade in hand, and land on my back a few feet away.

I shake off my pain and start to rise again.

He opens his mouth to blast me.

Two crossbow bolts fly into G'suul's open mouth.

He steps backward and lowers his head, yanking out the bolts with one hand and shaking his head. G'suul raises his head and fires off a bunch of energy bolts at Rachel. I can't see if they hit her or not.

I hold my flaming blade before me as I rise. I don't have the energy to leap, so I slowly trudge forward, concentrating on not falling over.

He turns toward me and inhales.

I bend my legs, preparing to dive right or left, depending where he spits.

From the side, Zaebos springs as high as his wounded body can muster and locks his muzzle on G'suul's left thigh.

I trudge another step forward.

G'suul leans over to fire an energy blast down at Zaebos.

I lunge and impale G'suul just under the ribs. With Boudicca's help I force my blade deep into his gut.

G'suul kicks out and sends Zaebos flying. Then he slashes down with both his right claws, slicing my face and neck. My skin may be hard as concrete, but he still penetrates to my cheekbones and windpipe. I stumble backward a few steps, Sedu blade in hand.

My vision blurs. All I can feel is blood pouring out of my throat. I fall to my knees, one hand on my blade, the other trying to hold my throat closed as I choke on my own blood. I try to concentrate on healing myself but I can't concentrate on anything. I can't concentrate on reaching Boudicca and trying to add her spirit to mine. I can't reach into the spirit of our House. All I can do is bleed—and pray.

Please, God. Life depends on me. These spirits from Sediin depend on me. Just let me last long enough to finish G'suul. That's all I ask.

G'suul reaches out with his lower-right claw and wraps it so tightly around my throat that it seems to slow the bleeding, but crushes my throat in. His upper-right claw pulls back my flaming hair so I'm looking into his eyes, some nine feet above my head.

"I'll heal," he sneers. "But you, your family, your House, and ultimately your world, will all die by my—"

Leeik grabs hold of G'suul's lower-left claw and uses it as leverage to kick his way up the Rishon's body. Leeik then wraps both of his legs around G'suul's head and bites down on one of the monster's dozen eyes. G'suul screams in pain and drops me as his two right arms grab at Leeik.

I strain with all my might until I'm standing. I can't see straight. The flames in my eyes and hair are short and dull. My blade feels like it weighs as much as a truck. I'm so wobbly a strong wind could blow me over. But I can't fail. I have to reach G'suul.

Leeik spits out the eye and goes to bite another. G'suul grabs Leeik's leg with his razor-sharp upper-right claw. He holds the Mazzik in front of him.

G'suul fires an energy blast directly onto Leeik's gorilla-like head.

I scream as Leeik's head bursts apart. I'm too shaky—and shaken—to do more than that. G'suul lets Leeik's corpse fall to the ground.

G'suul turns back to me. He opens his mouth. I dive left to avoid the blast. As my chest slams against the dirt, I feel a massive gush of blood pour out of my throat.

My vision starts to go dark. I can barely hear the battle around me. I don't have enough energy left to move.

Please, God...

I look up at G'suul. With my fading sight, I can just make out two crossbow bolts bouncing off his tentacles. G'suul growls furiously.

I inhale, the air bubbling in my bleeding throat. I try to push myself off the dirt but I don't have the strength.

Suddenly, I am lifted off my feet.

I feel a jolt of healing. Of energy. Of rage.

"Together," my wounded brother gasps into my ear.

I have enough strength to nod. I grip my Sedu blade tightly.

Garz stumbles forward toward G'suul.

G'suul inhales to blast me.

I shove my blade up through his mouth tentacles into his head.

He glares wide-eyed, unable to speak with my blade sealing his mouth shut. I can feel the souls he has devoured fighting desperately with Boudicca's spirit. I feel the pressure, like a magnet trying to expel my blade, but Boudicca won't let them win.

And neither will I.

"If you meet your maker," I wheeze. "I hope he hates you as much as I do."

G'suul grabs my blade with both of his claws. Garz leans over me and breathes fire on them, roasting both of them. G'suul lets go when his hands start turning to charcoal.

He tries to scream, but my blade has forced his mouth shut. As scared as he is, I don't feel him dying.

"Hold on tight," I tell Garz. My brother tightens his grip around my stomach and holds me above his head.

I yank my Sedu blade out of G'suul's chin and wind my arms behind me.

With as much of a battle cry as I can muster, I put every last ounce of energy, every muscle, every bit of focus and concentration I have left into swinging upward as hard as I can. When my blade connects with G'suul's thick neck, my arms buckle like I'm trying to slice through the side of a building, but I have enough momentum to cut through. Blue goo splatters everywhere as G'suul's huge head falls to the ground.

45

IT'S DONE.

I can't feel the blood seeping out of me.

I can't hear.

My vision fades.

I'm sorry for leaving you, Rachel. I'm sorry I'll miss your Bat Mitzvah. I know you'll be an amazing heroine. Thank you for helping me keep my promise to Matka. I love you.

I love you all.

See you in Merkaba, Jake.

I can't feel Boudicca. *If any of your spirit is left, thank you for fighting with me, champion.*

My arms don't have the strength to hold my Sedu blade anymore.

But it's okay.

My job is done.

I let it go.

I can finally let go....

46

BLACKNESS SLOWLY—very slowly—gives way to grainy brightness. The brightness becomes blinding. I tell my arms to cover my eyes, but I can't make them move. Squinting and turning my head is all I can manage.

When my eyes adjust to the morning light, they focus on Garz, looking down on me as he holds me horizontally against his chest. He's smiling—his closed-mouth grin quivering slightly—and behind the flames emanating from his eyes, I can see they're wet.

"Welcome back, my sister."

"Have I been out long?"

"Not long. But too long."

"Yeah—remember, I told you you're not allowed to die. Don't scare us like that, okay?" Rachel sobs, rubbing my shoulder.

Being in Garz's healing arms must be why I'm alive. My throat is still slashed. I'm still impaled and missing flesh off my side and ripped to hell. But my bleeding has slowed to the point that I'm not dead. At least not yet.

"I'm sorry," I whisper, turning to Rachel and trying to smile. She's standing with one charred leg off the ground, battered, scarred, and bruised. "Thank you. Thank all of you."

"It was nothing," Rachel cracks, drying her huge, glowing eyes. "Just trying to save your ass. Again."

My eyes catch the remains of Garz's chief lieutenant, and one of the most powerful Mazzikim that ever was. His body is half disintegrated, as without his spirit, there is nothing left to maintain the manifestation of his body.

"Garz...Leeik—I know how much—"

"You avenged him," Garz says, swallowing his emotion.

"He could have lived forever..." I feel my eyes getting hot. "He's dead because of me."

"Many times he told me how proud he is of you and Rachel. He may have lived for millennia, but he felt more alive in these recent years than ever before. He was a warrior who gave his life for a noble cause and for the beings that he loved."

"He was your friend," I gently lean my cheek against Garz's chest.

"Yes," Garz lowers his head. I can feel his deep sorrow like a weight in my chest. "Now we collect our wounded and return to Sediin. We shall mourn our friends in due course. I will...I will miss him dearly."

"We all will." Rachel runs her fingers tenderly through my flaming hair and pats Garz's arm.

I smile pensively at her, then turn back to Garz.

"Jake...?"

Garz twists me around so that my head can see Jake. Pelegor, his beautiful silver fur completely matted with dirt and grime, lies on the ground while a wounded Zaebos scoots along the dirt and tries to shove what's left of Jake onto Pelegor's back. It would be comical if everyone wasn't so bloody and broken.

"I can help." Vetis slowly hobbles over, his right leg dragging behind him. His lower-left praying mantis–like arm has been completely blown off, and his lower right holds his chest. With a loud grunt of pain he wraps his upper arms around Jake's head. He pulls as Zaebos pushes, and eventually they get Jake's limp, fractured body across Pelegor like a saddlebag.

I know that Jake can't die, but he sure doesn't look alive.

Zaebos slides himself onto Pelegor, and my Mazzik mount painfully rises to his feet, his armor blasted away and his side shredded with searing wounds. With a broken, halting trot he approaches us. Vetis accompanies him.

When they near I can see Jake's pulverized, bleeding limbs are all twisted in the wrong directions, most with shattered bones sticking out of his skin. His chest has collapsed inward. His neck is broken, and he's looking at me sort of backwards and upside down.

"Honey, you don't look so good," he wheezes, each breath clearly agony.

"You married well, Alex," Garz says. "Jacob Harman is among the bravest of humans."

"Thanks, Garz," Jake pants. "But is it really that brave if I know I can't die?"

"A coward fears not just death, but pain."

"Yeah, well, right about now, I really wish not dying also came with not hurting," he groans.

"I know what you mean," I agree.

"I'm glad you're still with us, Alex," Vetis says as he limps around to put his remaining arms around his daughter. "I was worried."

"Your arm..."

"Will heal when we return," Vetis winces.

"We all will," Garz adds. "Come, let us—"

"The battle," I interrupt. "Is it over? Can I see?"

"It winds down but still rages," Garz informs me as he twists again so I can watch the fighting. Just down from the side of the low hill we're on, Mazzikim and Ruhin are engaging black-clad Nephilim all over. It's too chaotic for me to see who's winning; Ruhin open portals all over and shove Mazzikim back to Sediin.

"Kydriss...?" Jake wheezes.

Pelegor swings his eagle head around. If beaks could quiver, his would be.

"When I picked you up, I saw his body...he did not make it."

"Aw, hell," Jake closes his eyes. "I'm sorry, Pelegor. I'm glad I got to know him a little bit. I'm sorry I won't get to know him better."

"Thank you," Pelegor lowers his head. "It is as Lord Garz says. We all knew the risks, and—"

"I hate to interrupt, but I can feel my consciousness fading. Are we winning?"

"The battle is fierce and cruel. Lord Mog had to be rushed into a portal by his Ruhin and Mazzikim. Lord Gryx marshals all who remain. His skill as a warrior and a dozen Mazzikim keep him from suffering the same fate. But it looks to me like the Nephilim's will is broken. I felt it breaking when Kesed killed H'ythiis. I burned her to ash."

"Can we break more of their spirits? What about G'suul? Do you think they know about him?"

"Some saw G'suul fall on this hill—they know that their hold on this world is forever broken. Word will reach the others soon. That is, those not already engaged..." Garz twists me to another angle of the battle.

"Oh my God!" I gasp.

I see Kesed, screaming like a crazed berserker, steamrolling through the Nephilim in front of him, ripping one in half and grabbing another. A swarm of flying, torch-wielding Ruhin behind him burn the dismembered corpses in Kesed's wake. Above him, Zedek strafes the Nephilim with jets of deadly blue flames.

"How..."

"The Greater Sedu are beyond life and death in any and all realms—they are avatars," Garz explains. "Kesed *is* Mercy. As long as Mercy exists in this or any realm, so will he. Zedek retrieved Kesed's reformed body in The Nothingness, and the pair then rejoined the fight. It seems Kesed's mood is quite foul after being killed."

"Mine would be, too," Rachel says. "Besides, the Nephilim are totally merciless. Everything he hates."

"Yes. Remember also, he blames himself for all this, which I'm sure fuels his rage."

I watch Kesed race around, stepping on Nephilim like roaches who have been crawling all over him and making him crazy.

"Are those people?" A bruised but intact Zogo slowly joins our group. He points upward into the sky behind us as he approaches, careful to walk around G'suul's corpse. "Up there? Are those the metal flying machines you've told me about?"

I don't have the strength to lift my neck, but Garz cranes his demon-like head and searches the sky where Zogo pointed. He sighs heavily. "Helicopters."

"Two of them," Rachel says to me. "Like the ones we've been hitching rides on. They're still far away, but pretty soon they'll be overhead."

"Hey...that's a good idea, Rachel," I groan. "Over*head*... Can we get Qwyll to fly over the enemy with G'suul's head before it disintegrates? Seeing their Watcher dead and turning to ash would have to make them reconsider their life choices."

"Um..." Rachel's voice quivers. "Where's...where's Qwyll?"

A shudder runs through me. Qwyll is as close to Rachel as Zaebos is to me...

"He was critically wounded. Shot out of the sky," Garz explains. "A flying Ruhin opened a portal underneath him and he fell into it."

"There's a chance, then..." the plea in Rachel's voice is unmistakable.

"Yes," Garz says.

I still can't move my arms, but I try to nudge my head toward Rachel's hand to comfort her. I hope Qwyll lives, too.

"Perhaps I can be of help?" Lord Stygg staggers toward us, his two upper arms resting on the shoulders of two of his tall, bipedal, gorilla-like Mazzikim who hold onto their lord and help him walk. The blast that knocked him out of the sky completely burned away his armored jacket. What I can see of Lord Stygg's torso is more scar than tissue. His two lower arms hang limply by his side.

"Lord Stygg! I'm so glad you're alive!" I smile.

"Forgive me for letting you all go. I was hit hard; I fell hard. But it isn't so easy to kill a Sedu, wouldn't you say?" The sides of his mandibles curve upward, almost like a spider version of a smile. I think. I'm not really good at reading emotions on spider-like mandibles.

"There's nothing to forgive. I'm just glad you're going to make it back to Sediin."

"Seriously, you were awesome," Rachel agrees.

"So were you, little bug," Lord Stygg praises his protégée.

"But to the task at hand." He turns back to Lord Garz and me. "You have a head, a very large head, that you wish to propel over the melee."

Rachel limps over to G'suul's head, picks it up, and turns toward Lord Stygg.

"Here," Garz calls out. Rachel stops and holds up the head. Garz blows a long and hot jet of flame over the head, and soon it burns hot and bright.

Rachel nods with a smirk; I think she enjoys the idea of one final indignation to the horror that caused so much death, destruction, and pain to our world and our lives. She limps as fast as she can over to Lord Stygg, I assume to be sure Lord Stygg gets a chance to throw G'suul's head before it burns out.

"Thank you, little bug," Lord Stygg says, another one of those spider-smiles on his face. He lifts his arms from both Mazzikim and they step back. He takes the head from Rachel, crouches, and twists into a stance sort of like a shot putter. He launches himself into the air with a grunt of extreme effort, twisting as he ascends. When he reaches maybe twenty-five feet in the air and has spiraled so that his arm is at the right trajectory, he releases the flaming head over the battle.

It has the desired effect, catching everyone's eye below. As it starts to arc down, Zedek flies over, grabs it in one of his talons, and precedes to scream and fly with it over the battle, breathing flames as he does.

Lord Stygg, spent, doesn't position himself for landing; he just drops. One of his large Mazzikim catches him.

"You did it!" Rachel smiles.

"Thank you, Lord Stygg," I add. "I am so proud our Houses are allied. I love you and all your family. And I love that you're building with me a Sediin in which love is not a weakness. And speaking of weakness..."

"Yes, my sister," Garz nods. "We are done here. The Greater Sedim and Lord Gryx will remain to direct what remains of our troops."

"What about dealing with the humans?" Jake grunts haltingly. "It's morning. Choppers just landed near; I heard 'em. Someone needs to explain what happened and manage the cleanup."

"We're gonna have to leave it for another day, Jake," Rachel shrugs. "You're twisted a million ways and in no shape to hang out. My girl here needs some chicken soup and a year of sleep. Everyone else looks like a demon or monster."

"Leave that to us," the huffing old man running up to us says. "General Patrick and his squad are disembarking from the Chinook now; I ran ahead to see you off."

"Uncle Mort!" Rachel exclaims, and I more like enthusiastically wheeze.

Mortimer Stygg tenderly places a hand on Rachel's head, then my head. He nods to Garz.

"Klara took a moment to return to Earth and inform us when the battle had begun," Mort explains. "We assembled and came out as soon as we could, knowing that the tribal police and US military would be here eventually."

"Good ol' Klara, always finding ways to help," I smile.

Mort nods as he walks over to his father. He puts a hand on Lord Stygg's spider-like cheek. Lord Stygg's eyes well, and he gently raises a claw to caress his son's hand. It's as beautiful as a scene with a giant, wounded, humanoid spider can be.

One of Lord Stygg's Mazzikim takes a Sedu blade from Stygg's belt and carves a portal in the air. "Heal well, my friends." Lord Stygg waves, and his Mazzikim carry him through.

"Our turn," Garz says.

"I can grab your blade?" Rachel asks me.

"I give Rachel permission to wield my blade," I pronounce.

She reaches down and picks up my Sedu blade. She holds it as high above her head as she can so that it's tall enough for Garz if he crouches, and tears a portal from there to the ground.

"I'll see you soon," Mort smiles. We nod, or give whatever level of acknowledgement our various battered and bruised bodies are capable of, and turn to the portal.

"Hey! Stop! What is all this? What's going on?" demands a rather gruff-sounding voice I assume is military or police.

Rachel rolls her eyes and huffs. "Seriously?"

And just like that, I can feel Garz's rage go from quenched to thermonuclear.

"We're leaving—before I burn him and his army to ash," Garz growls to Mort. I can't help but smirk.

Mort nods and motions toward the portal.

Pelegor, Jake, and Zaebos are the first to cross into our House.

"What the hell is—"

"Hello, Major; I'll explain everything," I hear Mort say.

Vetis and Rachel and Zogo step through, with us close behind.

"On whose authority—"

"On their own authority," I hear General Patrick say as we cross over. "And if that's not enough for you—mine."

47

"Garz wasn't really gonna fry the major, was he?" Josh asks, sitting on one of the low rocks at the rightmost boundary of Little Corona beach.

"Hell, *I* was going to fry the major," Rachel snorts, sitting right next to Josh on the same rock.

At the shoreline directly in front of us, children and Ruhin play with each other at the edge of the gentle waves. Each marvels at the other's weirdness as Mazzikim and parents stand nearby, watching over them attentively. Some parents look as excited as their children. Others look worried. The Mazzikim stand like statues, calm and powerful.

Zaebos and Daeba lounge on a towel on the sand next to us, their five nearly grown puppies running around them joyously, and sometimes running up to the smiling human children and running back. They've grown so much since the days I'd play with them as they frolicked around Firebird Manor. At the time, only Zaev could breathe fire, which is why we called him "Little Flamey." Now all of them can breathe fire. Their parents, however, are making very sure that they don't breathe any fire this evening. We don't want the hellhounds scaring the kids.

At the entry to Little Corona beach, Sergeant Franklin and the Newport Beach police have been welcoming people at the top of the walkway, thanking them for coming and explaining to them who all is here and what we look like, along with some basic common-sense instructions, like don't let your kids pull on a Ruhin's or Mazzik's fur. One of the local gelato stores from Pacific Coast Highway has been handing out free ice cream to everyone. Well, free for them; as soon as the store volunteered to be part of our community event I offered to pay them.

The people all over the beach steal glances our way. We all do our best to look inviting and friendly. That was the whole reason I set this up with the Newport Beach Police Department and city council—to show that we're friendly, we're part of the community, and we're pro-law-and-order. I'm really happy that there's so many people here at the beach with us. And they keep coming.

People seem the most weirded out by Garz. Rachel and I are in our human forms, but he's in his Sedu form, looking like an eight-foot-tall reptilian, horned demon, sitting along with Pyza—also in Sedu form—on a huge boulder just above Rachel and Josh. Jake and I are relaxing on a boulder to the left and a little below Garz and Pyza. Klara and Captain Jeffers relax on a towel next to us on the sand.

"I mean, I know, but—"

"Seriously, Josh," Jake admonishes his little brother. "It's cool. Let it go."

Garz looks down at Josh. "Alex did not save the life force of this world only to have her own life drip out while an ungrateful toy soldier interrogated her."

"But how do you really feel," Josh cracks. Garz nods at the young Harman, the corners of his mouth raised in a little smirk.

"Hey, Klara?" I call down to the towel below me that Klara is sharing with an off-duty Captain Jeffers.

"Alex?" Klara turns around and looks up, a huge smile on her face. The same smile, actually, that Captain Jeffers wears on her face. It makes me happy to see them happy. They deserve it.

"As ever, you managed to help save the day. I couldn't have handled being on Earth much longer, and Garz would have created a national incident if Mort hadn't arrived with General Patrick and his squad to deal with our mess. Thanks for alerting them."

"I'm glad I could find a way to help," Klara says.

"It was our pleasure as well, Alex," Jeffers adds.

I'm about to answer when I look up and see Terry and a bunch of his elders and their families walking toward us. Well, the adults, anyway. The kids are enjoying their gelato, splashing around in the waves, or playing with Ruhin.

"It's as beautiful out here as you say, Firebird," Terry Miles says as he stands next to the rock Jake and I share. "Never been to Orange County, California, before."

"Ooh, you gotta take the kids to Disneyland!" Rachel leans over to say.

"They're way ahead of you, Stinger," Terry grins. "They were already excited about Disneyland on the plane ride."

"Can I pay for it? I'd love to make it our treat."

"Not necessary. You've already paid for our airfare, food, and lodging, as part of the conference and memorandum of cooperation signing you and your team organized. Paying for us to bring out our families was unexpected and generous enough. You don't have anything to prove," Terry says.

"It's not that I want to prove anything. Well, maybe I do, but not out of guilt for your reservation being all ripped up. And we will help you heal the earth, we promise."

"And we believe you," Terry says. The elders with him all nod their agreement. "We wouldn't have been willing to come this way if we didn't."

"Thanks. I wish it was this easy dealing with the rest of the world."

"You seem to do okay." Terry flashes me a wry grin. "You have a very good relationship with your local authorities here."

"I do, but I'm still worried," I admit. "Those are good people, with their heart in the right place. But in Spain, a police chief accused me of fomenting anarchy, that the Nephilim and their cult are too intertwined in Western institutions, and if I bring them down I risk eroding everyone's trust in society and bringing everything down."

"Then bring it down." Terry waves his hand dismissively. "Earth-Daughter builds great canyons by bringing down mountains. Maybe that's your role as well, Champion."

"Uh...I'm not sure that this is making me feel better."

Terry laughs. "I'll admit, the dominant culture hasn't been good to my people, so I have no love for it. But I tell you sincerely, Firebird Champion, as one leader to another, if we are not happy with what exists, it's up to us to build something better. You have done well to find authorities you can trust. Work with them. Create a new, more truthful and inclusive society. You are not beholden to the corruption of old. You are the new."

Rachel leans over and gently punches my arm. "He's right, you know. We can do for Earth what you're doing in Sediin. You know I'll help."

I slowly nod.

"I've been so worried I might be bringing down the system, I've forgotten that some parts of the system *should* be brought down."

"Build something worthy of your kind, Champion—both your kinds."

"I'll try. Maybe the people of this world having common enemies and challenges will help. Maybe Team Firebird can help set an example of getting along with all peoples."

"I think you can. We can start here, with our peoples." Terry holds out his hand.

"Yes, we can." I take his hand and we shake on it.

"We shall rejoin our families. But I wanted to thank you again and express our relief that you are well and healthy."

"It has been our honor, and thank you for the kind words," I smile. Terry and all the elders wave and return to their families by the water.

As soon as they leave, Josh speaks up. "He's right, Alex, you look really great after everything Rachel told me you went through. I mean, it's just a week and you look good as new!"

"Thanks, Josh. But remember, a week here is seven months in Sediin. So it's not quite as overnight as it seems," I grin.

"Oh yeah...man, that time difference still throws me for a loop."

"You'll get used to it." Rachel pats his arm.

"Seriously, Josh, my House really took care of me, in the best way. I couldn't have asked for more. I passed out from crossing back to our House, and when I woke up, I was lying on my bed, a crisp white gown placed next to me. Pyza and Zogo were washing me—"

Josh raises his eyebrows and turns to Rachel.

"Get your mind out of the gutter, goober." Rachel smacks his arm playfully.

"The blasts melted her uniform onto her body," Zogo, who's been nearby policing the other Ruhin, walks over to explain. "While she was still unconscious we sliced her out of her destroyed clothing, and then I brought the water for Pyza to bathe her."

"And thank both of you." I reach my arms out toward him. He walks up the rocks to me, a big smile on his beak. I embrace him and kiss his head.

"It was my pleasure, Alex," Pyza leans over Garz to address me.

"I have never been a fighter, but it feels good to help those I care about heal. Your House has come to mean a great deal to me," she says, gently caressing Garz's arm. He remains silent, but the barely contained smile says it all.

"My lady," Zogo points down the beach to Vetis, in his full insect-Sedu form, kneeling on the ground while two children feel his claws and arms and poke his head. Vetis has the biggest smile, clearly loving it. The mother looks like she might have a heart attack, but to her credit she's letting her children have their moment with the insect-man.

"The younglings seem fascinated with us. Vetis wanted me to ask, if it's alright with you—"

"Oh my god, yes!" Rachel laughs. "It's totally fine! I want you guys to have fun!"

"Me too." I scratch Zogo on his smooth, turtle-like head. "You and Vetis meet people and enjoy yourselves. Tell Vetis we all approve of him in Sedu form. And you're a great ambassador for Ruhin-kind."

"Thank you, my ladies." Zogo bows, a humungous smile on his beak. "We'll be back when it's time."

I nod, and Zogo skips toward Vetis.

I turn back to Josh and continue. "For two months I got stronger, while Zogo, Pyza, Garz, Vetis, and Rachel took care of me and Jake. Mazzikim would come by my open door to look in on us and wish us well. Eventually even Qwyll—who was wounded so badly we feared he didn't make it— popped in with Rachel, too."

Rachel instinctively turns down the beach to smile at Qwyll, who is standing watch over a few four-legged Ruhin running around with a pair of little boys.

"Zogo and other Ruhin would bring us really delicious, fully prepared meals," I continued. "We'd get cheers when we went out with the others for a walk around the House or the grounds. It was really sweet. Once I had healed enough that I could heal Jake, I did."

Josh turns to Jake. "I know that you're married and all, but you could have come home.... I mean, if Rachel hadn't come by to tell us you were okay..."

"Hey, you said it yourself—I'm married. I wanted to be with my wife. Besides, you know how Dad gets. The condition I was in, even though he knows I can't die, it would have given him an aneurysm. Trust me, if the House of Keroz and Alex didn't have the power to heal my body faster than normal, right now you'd be talking to me in a bowl."

Josh swings his head to Rachel. With a most sympathetic expression, she nods and caresses his arm. Josh shudders.

"Besides, other than giving me some choice painkillers, there's really not much modern medicine could have done compared to what Alex did."

"I'm sorry it took me so long to heal you fully." I kiss him.

"It just meant I got to spend more time with you. In excruciating pain, but still..." Jake cracks.

"Get a room, you guys!" Josh smirks.

"We're building it," Rachel quips.

And she's right. Above us is the walkway up from Little Corona beach, and toward Poinsettia Street is where Firebird Manor used to stand. Wyatt had already started the process of getting an architect to design the new house, and Garz is taking those plans and turning them into bulletproof and bombproof materials made out of the spirit of our House. When it's finished, Firebird Manor will truly be the earthly extension of the House of Keroz.

I'm so sorry, Wyatt....

"Hey," Jake caresses my back, attuned to my changes in expression. "Something the matter?"

Before I can answer, we hear Raya's voice.

"Is...is this your dog?" she shouts at us as she steps off the walkway and starts heading across the sand toward us. An over three-foot-tall, majestic, sturdy but still slender Irish wolfhound with a thick, brown leather collar over its red wiry fur trots in front of her.

Klara and Jeffers both comment about how beautiful it is. The dog nuzzles Klara as it passes by her.

"Aw," Klara coos, completely charmed.

Zaebos eyes the dog suspiciously.

"Raya! Hi! Thanks for coming!" Jake scoots over to give her room.

"Oh...I'm only here for a moment. I saw this dog lingering by Firebird Manor, looking for something—you, I guess—and it walked over to me."

Raya looks so sad, it breaks my heart. Nothing I do can ever bring Wyatt back, but I wish I could.

"Still, it's so awesome you're here," Rachel says.

As Raya walks by Klara and Captain Jeffers, Klara reaches up and gently cups her hand around Raya's calf. Raya looks down with a kind but melancholy expression.

"Why would you say this is my dog?" The dog turns to me as if it under-stands, steps up the rocks with his two front paws, and gives me a huge lick across my entire face. It's kinda gross but awesome, too.

Zaebos growls.

"No, no, it's fine, Zaebos, thanks for looking out for me," I giggle. I can't help but laugh and put my hands on the dog's neck and caress him. Jake does the same. The wolfhound shoves its muzzle right in Jake's face and licks him. Rachel reaches across Jake, and the dog dutifully licks her hand, too.

"I like him," Rachel smiles.

"So you're not familiar with this dog?" Raya asks, sounding quite con-fused. "I mean, I didn't think you'd had time to get another dog after Jesse, but then I read his tag."

"Tag?" I reach under his collar and hold up the silver tag. Like the collar, the tag is adorned with detailed, gorgeous Celtic design work.

The front of the tag says "Reilly," and on the back it says "Lady Firebird" with my private, secure phone number.

What the hell?

"I've never seen this gorgeous boy before," I shrug. "None of us have." I look around at everyone, and they all nod. Garz is careful not to make a scene that might scare anyone, but he's clearly on guard now.

"Well, I can communicate with life, right? So let's see..." I begin. "Reilly, what's your story?"

I close my eyes and reach out to Reilly, imagining a scene with someone securing this collar to his neck, trying to impart the idea that I want to see through his eyes who that person is.

Suddenly, my mind is filled with an image as vivid as if I were watching it on television. Right here, in Corona Del Mar, on the grounds of Firebird Manor, Reilly looks into the eyes of an extremely beautiful, tall, voluptuous woman wearing a strapless, ankle-length, sheer, flowing green dress. Her thick, luscious red hair falls nearly to the ground, covering her huge breasts as she buckles the collar. And those eyes...I'd recognize the glowing green fire of her eyes anywhere.

"Thank you," the woman smiles at the dog—at me–with the same warm smile I saw in Broxton.

"Matka?" I breathe.

The image fades and I open my eyes—and for a moment, it looks like Reilly's irises are lit from the inside the same as Matka's.

"So...did anyone else see green flames in Reilly's eyes?" Raya asks ner-vously.

We all turn to each other and nod.

"I'm glad it's not just me. Even after everything, I'm not used to things like this."

"Oh, trust me," Josh tightens his lips to suppress a wry grin. "With this bunch, an Irish wolfhound with flaming green eyes is downright normal."

Even Raya can't help but smile.

"Alex, what else did you see?" Jake asks.

"Reilly here is a gift to us, from Matka. Or maybe we're a gift to you?" Reilly sticks out his tongue and nuzzles me, a huge smile on his muzzle.

"Oooh, killer!" Rachel says. She scoots closer to the dog. It turns to Rachel and licks her too.

"You mean, the Earth goddess?" Raya asks.

"That's exactly who I mean," I nod.

"I...I saw her too, Alex," Klara whispers, tears in her eyes and a quivering smile.

I reach down to Klara, who reaches up and takes my hand for a moment.

"Everything I've done, Raya. Everyone who's fought with me, we've all been part of Mother Earth's army. Everyone," I emphasize, not saying his name, but she knows who I mean.

Raya offers a faraway smile. "And so Matka entrusts you with one of her wolfhounds, for a job well done."

I stand up and hug Raya tightly. "Raya, this war had dear casualties. We lost loved ones, on Earth and from our House. If I could have shielded—"

"Oh, I know," Raya quickly interrupts. "Wyatt would never have stood for those monsters quietly killing people for centuries. With so much modern surveillance, it was only a matter of time until they were exposed, and he would have gotten in their faces about it. I'm glad you were able to win the day, so he didn't die in vain."

I nod and hug her even tighter.

"So what are you up to now?" Rachel asks, as Raya and I end our embrace.

"Well, I'd actually come to say goodbye. I can't afford to live here in Corona Del Mar, so I'm going to move in with my sister and her family in Fullerton, at least for a while. We haven't always seen eye to eye, but there's love there, and she reached out to me and offered me a bed."

"Sounds nice," I say. "But always know that we can afford the rent if you want to stay in town for a while, or when Firebird Manor is reconstructed, you can stay with us."

"Thanks for the offer, but I think I need to be with family for a while," Raya says. "I do want to see the new Firebird Manor when it's finished, though. We'll keep in touch?"

"Yes, we will," I say and take her right hand in both of mine.

"Can I invite you to my Bat Mitzvah?" Rachel asks. "Now that the Rishonim are gone and the surviving Nephilim scattered, I can finally set a date. Assuming Congregation B'nai David has an opening, I'm thinking maybe three months from now. Is that cool?"

"It is," Raya smiles weakly. "Alex will have my new address, and all my other contact information will be the same, so you'll be able to send me an invite. I'd love to come."

"Awesome," Rachel smiles.

"Anyway, I should go. I love you all," Raya says.

"We love you too," Rachel says. She rises from her rock and I scoot over so she can hug Raya. Jake hugs her next. We all sit down on our boulders as Raya turns, hugs Klara, and heads toward the paved path out of Little Corona beach to Ocean Street.

"It's setting," Jake says, looking at the horizon.

We quiet down. Ruhin playing with children slowly stop, their gaze hypnotized by the reddish-yellow glow radiating through the sparse purple clouds as the deep orange sun begins to sink below the Pacific.

The waves gently wash onto the sand. Ruhin, Mazzikim, and people all stand next to each other. I put my arm around Jake. Klara walks up and puts one arm around me and another around Jeffers. Vetis and Zogo come up and stand with all of us—and Reilly—as we look out into the twilight, transfixed.

There are still Nephilim out there, hiding somewhere. Still people who hate us. Still forces of chaos.

We need to finish rebuilding Firebird Manor. I need to return to those areas where the Nephilim have destroyed the ground and see if I can help bring it back to life. Matka said that she had a role for Klara to play. Maybe this is part of it.

Now that the Nephilim are no longer numerous enough to be a threat and our loved ones who went into hiding are coming home, I need to talk with Hector Godinez and figure out what my relationship to the American government is, if I still have one.

I'll figure all that out later. Right now, for the first time ever, an entire community of human beings and an entire House of spirit beings take in a gorgeous Pacific sunset together. And for this one, beautiful moment, everything seems right.

Don't Miss:

The Dawning of Firebird Alex

The Dawning of Firebird Alex collects The Sedumen Chronicles Books 1-3, the *Firebird Manor* novelette, and a glossary of terms used in the books.

Firebird Alex (The Sedumen Chronicles Book 1)

Alex knows she's different; other girls don't burst into flames when they get angry. After she nearly burned the house down when she was twelve, her mother confessed that her father was a demon.

Now eighteen and mourning the death of her mother, Alex sinks inside herself until she discovers a dagger that can open a portal into her father's realm. Although she yearns to meet her father, nothing terrifies her more. When an unknown threat from across the portal menaces her friends and her loved ones, Alex knows she must act.

Alex will do anything to save her friends—even risk appealing to her father in his strange universe of bizarre creatures, unfamiliar alliances, and unimagined power. She knows that to face a tormentor from across the portal, she'll need to learn to fight fire with fire.

Lady Firebird (The Sedumen Chronicles Book 2)

Alexandra Gold leads two lives.

In a universe filled with powerful spirit beings, she is the half human, half-demon Lady Firebird of the House of Keroz. She stopped Dirk Raum from murdering humans whose fresh souls he fed the House of Raum. This won her the respect of some but the enmity of others.

On Earth, she appears to be like every other eighteen-year old girl, but she longs to step forward as Lady Firebird, and let people know that she will protect them—but she worries that once people see her flaming hair, eyes, and long fangs, she will terrify those she wants to help. When Dirk returns and starts a kidnapping spree as part of his plan to conquer both universes, Alex races to the rescue.

She is ready to meet the challenge; but is the world ready to meet Lady Firebird?

Firebird Vengeance (The Sedumen Chronicles Book 3)

When half-demon Alexandra Gold uses her innate grace to save the soul of a murdered girl, it brings her to the attention of the most powerful beings in her parallel universe.

At first, she believes this is a blessing. When she discovers that she has been the unwitting pawn of an ancient vengeance that intends to destroy every living human and demon in both universes, she realizes that she's been cursed. This ancient vengeance has the power to re-animate the dead and use them to murder the living—and for each of the thirty-six most righteous human beings it murders, the more powerful it becomes.

All Alex has is her blade, her power over fire, and her wits. For her to stop this vengeance, she must convince those humans and demons who are terrified and blame her for this catastrophe to help her fight back.

Stinger and Bow (The Sedumen Chronicles Book 4)

Stinger needs a new crossbow.

Thirteen year-old Rachel Silver—or as she's known to the world, Stinger—needs a new crossbow. Her last bow failed her when she needed it most. Besides, Firebird Alex, her aunt and fellow Seduman—half-human, half-spirit being—wields a Sedu blade, made with spirit magic.

So Stinger designs herself a magic crossbow, then convinces her best friends to accompany her around the world and into the universe of Sediin to find the right craftsmen to have it made. Trouble is, warriors attract people who want to challenge them, whether they're ready or not. Stinger is still tormented by her last battle—she's suffering night-terrors, shakes, and cold sweats. When the situation turns deadly, will she be able to come to grips with her trauma and become the warrior she needs to be to save her friends?

Watcher and Firebird (The Sedumen Chronicles Book 5)

Firebird Alex didn't know much about the Nephilim until they assassinated her friend in the United States government, kidnapped the man she considers her uncle, and tried to murder her—twice. Now she's learned that they, and their leader "the Watcher," will stop at nothing to kill her, everyone she loves, and every Seduman on Earth.

Alex must stop their murderous plans even if it means compromising the heroine she's become.

About the Author

Orren Merton started writing fantasy and science fiction at an embarrassingly young age, mostly for his own amusement. In high school, he listened to a lot of dark and moody rock, which inspired him to pick up guitar and start playing up and down California in a few bands, culminating in his Industrial rock group Ember After. During that time, magazines, developers, and corporations began to pay him to write and edit music software related articles, manuals, and books. Since then he has written the urban fantasy novel *The Deviant* and the science fiction novel *Skye Entity* before working on his current series, *The Sedumen Chronicles*. He lives in Southern California with his family, pets, collection of sci-fi/fantasy memorabilia, and curiously large stuffed animal collection.

Follow Orren Merton Online:
Web: www.orrenmerton.com
Email: info@orrenmerton.com
Twitter: @orrenmerton
Facebook: www.facebook.com/OrrenMertonOfficial
Instagram: www.instagram.com/orren_merton/
Tumblr: orrenmerton.tumblr.com